Praise for *New York Times* and *USA TODAY* bestselling author Vicki Lewis Thompson

"Vicki Lewis Thompson is one of those rare, gifted writers with the ability to touch her readers' hearts and their funny bones."
—#1 *New York Times* and *USA TODAY* bestselling author Debbie Macomber

"This modern cowboy tale expertly balances sex and emotion with a touch of humor. It's one of the hottest western romances of the year!"
—*RT Book Reviews* on *Claimed!*

Praise for *New York Times* and *USA TODAY* bestselling author Jill Shalvis

"Shalvis thoroughly engages readers."
—*Publishers Weekly*

"Shalvis's writing is a perfect trifecta of win: hilarious dialogue, evocative and real characters, and settings that are as much a part of the story as the hero and heroine. I've never been disappointed by a Shalvis book."
—*SmartBitchesTrashyBooks.com*

Praise for *USA TODAY* bestselling author Julie Kenner

"[Julie Kenner has a] flair for dialogue and eccentric characterizations."
—*Publishers Weekly*

"Julie Kenner's characters and their sexual adventures will win your heart."
—*RT Book Reviews*

NEW YORK TIMES AND USA TODAY BESTSELLING AUTHORS

Vicki Lewis Thompson
Jill Shalvis

USA TODAY BESTSELLING AUTHOR

Julie Kenner

Holiday Hideout

™ **Harlequin**®

TORONTO NEW YORK LONDON
AMSTERDAM PARIS SYDNEY HAMBURG
STOCKHOLM ATHENS TOKYO MILAN MADRID
PRAGUE WARSAW BUDAPEST AUCKLAND

ISBN-13: 978-0-373-83762-5

HOLIDAY HIDEOUT
Copyright © 2011 by Harlequin Books S.A.

The publisher acknowledges the
copyright holders of the individual works
as follows:

THE THANKSGIVING FIX
Copyright © 2011 by Vicki Lewis Thompson

THE CHRISTMAS SET-UP
Copyright © 2011 by Jill Shalvis

THE NEW YEAR'S DEAL
Copyright © 2011 by Julie Kenner

Recycling programs
for this product may
not exist in your area.

Printed in U.S.A.

CONTENTS

To the memory of Christopher Reeve,
who was the epitome of Superman.

THE THANKSGIVING FIX

New York Times and USA TODAY
Bestselling Author

Vicki Lewis Thompson

PROLOGUE

Once upon a time, a middle-aged couple named Ken and Jillian Vickers rented a cozy cottage overlooking Lake Tahoe in hopes that a weekend away would revitalize their marriage. The plan worked so well that they bought the cottage. But it was far too small to accommodate their children and grandchildren, so on Thanksgiving, Christmas and New Year's, it sat empty.

Ken suggested renting it out for those holidays, which made financial sense to Jillian. But after several seasons, an unusual pattern emerged. Renters routinely left notes expressing their joy at either rekindling an old love or finding a new one during their stay at the cabin.

The consistent theme of the notes fascinated Ken and Jillian, both sociology professors at the University of Nevada in Reno. Perhaps the little cabin had a special effect on couples. If so, Ken and Jillian vowed to collect enough evidence to uncover its secret....

"I STILL SAY you're taking the concept too far." Ken Vickers paced the small kitchen. "This is a blatant matchmaking attempt, which will skew the data we've collected so far."

"And I say it's the ultimate test." Jillian scooted under the kitchen sink. "Hand me the wrench."

"But—"

"With this renter, we have a golden opportunity to see if the cabin's effect is strong enough to override a renter's preconceived objective. Beth insists she's stopped searching for Mr. Right. I want to see what happens if we bring Mr. Right to her doorstep." She wiggled her fingers. "Wrench, please."

Ken sighed as he leaned down and placed it in her outstretched hand. "You don't know that Mac is Beth's Mr. Right."

"Yes, I do. Besides being a terrific handyman, he's a nice person. Beth was one of those great students you never forget. They're perfect for each other."

"Aside from the fact that he loves it here and her job's in Reno."

"So they'll drive back and forth. It's doable. And they'll make beautiful babies."

"Babies? Jillian, for God's sake. They haven't even met and you're already envisioning babies?"

"You have to admit they'd make a handsome couple, Mac with his dark hair and those startling blue eyes, and Beth with her reddish-brown hair and green eyes. Their kids would be absolutely—"

"What if she doesn't notice the leak and we end up with water damage?"

"C'mon, Ken. She manages one of the largest hotels in Reno. She'll notice."

"I still don't think this is a good idea. Something could go wrong."

"I promise you, it won't." Jillian loosened the pipe fitting. "Would you please turn on the water?"

With another martyred sigh, Ken complied.

"Good—we've got a leak. It's just enough to get her attention. You posted Mac's number on the refrigerator, right?"

"I did, but...I don't know if I can just walk out of here with that pipe leaking. It goes against my instincts."

"Not mine. She'll be here in the next hour, and it's starting to snow." Jillian eased out from under the sink. "Let's get going before the roads get too icy."

CHAPTER ONE

A<small>FTER UNPACKING AND TAKING</small> a long soak in the claw-foot tub of her Lake Tahoe rental cabin, Beth Tierney put on an old sweatshirt and sweatpants along with her sock-monkey slippers. Then she settled down on the living room couch with a glass of wine, a pen and a yellow legal pad.

Before she left the cabin on Sunday, she would have a Single and Proud of It speech for her well-meaning yet interfering family when they gathered for Christmas. Never again would she face a holiday dreading that they'd try to fix her up with a marriage prospect. Pen poised, she debated how to begin.

Now that I've turned thirty, I— She scratched that out. No sense in calling attention to her age when that was the first thing they mentioned when they broached the subject of her singleness. *As you all know, I used my Thanksgiving break to take stock of my life.*

That was better. Her father was fond of telling his children to "take stock of their lives." She'd reminded her mother of that when announcing she wasn't going to be attending the family Thanksgiving celebration in Sacramento this year. Her two brothers and one sister—all married even though they were younger than she was—had thought hiding away in a cabin for the Thanksgiving weekend was stupid, and had called her to say so. But her mom and dad had given their blessing.

She glanced out the window where a light snow continued to fall. Good thing she'd made it before the roads got bad. Returning her attention to the yellow legal pad on her lap, she chose her next sentence carefully.

After much consideration—her dad would love that part—*I've decided to embrace my single status*. Brilliant opening. She tapped the pen against the paper, pleased with herself.

This getaway had been such a great idea. Besides writing the speech to give to her family on Christmas, she planned to spend the long weekend appreciating all the enjoyable things about being unattached. She sipped her wine and stared into the fire.

These days, being single no longer carried a stigma. The words *spinster* and *old maid* didn't apply to an educated woman with a terrific future in business. She had a loving family, many close friends and a spacious condo.

She didn't need a man to keep her feet warm at night. Wearing wool socks to bed was a far simpler solution.

She didn't require a ring, a wedding and a home in suburbia to feel complete. Her life was full, and her family might as well give up the quest for a fairy-tale ending. It wasn't going to happen.

She wasn't bitter about that. No tragic love stories had turned her against marriage. Besides her family's endless matchmaking attempts—which had never gone well—she'd dated some almost-right guys over the years. Two had even proposed.

But neither of those relationships had measured up. She wanted to be madly in love, of course, but she also needed to be respected as an equal partner. Her ideal man wouldn't take himself too seriously, but he would take the nurturing part of their relationship *very* seriously.

For example, he would remember her birthday without being reminded. She would love to meet the man who believed that remembering birthdays and anniversaries was important. If a guy could tell her, without a cheat sheet, the birthdays of his parents and siblings, that would make her sit up and take notice.

Everyone said her expectations were too high, which meant there was a good chance no man would make the grade. She was okay with that. Some people were meant to be married, and some weren't. She fit into category B. She was perfectly fine as she was, and she was going to give them a detailed list of all the reasons why. Maybe then her well-intentioned family would get off her back.

The fire needed tending, so she got up to add another log. Once she had it crackling nicely again, she decided she could do with some brain food to help her list along, walked over to the tiny kitchen area adjacent to the living room, and opened the refrigerator. Cheese and crackers sounded good.

She found a wooden cheeseboard on one of the shelves, and used a knife from the well-stocked drawer of kitchen utensils to slice the cheddar she'd brought. Ken and Jillian had thought of everything, but then, they would have since they spent many weekends at the cabin during the rest of the year. She rinsed off the knife and left it in the strainer.

But as she picked up the cheeseboard and started back to the couch, she heard water dripping. Returning to the kitchen, she opened the doors and examined the pipes under the sink. Near as she could tell, a pipe fitting had worked itself loose. She tried tightening it by hand and then tested it by running more water in the sink. Still dripping.

She could call the handyman whose number was posted on the refrigerator, but that seemed silly. She'd carried a toolbox in her trunk for years, a habit instilled by her dad. He always said a person should be prepared for life's little hiccups. Handling this herself would be symbolic: Beth Tierney proves that she doesn't need a man around.

After donning her jacket and pulling boots over her monkey slippers, she hurried outside, fetched the toolbox and ran back in. The handyman shouldn't have to come out in this weather, anyway. He was probably some old guy who was at that moment helping his wife with the pumpkin pies or hauling in folding chairs for the extended family that would arrive tomorrow.

Beth battled a wave of nostalgia. By doing the hermit thing this year, she'd miss the carving of the turkey and the Thanksgiving Day toasts. Her mother, sister and sisters-in-law would gather in the kitchen for girl talk while her dad, brothers and brother-in-law watched football and her nieces and nephews ran around fighting over who got the wishbone.

Holidays were chaotic in her family, and she loved every minute, except…they would always, *always*, drag some single guy into the mix, hoping Beth would hook up with him and instead add a sour note to her holidays. If she ever expected to enjoy another holiday with her nearest and dearest, she had to put an end to their matchmaking.

After taking off her coat and boots, she chose a wrench from her toolbox and wriggled into position under the pipe. A few twists of the wrench and the dripping stopped. Scooting out from under the counter, she tested her job by running water into the sink. All fixed. Beth Tierney, single girl, had triumphed over another household emergency. Who needed men?

Although she had to admit there was one thing she did need a man for. She wasn't ready to give up sex at the ripe old age of thirty. But a girl could have sex without expecting it to lead to white lace and promises. In fact, sex would be much more honest if both parties agreed that it wasn't a prelude to courtship and marriage.

Putting away her wrench, she picked up the cheese-board and returned to the couch. Maybe she'd write out that conclusion in her speech, although her sex life wasn't exactly a subject she shared with her parents. Still, she needed a manifesto that would remind her of why she'd made this decision to give up on wedding bells. She picked up her legal pad and began to write again as the fire blazed in the hearth and snow fell outside the window.

"MOM, *please* DON'T FIX ME UP with someone for Thanksgiving." Mac McFarland cradled the cell phone against his shoulder as he pulled off his boots. Once he'd finished this call, he'd build a fire and pop open a beer. Snowy weather was a perfect excuse to relax by the fire with a cold one.

"It's not a fix-up," his mother said. "She's a friend of the family."

"Since when? I've never heard of this Stephanie person."

"A recent friend. Your father hired her last month as his new receptionist. There's no harm in meeting her, Conneach."

He cringed. Although he'd trained everyone else in his life to call him Mac, his mother insisted on using his given name, which had been a burden to him from the moment he'd realized other boys had names like Bill and Pete and Sam.

In print, his name stymied people. When he pronounced it for them, they thought he was saying cognac, and they teased him about being named after a type of brandy. Self-preservation had prompted him to change his name to Mac McFarland, and that had worked for everyone—except his mother.

"Mom, I'm sure these single women you round up are embarrassed to be paraded in front of me as if you're trying to marry me off."

"There's no *as if* about it. I *am* trying to marry you off. You're thirty-one years old. It's time. And I don't have to remind you that you're the hope of the McFarlands."

"No, you don't have to remind me." But she did at every opportunity. As the only son, he was supposed to guarantee that his father's branch of the McFarland clan would continue. His younger sister had no such responsibility, and frankly, that was unfair. The whole charade was so three centuries ago.

"You intend to get married at some point, I hope?"

Mac set his boots aside and wiggled his toes inside his wool socks. "Maybe. I suppose. I'm in no rush, but someday, when I meet the right woman."

"And how do you intend to do that? You're either working or camping alone in the woods."

"That's not true. I have dates."

"With who?"

"Like with…Kathy."

His mother made a dismissive sound. "That was months ago, and you were never serious about her. I could tell."

"Mom, I love you, but you have to stop pushing."

There was a pause on the other end. "I can't uninvite her."

"I suppose not." His phone beeped. "Listen, I have another call."

"I'll see you tomorrow, then."

"Yes, you'll see me tomorrow. Bye, Mom." He disconnected and picked up the new call, which turned out to be Jillian Vickers, one of his favorite people. He wished her a happy Thanksgiving.

"Same to you, Mac," she said. "Hey, have you heard anything from our weekend renter, Beth Tierney?"

"No, I haven't." He frowned. "Why, is there a problem?"

"I'm not sure, but I would really appreciate it if you'd go over and check on her." Noise in the background indicated Ken was mumbling something. "Last time we were there, we thought we heard a leak in the kitchen, maybe under the sink."

"Really?" Mac sat up straighter. "You should have called me. You don't want water damage on those oak cabinets."

"I know, but I…I sort of forgot about it. I'm sure it's nothing, but could you take a quick run over there and check?"

"Sure." Mac reached for his boots. Something about this situation wasn't adding up. Ken was a stickler for details. Jillian might have forgotten about a leak, but Ken wouldn't have. He'd either have made sure he'd fixed it himself or phoned Mac. Still, Mac wasn't about to refuse a request from such great customers.

"I realize I'm sending you out in the snow," Jillian added. "I'm sorry about that."

"Gives me a chance to try out my new snow tires." He pulled on one boot. "I'll give you a call after I go over there."

"Thanks, Mac. You're the best. Talk to you soon. Oh, and her name is Beth Tierney." She hung up.

I know, Mac thought. *You already told me that.* He was halfway over to the Vickers' cabin before he figured out what was bothering him about this errand. Instead of calling him, Jillian could have called the renter. No doubt the woman had a cell phone with her, and the rental agreement would have that listed.

Oh, well. Maybe Jillian hadn't thought of that. No doubt she was cooking and cleaning in preparation for the big Thanksgiving dinner with her family and she was distracted. He was nearly at the cabin, anyway, and he was pleased with the way his new tires gripped the road. This really did give him the chance to test them out, so it wasn't a wasted trip.

Anyway, if it turned out there was actually a leak, he needed to fix it before those beautiful cabinets suffered. He'd refinished them just last summer, and the image of water dripping on them made him wince.

Parking the truck in front of the cabin, he turned up his coat collar and grabbed his toolbox out of the camper shell in the back before going to the door. He smelled wood smoke, which meant she'd built a fire.

He pictured the roaring fire he would enjoy once he finished this chore. The temperature had dropped significantly in the past hour, and he was ready to go home and settle in for the night. He knocked briskly.

When the door opened, he blinked in surprise. He hadn't thought much about who was renting the cabin, but in the back of his mind he'd wondered what sort of woman would deliberately spend Thanksgiving weekend alone in a mountain cabin. He might have expected some eccentric old lady who'd had it with the Thanksgiving Day hype and wanted an escape. He certainly hadn't expected Beth Tierney to be young and beautiful.

Not that she was trying to be beautiful. She wore a faded UNR sweatshirt, baggy sweats, and—he couldn't help smiling when he saw them—sock-monkey slippers. Her dark brown hair was caught up in a haphazard ponytail, and her face was bare of makeup, which only emphasized the soft green of her eyes. Any woman who could look that appealing without trying captured Mac's attention.

"I'm Mac McFarland, the handyman," he said. "Ken and Jillian called me about a potential leak."

"Oh!" She glanced at the toolbox in his hand. "I'm sorry you've made the trip, especially in this weather. I fixed it."

"So there *was* a leak?" He didn't want to insult her by implying that she hadn't fixed it, but he loved this cabin and he was crazy about those oak cabinets. A leak that could threaten the finish he'd painstakingly applied had to be investigated. By him.

"Yes, but I handled it. Thank you for coming by, but everything's under control. Happy Thanksgiving." She started to close the door.

He put his hand on the door. "I believe you…" Although he didn't, not really. "But would you mind if I double-check the situation to see if it's dripping again? Leaks can be tricky."

"You don't think I fixed it, do you?"

She seemed pretty confident, but he still wanted to look for himself. "I'm sure you did, but I promised to report back to Ken and Jillian after I checked on things." He smiled. "It's what they pay me for."

She hesitated and finally shrugged. "I suppose you wouldn't want to jeopardize your work relationship with them."

"I'd rather not. They're good customers." He gave her points for being understanding.

"Okay, then." She stepped away from the door with obvious reluctance. "I'm sure the pipes are fine, though, and I'm kind of busy right now."

He glanced at the cozy fire, the glass of wine, the cheese and crackers, and a yellow legal pad with some things scribbled on it. "Are you a writer?"

"No."

So much for that attempt at conversation. Damn, now he was curious. Maybe she'd recently broken up with someone and this was how she was dealing with it. He couldn't imagine anyone giving up on a woman who looked like her, but she could have a boatload of bad habits.

As he walked into the kitchen area he noticed a toolbox sitting on the floor beside the row of cabinets. He gave her more points; no women he knew traveled with a toolbox.

And it was definitely hers, because Ken and Jillian kept whatever tools they needed hanging inside a locked closet by the back door. Ken had made the decision not to give renters access to the tool closet, which Mac thought was a wise move—not so much for fear of theft as for incompetence.

Mac took off his heavy parka and draped it over a kitchen chair. Then he crouched in front of the sink and opened the cabinet doors. They moved smoothly on their hinges, exactly as he'd intended when he'd put in all-new hardware last summer.

Nothing was dripping now. He rolled onto his back and scooted under the sink to examine the pipes and fittings. All was well. "Would you turn on the faucet for me, please?"

She walked over, her monkey slippers whispering against the wooden floor, the scent of cinnamon arriving with her. Water splashed into the stainless-steel sink, but none of it dripped from the fitting.

"Thanks, that's good."

The splashing stopped and she walked away again.

He waited. Still no drip. That left him with no reason to stay, no reason to satisfy his curiosity as to why this beautiful woman was here during what was, for most people, a family holiday. He certainly would be dealing with his family tomorrow—along with Stephanie, the woman his mother hoped would become the bearer of McFarland sons.

Easing out from under the sink, he sat up and leaned his arms on his knees.

Beth stood looking at him, her expression more open than it had been a few moments ago. "No leak?"

"Not that I can see." Something else was different about her, too. Then he realized she'd taken her hair out of the ponytail. It fell to her shoulders in soft waves and he noticed tinges of red mixed with the brown. "Whatever it was, you've obviously taken care of it."

"Thanks."

He stood. "Guess I'll let you get back to your fire. I appreciate you allowing me to come in." He walked over to the chair where he'd hung his parka.

"It seems a shame that you drove over here for no reason."

He picked up his coat and turned toward her. "No worries. It's okay."

"I don't know if you have somewhere you need to be, but…would you like to stay for a glass of wine?"

He had no idea what had prompted that invitation after her initial chilly response, but he wasn't opposed to her idea. At all. "I have nowhere I have to be, and that sounds great. Thanks."

"I hope you like red."

"Absolutely." And this would give him a chance to

stay a little longer and try to unravel the mystery that was Beth Tierney. "But I should call Jillian and let her know the leak's not a problem."

"Sure. While you do that, I'll pour you some wine."

"That's a deal." He pulled his phone out of his jeans pocket and punched in Ken and Jillian's number.

Jillian answered on the first ring. "Mac? Did you take care of the leak?"

"No, Beth did and it's fine now."

"Oh. I see. So I guess you didn't need to go out in the snowstorm, after all. Sorry about that." Jillian sounded a little subdued.

"Guess not. You have a capable renter here."

"Right. So you're heading home?"

"Not quite. Beth offered me a glass of wine, so I'm taking her up on it."

"Oh! That's great! I mean…how nice of her."

The puzzle began to click into place. "Jillian, what's up?"

"Nothing, nothing. I just think you two might have some things in common. She's Irish, too, you know."

Turning away from the living room, Mac lowered his voice. "Did you arrange this?"

"Not exactly. Well…sort of."

"Honestly, I'm beginning to think you're in league with my mother." But Jillian was a customer, so he couldn't be too hard on her. Still, it was an underhanded trick.

"Mac, it's harmless. I just thought you two might get along. If you don't, no harm done."

He glanced toward the living room where Beth sat on the couch with her wineglass on one end table and his on the other. She'd put the plate of cheese and crackers on the couch's middle cushion. A guy would have to be dead to turn down the chance to spend time in front of a fire with a beautiful woman on a snowy night, even if it was technically a fix-up.

He angled away again, once more shielding his conversation with Jillian. "I'll say this," he murmured. "You have good taste. Talk to you later." He disconnected the call and tucked the phone in his pocket.

Now to solve the mystery…

CHAPTER TWO

INVITING THE HANDYMAN TO STAY for a glass of wine hadn't been part of Beth's game plan. But Mac Mc-Farland was serious eye candy, a fact she hadn't been able to ignore, especially after he took off his coat and started to inspect the pipe. Between the faded jeans that showcased his tight buns and a blue chambray shirt that required no padding to emphasize his broad shoulders, he was outfitted like a certified hunk.

His dark, wavy hair brushed the back of his collar in a most attractive way, and his eyes were the kind of startling blue that won guys modeling and movie contracts. On top of all that, he smelled good. From the moment he'd come through the door, she'd breathed in a heady combination of pine boughs and wood smoke.

Even though she was concentrating on the joys of singlehood this weekend, that didn't mean she couldn't invite a guy for a drink.

She wasn't exactly dressed for company, though. It was too late to apply makeup, but at least she'd spritzed a little of her favorite spice body mist on after her bath.

Maybe she'd share a drink with Mac and then he'd go on about his business. But if not, and his arresting blue eyes continued to fascinate her, she might try out the new ground rules she'd devised for her sex life and see what his reaction might be. Assuming he was interested in her and didn't have some sweetie in the wings, that was.

Once he'd joined her on the couch, she picked up her wineglass and searched for an icebreaker.

He took a sip of the wine. "Good stuff. Thanks."

"You're welcome. So…did you decide in kindergarten that you wanted to be a handyman and that was the end of that?"

He laughed. "No, I wanted to be a superhero, but sadly my superpowers never developed, so I had to settle for household maintenance instead."

She could imagine him in spandex and a rippling cape. He had the classic square-jawed superhero look about him. "I'll bet your customers think you're heroic. A good maintenance man is hard to find." As she knew from her experience as a hotel manager.

"That, as a matter of fact, is true. Just about anyone can hang out a shingle. But I learned from an expert— my dad. I worked for him all through high school and college." He reached for a cracker and put a piece of cheese on top of it.

"But now you don't."

"Nope. I developed an independent streak. But at least by working on this side of the mountain, I'm not in direct competition with him." He popped the cheese and cracker into his mouth and began to chew.

"So he's in Reno?"

He finished chewing and swallowed. "My folks live there." He picked up his wineglass and gestured in her direction. "Your turn."

"I manage the High Sierras Hotel."

He nodded. "I can see you doing that."

"You can?" She glanced down at her sweats. "I don't look much like a hotel manager at the moment."

"No, but you act like someone who makes plans and carries them out, which would make for a good manager."

She gazed at him, intrigued. "How can you tell?"

"The fire, the wine, whatever you were writing when I got here. That looked like part of a plan to me."

"It was." She was impressed that he was so observant and wondered what he'd think of the manifesto she was creating.

But she didn't know him well enough to talk about it, at least not yet. When she didn't offer to tell him her purpose in coming here, he didn't ask. She took that as a promising sign that he respected boundaries.

He swallowed another sip of his wine. "I'd think this would be a busy week for you at the hotel."

"It is, but my assistant is excellent and he has my cell number in case anything unexpected crops up. I can get back there fairly fast if necessary."

Mac glanced out the window where snow continued to come down. "Or not."

"Or not." She smiled. "To tell the truth, I wouldn't mind being snowed in. I'm a bit of a workaholic, and a heavy snow would force me to stay away from the hotel for the whole weekend." She swirled her wine in the glass. "I love my work, but I have a tendency to obsess over it."

"At least you have an assistant." He helped himself to another cracker and piece of cheese. "I'm the whole show, and sometimes that means working 24/7. Well, not quite, but it can feel that way."

"So why don't you have an assistant?" She had an idea of the answer, but was curious as to whether she was right.

"Damned if I know. I should hire one, but..."

"A good maintenance man is hard to find?"

"I just think I can do the job better than anyone else. I have a bit of an ego, I guess." He grinned at her.

Her heart rate picked up. That smile of his was killer. "So I'm lucky that you're not rushing off to repair someone's broken pipes or faulty light fixture tonight."

"It could still happen. I've notified all my customers that I'll be in Reno tomorrow at my folks' house for Thanksgiving dinner, but I'll be here until morning, and my people know that." There was a note of pride in his voice.

She thought of his childhood ambition of becoming a superhero. He hadn't strayed all that far from his dream, after all. "Which is why Jillian Vickers called you."

He nodded and swallowed a mouthful of wine. "About that." He glanced over at her. "You should probably know that Jillian loosened that fitting on purpose."

Beth stared at him. "On purpose? But why would she… Oh, my God." She started to laugh. "Oh, my *God*." She put her wineglass on the end table so she wouldn't spill on the couch, a real danger because she was shaking with laughter. "That's hysterical!"

"Care to tell me why?" He sounded a little miffed.

"Because…" She gasped for breath and realized her hilarity might have offended him. "I'm sorry. It's not hysterical that she'd try to fix me up with you. You're gorgeous."

His eyebrows lifted. "Well, I wouldn't go so far as to say—"

"It's just that the reason I stayed away from my family's Thanksgiving celebration in Sacramento is because I knew they'd have a blind date for me there. Then Jillian pulls this trick." She threw both hands in the air. "I can't get away from people trying to find me a man!"

He frowned. "And you prefer women?"

"Heavens, no!" She suppressed another fit of giggles. "I like men just fine. But I'm sick of my family trying to marry me off, which is what these blind dates are all about. My three siblings are married, and I, the eldest, am not. Apparently that bugs them." She wiped her eyes and gazed at him. "Sorry. I didn't mean to lose it like that."

"No need to apologize. Actually, we're in the same boat."

She cleared her throat. "How's that?"

"My mom is determined to find me a wife. In fact, she's invited someone named Stephanie to dinner tomorrow."

"Oh, dear. I know exactly how awkward that can be. You have my sympathies. And on top of that, Jillian's trying to play matchmaker." She looked at him. "You don't have to stay, you know. I mean, first I'm dumped on you, and then tomorrow you'll be dealing with Stephanie. I'll bet you'd rather spend the night on your own."

"Actually, it's comforting to be with somebody who's stuck with the same problem." He polished off his wine.

"In that case, would you like a refill?"

"Sounds good."

"All right, then." She stood. "Be right back."

"Do you mind if I stoke up the fire while you do that?"

She paused for a moment to absorb the fact that he'd asked instead of assuming that, as the guy, he had dominion over the fire. Interesting. "That would be very nice. Thank you."

As she walked back into the living room with the wine bottle, she admired how good he looked tending the fire. She'd never dated a handyman before, and the idea of being with someone who was good with tools had an erotic component that she liked. Still, she couldn't lose sight of the fact this was a fix-up, and this weekend was supposed to be about putting an end to those.

It helped that he was tired of being fixed up, too, and after all, he'd been inconvenienced by Jillian's meddling. She glanced at the nearly empty cheese-and-crackers plate, and her natural tendency to be hospitable kicked in. He was a big guy, and big guys usually had appetites to match.

She refilled his wineglass. "I have a large frozen pizza I was going to cook for dinner. Want to share it with me?"

He looked up, fire tongs in one hand. "I hate to eat your stash of food."

"Don't worry. I brought plenty. I'm planning a single girl's version of Thanksgiving dinner tomorrow—Cornish game hen, sweet potatoes and some other veggies. I'll have leftovers to take me through the rest of the weekend."

After positioning another log on the fire, he replaced the screen and stood. "Pizza sounds great."

She set the wine bottle on the end table next to his glass. "Then I'll go pop it in the oven."

Mac followed her into the small kitchen area. "Matter of fact, your whole plan sounds great. I envy you having the guts to tell your family you weren't going to play their silly game."

"If I can't do it now that I'm thirty, when can I?" She opened the freezer, took out the boxed pizza and opened it.

"You're a very young-looking thirty, Beth."

"You didn't have to say that, but thanks." She appreciated a man who knew how to give a well-placed compliment. She'd decided not to be paranoid about being thirty, but it didn't hurt to have someone claim she didn't look it.

"I'm thirty-one, and I haven't been that bold. Then again, my mom keeps reminding me I'm the 'hope of the McFarlands.'"

She turned to him. "You're what?"

He leaned against the counter—six feet and a couple of inches of heart-stopping masculinity. He stuck his hands in the front pockets of his jeans, which stretched the material over his package. "If my father's line is to be continued, I'm the only one to do it."

A sudden image of *how* he would do it crossed her mind, and she resisted the urge to fan herself. "You're an only child?"

"I have a younger sister, but in my father's worldview, the son is the only one who can carry on the family name. According to my mother, my dad lives for the thought of me fathering a son."

"I see." She wondered if he had any idea how sexy he looked standing there talking about doing his familial duty. "Sounds sort of medieval."

"I absolutely agree. And I've said that, but it doesn't seem to make any impression."

"At least I don't have that kind of pressure. My two brothers and my sister are providing the next generation of Tierneys." She ripped the plastic off the pizza.

"Do you happen to know if there's a pizza pan any-where?"

"There should be." He started opening doors. "I seem to remember seeing one when Jillian unloaded cabinets so I could refinish them. Yeah, here it is." He pulled a large flat pan from a bottom cupboard.

She took the pan from him and deposited the frozen pizza on it. "You refinished the cabinets?"

"Last year. They needed it."

Gazing around, she had new appreciation for the honey glow of the oak. "Nice job."

"That's the kind of work I like the most, the kind where you can see a difference after you're finished. Wiring and plumbing are sort of fun, but they're not as creative."

In her preoccupation with Mac, she'd forgotten to turn on the oven, so she did that. The pizza had to thaw a little bit, anyway. "So you enjoy your work."

"I love it. Maintaining vacation homes around the lake is my idea of paradise. I set my own schedule and the views are amazing. Sometimes I'm crazy busy, but when there's a lull, I go camping and chill out."

"And you're happy."

"Hell, yeah, I'm happy."

"You don't feel that you need a woman to complete the picture?"

He scrutinized her. "Is that a trick question?"

"No, it's a serious question."

"You mean, do I think I have to get married to be happy?"

"Right."

"The answer is no, I don't."

"Hallelujah!" She punched her fist in the air. "I knew I wasn't the only oddball out there!"

"I take it you don't have the need to rush to the altar, either?"

"Definitely not. Hotel management is demanding, which is fine, because as a single person I can devote myself to it. But if I had to work around a husband's expectations, I'd feel torn."

"Depends upon the expectations."

She gazed at him and realized she'd never felt free to discuss this with a man before. "I work very weird hours sometimes, and I couldn't be counted on to cook and clean, let alone take care of a baby."

"I hate to think that's the current definition of what a wife does. I'd like to believe we've made some progress."

"There are guys who would do those jobs, or would be happy to hire a cleaning lady and a nanny, and eat out a lot. But they'd still expect my attention some of the time."

He smiled. "Yeah, that's fair to say."

"I just don't know if I have that time—not to mention the energy—to give the proper amount of attention to a partner."

He studied her. "You would if it mattered enough."

"Then maybe it doesn't."

"Does your family get that?"

She shook her head. "My family is into marriage.

That comes before everything else, as if a person must be coupled up to have a fulfilling life. I just don't believe that."

"For that matter, neither do I."

"Then let's get this pizza in the oven so we can sit by the fire and drink to that." Beth slipped the pizza pan into the hot oven, set the timer and walked back into the living room where Mac was filling both their wineglasses. She felt euphoric. She'd found a man who agreed that marriage wasn't the be-all and end-all of existence.

She picked up her glass from the end table and touched it to his. "To being single and loving it."

He looked into her eyes. "To making our own choices."

"Exactly. Down with blind dates." Then she remembered he still had one to deal with and made a face. "Sorry."

"Don't be." He glanced out the window. "Something tells me the weather is going to keep me from making it to Reno tomorrow to meet Stephanie, anyway."

"Really?"

"Well, not really. I have new snow tires and I'll bet I could make it if I wanted to, but I don't. My mom said she couldn't uninvite Stephanie, so I've decided I just won't be there. The roads are going to be too dangerous. I'm sure of it."

Beth had a moment of misgiving. "I'm probably a bad influence."

"No, you're a good influence." He lifted his glass in her direction. "Thanks, Beth."

"You're welcome." She sipped her wine and tried to ignore the guilt whispering through her mind. What if Stephanie was perfect for him? His mother knew him well and she might have found his ideal mate.

Once they were settled on the couch, she turned to him. "Have you liked any of the women your parents have fixed you up with?"

"I've liked most of them. But that doesn't mean any of them was someone I envisioned spending my life with."

"Yeah, same here with the men my folks have brought around."

"To start with, there has to be plenty of chemistry. You know, a certain zing."

"Right." She wondered if anything was zinging for him when he looked at her. She was experiencing some serious zing regarding him. But if he didn't go to Reno, he might miss out on a fabulous meal. "Is your mom a good cook?"

"Do bears live in the woods?" He grinned as he relaxed against the cushions with his wineglass cupped in one large hand. "Yeah, she's great."

"So she's a wonderful cook, which means you would be able to enjoy a feast tomorrow."

"Granted, I'd be well fed, but I'd pay for it. Believe me, turkey with all the trimmings doesn't taste nearly as good when you're expected to entertain someone you've never met who has been carefully selected as a potential fiancée."

Beth sighed. "I know. Believe me, I know." She hesitated. She was only a mediocre cook at best, but what the hell. "You could come over and share my Cornish game hen, although I warn you, it won't be anything like a full Thanksgiving dinner, and I'm no gourmet chef."

His eyes lit up, but then he shook his head. "I don't want to interrupt your plans. You probably had it figured out so you wouldn't have to go shopping while you were here. I can't believe you have enough to feed me, too. I eat a lot."

"So what if we do use up what I have? It's not as if we're that far from civilization." She gestured out the window. "Down the road a bit are a whole bunch of hotels and casinos. If those snow tires work as well as you say, you can always buy me dinner if the provisions give out here."

"I could do that."

She realized then what she'd said and her cheeks warmed with embarrassment. "Wait. I'm sounding pushy. I wasn't implying that you would stick around that long, and I certainly didn't mean to suggest you had to invite me out." *Way to go, Tierney.*

"Easy, Beth." He smiled. "You're not being the least bit pushy, if that's what you're worried about."

"I am worried about that. First I talk you into abandoning your mother's turkey-day feast, and then I invite myself on a dinner date. I may be in management, but I swear I'm not a bossy person."

"You didn't talk me into anything. You inspired me to take my destiny into my own hands for a change. If I accept your invitation for Cornish game hen, then I'll damn well be sure to return the favor with a dinner at a restaurant later on. For that matter, we could eat out tomorrow, if you want. The casino restaurants will be open."

She gazed at him. "No, I think we should cook our own version of Thanksgiving dinner right here, as part of our new declaration of independence from family meddling. We'll count all our blessings for the life we have, not the one everyone else thinks we should have." She took a deep breath. "That is, if you want to."

"I do. It's a great idea."

"I like it, too."

And she liked him. So far, she liked him better than any man she'd met in a long time. If she were in the market for a serious relationship… But she wasn't. That was the whole point.

She probably felt more free and at ease with Mac because she'd decided that marriage wasn't for her. No pressure. They could discuss this issue without it being a loaded topic. "Have you ever come close to getting married?"

Mac sipped his wine and stared at the flames licking at the dry wood. "A couple of times, but then other things weren't right about the relationship. In one case she was determined to make it on Broadway, and neither of us wanted to change our lives to accommodate the other one."

"How about the second person?"

"She was a lot of fun, but not quite what you'd call mature. Eventually I got tired of being the only grown-up in the relationship." He sighed. "Marriage is a big deal and I'd want to get it right. I guess maybe I'm too picky."

"That's what my family says about me, too." From the corner of her eye she could see that he was looking at her instead of the fire, so she turned to face him. "But how can you not be picky when the stakes are so high?"

"That's what I think, too. But how about you? Ever come close?"

"I've had two different guys propose."

"That's pretty damn close. I mean, usually a guy won't ask unless he thinks you're likely to say yes."

Beth groaned. "I know, and I felt awful each time because I turned them down."

"So I figured."

"But I swear, Mac, neither of them listened when I said how much I love my job and how it monopolizes my life. One of them suggested that because I love the hospitality industry I'd make a great hostess when he had to entertain out-of-town clients. He expected me to cut back to part-time so I'd be free to do that."

"Marriage shouldn't be about giving up things you love to do."

"No."

"But there's..." He paused to clear his throat. "There's one small problem with the concept of a happy single life."

"What's that?"

He took another drink of his wine. "How does sex fit into the plan?" He glanced over at her. "Or are you saying you're willing to give that up?"

"I'd rather not." When she met his gaze, she felt that zing again. It scooted through her body and ignited various significant parts of it. Unless she was mistaken, the feeling was mutual.

"I don't want to give it up, either." After another charged moment, he broke eye contact and stared into the fire, as if realizing they might each need a moment to decide where to go from here.

Maybe she should drop the subject, which was becoming quite personal. But she found she couldn't let it go. This was a question she'd wrestled with and never had the chance to discuss with a guy, especially a virile one like Mac. "I mean, we're both pretty young to be celibate."

"I know, but I'm not crazy about one-night stands, and deciding to go beyond that implies a certain level of commitment, doesn't it?" He looked over at her, his gaze reflecting his uncertainty.

She swallowed. This discussion was heating up faster than the blaze in the fireplace. "Yes, I suppose, but the commitment can be limited."

"Can it, really? In my experience, the more you

have sex with someone, the more they start thinking of making the relationship permanent."

"I wouldn't." Now, how had that popped out? She took a deep breath. "Speaking hypothetically, of course."

"Of course." He studied the fire some more, and drummed his fingers softly against his knee.

She hoped he hadn't thought she was propositioning him with her remark. She hadn't been, but if she tried to explain, it would be even more awkward.

As she tried to figure out how to reestablish the casual mood they'd enjoyed before they'd started discussing sex, he put his wineglass on the end table and stood.

"Listen, before I drink more wine or the roads get any worse, I need to make a quick trip to my cabin."

"Uh, okay." She waited for him to tell her why.

He retrieved his coat from the chair in the kitchen. "I'll be right back. Keep the pizza hot."

Still, she expected him to say what was so important that he had to take care of it immediately. "Do you have a dog?"

"No." He headed for the door. "See you soon. My cabin isn't far." And then he was gone.

She stared at the closed door for a long time and tried to figure out what was going on. Most men would have come up with some excuse as to why they were leaving, even if they didn't want to admit the real reason. Maybe he wasn't good at making excuses, which was actually kind of refreshing.

The timer dinged, telling her the pizza was done. She switched off the oven and hoped the pizza wouldn't dry out while he was gone. He'd said he'd be right back.

In the meantime, she could work more on her project to embrace her single status. She titled the next section of her notes "Reasons Why I Love Living Alone!!!" Setting down her wineglass, she made a long list. When she got home she'd type it up, print it and frame it to keep her focused.

CHAPTER THREE

NOT THE MOST GRACEFUL EXIT in the world, Mac thought as he drove carefully through the snowstorm to his cabin. He knew Beth had been expecting some sort of explanation, but his reasons for leaving were varied and complicated, and he wasn't prepared to give Beth any of them, at least not until he'd thought things through.

Although the heater was on, the engine wasn't warm enough to heat up the cab, which was fine with him. The cold air helped him think, and he needed to think. Because his gut was telling him that, after all these years of dating, all the fix-ups arranged by his parents, he'd just met the woman he was going to marry.

Which was crazy. He didn't believe in that kind of instant recognition. He'd known her for—he consulted his watch—less than two hours.

Amazingly, that didn't seem to matter. His strong reaction defied all logic, but the longer he was with her, the more certain he became that she was the one he could build a life with.

And yet that made no sense, considering she was the first woman he'd ever met who seriously didn't need him. She didn't need him to make her feel good about herself, and she certainly didn't need him to take care of her. She might need him in a physical sense, but she'd just finished saying that having sex didn't necessarily imply a commitment of any kind.

Parking in front of his cabin, he sat in the cab and took a few deep breaths as he tried to rationalize his crazy response to Beth. She was beautiful. True, but he'd dated beautiful women before without having this instinctive connection.

The chemistry was there, but he'd felt chemistry before. Maybe not quite this strong, but close.

He couldn't remember ever being in such a rush to close the deal and create that ultimate physical connection with a particular woman.

Maybe it was her self-sufficiency. He enjoyed fixing things for his clients, but what a relief to find someone who didn't expect him to fix anything. Yeah... Much to his surprise, he was drawn to her independent nature.

And, he had to admit, she presented a challenge. Maybe by stating that she was totally uninterested in finding a husband, she'd aroused a need in him to prove her wrong. He hoped to hell that wasn't true. He took the subject of marriage too seriously to make it into a game.

Not that it mattered now. She probably thought he was a nutcase after he'd blown out of there without an explanation. But he couldn't exactly blurt out that he'd needed some space to analyze his strong reaction to her.

And he definitely hadn't been willing to tell her his other, more practical reason for leaving.

Their discussion about sex had been going in one direction—toward the bedroom. If Beth asked him to stay the night, he wanted to be able to say yes, and that meant being prepared.

He could be wrong. She might not ask him…but then again, he had been sent over by Jillian Vickers. Jillian knew him pretty well, and her matchmaking efforts were uncannily on target, so chances were, she knew Beth pretty well, too.

Then he remembered the sociology experiment that Ken and Jillian had going on and groaned. Of course. He and Beth were part of the study. Now, there was a spooky thought. Was everything he was feeling just the cabin mojo screwing with his mind?

No. He'd rather believe in love at first sight than magic cabins. Ken and Jillian were convinced the cabin had saved their marriage, but Mac thought it more likely that all they'd needed was a secluded spot to concentrate on each other. They could have been in the middle of the Sahara or on top of Mount Rushmore.

And their renters were discovering romance in the cabin for the same reason—it created a sense of intimacy.

But that didn't explain his mind-set. He'd spent

time with women in similar cabins, including his own, and never felt this urgent compulsion to bond.

Still, the Vickers' cabin was a charmer. Whoever had designed it originally had made the front half open and cheery, with the living room and kitchen blending into each other, and the back half cozy and… yes…romantic, with only one bedroom and one bath opening off it.

The king-size bed was massive and rustic. Jillian had found a bedspread made out of soft velour. Mac had run his hand over it once and it felt incredible. For the bathroom, Ken had located an oversize claw-foot tub and Mac had installed it as an anniversary present.

Considering the amenities, not to mention the hot tub on the back porch, Mac could easily see why couples left feeling more loving toward each other than when they'd arrived. He'd mention all that when he explained the experiment to Beth. She deserved to know that they were guinea pigs.

For now, though, he should head over there before she wondered if he'd run off into a ditch. Leaving the engine running, he navigated around the snowdrifts on his front porch and unlocked the front door. Once inside, he walked quickly to the bathroom and took the box of condoms from the cabinet under the sink. He tucked them into his coat pocket and started to leave.

He was nearly out the door when he realized that he'd have to return with something else that would justify his trip home. Arriving at her front door with a box of condoms in hand was just not classy.

So what to take back to her? Wine would be great—if he had any, which he didn't. A six-pack of beer wouldn't work if she favored wine. His fruit bowl on the counter held two overripe bananas. They needed to be eaten, but showing up with a couple of brownish bananas didn't strike the right note.

His refrigerator wasn't much help. It contained half a loaf of wheat bread, six eggs, an open quart of milk, some leftover microwave lasagna and the beer. He'd deliberately let his food supplies dwindle because his mother always loaded him up with leftovers.

He didn't have much in his cupboards—crackers that were probably stale by now, a few cans of soup, a can of regular coffee and some boxed macaroni and cheese. None of that cried out Hostess Gift. Instead it cried out Bachelor Who Doesn't Cook.

He considered making up some story that he'd left his TV or his coffeepot on. But then he could have just said that as he was leaving her place. Instead, he'd dashed out as if his tail was on fire.

Turning on a light in his small living room, he glanced around. Reading material? That would be lame, as if he had to bring along his own entertainment. And then he spied his stack of board games.

She might not care for board games, but he did. He took the combination checkers/chess set and Sorry!, one of his favorites because it wasn't rocket science. She might think he was a dork for disappearing abruptly and then returning with board games, but he'd brave it out.

The return trip was hairy, and he almost skidded off the pavement twice. Not many vehicles were on the road, which was lucky because at times he needed to go smack down the middle of it. He could see the lights of snowplows down on the main highway, but they wouldn't get up here tonight.

That meant he could be snowed in all night with Beth, whether they wanted to be that cozy or not. If he'd guessed wrong about her interest in him, he could always take the couch. Maybe he wouldn't have to tell his mother a little white lie about road conditions, after all.

As he pulled up in front of the Vickers' cabin, he decided to make that call to his mother before he forgot. Particularly since forgetting was a distinct possibility once he focused on Beth. He got his mother on the first ring.

"Conneach, I've been thinking about you. How's the weather up your way?"

"That's why I'm calling, Mom. It's blizzard conditions. I doubt seriously I'll be able to get out of here tomorrow."

"Oh, Conneach. What a disappointment."

Guilt stabbed him, but he wasn't going to back down after proclaiming to Beth that he was joining her for a feast of independence. "I'm disappointed, too, but I know you don't want me on the road if it's dangerous."

"No, of course I don't. If anything changes, come on, anyway. We'll have plenty of food."

"I know, but don't count on me."

"We could postpone until the next day. Your dad's closing the office on Friday, which means Stephanie will be off, too."

Mac hoped he wouldn't go to hell for lying to his mother. He couldn't very well tell her he'd met the woman of his dreams, even if that turned out to be the truth. "I promised a customer I'd install some new bathroom lighting on Friday, Mom. Sorry about that."

"Then I'll package up the leftovers and keep them until you can make it down here. What's your food situation? Will you have enough to eat?"

"I'll be fine. The casinos will be open, don't forget. I can walk there if I have to."

"All right. We'll miss you, but you can meet Stephanie another time. Call if you get the chance, but if I don't talk to you, Happy Thanksgiving."

"Same to you, Mom." He disconnected the call, picked up the board games and opened his door.

A jolt of happiness hit him at the thought of seeing Beth again. It seemed like ages since he'd left.

WHEN BETH HEARD MAC'S TRUCK pull up, she took the pizza out of the oven, found a pizza cutter and shoved it through the slightly hardened crust. The pizza was a little dried out and not terribly hot, but his trip had taken way longer than she'd expected. She was curious about what he'd gone after in such a hurry, and she hoped he'd say.

But if he didn't, she resolved not to pry. After all, they'd just met. She couldn't expect him to lay bare all his secrets right off the bat.

Once she had the pizza cut, she stoked the fire, thinking he'd knock on the door any second. When he didn't, she wondered what was keeping him, but she'd be damned if she'd go to the window and peer out. She stuck the pizza pan back in the oven and poked at the fire some more.

This was exactly what she disliked about getting involved with a man. Instead of doing her own thing as she'd planned, she was hanging around waiting for him to come through the door. He'd given her no reason for his errand, and now he was sitting out in his truck while the pizza got cold.

She'd decided to take the pizza out and start eating, when his knock sounded. Annoyed at herself for allowing this situation to interrupt her plans, she walked over and opened the door.

He stood there, tall, broad-shouldered and beautiful as ever, his coat collar turned up and snow in his hair. His blue gaze was apologetic. "Sorry. Everything took longer than I thought it would. Just now I was calling my mom to cancel for tomorrow. She would have panicked if I hadn't shown up and not told her I couldn't make it."

Her irritation ebbed a little. She stepped back from the door. "How did she take it?"

"Fine." He walked in and she closed and locked the door behind him. "She's disappointed, but she doesn't want me driving if the roads are bad."

She noticed he was carrying something under his arm. "What have you got there?"

"A couple of games. I thought we might—"

Her irritation returned. "Mac, I don't want to get all up in your business, but this is getting weird. You leave abruptly with no explanation, and then you return a long time later with a couple of board games."

"You don't like board games?"

"That's not the issue, and besides, Ken and Jillian have a cupboard full of games. You've been here a lot over the years, so you must know about the games closet. This isn't adding up."

He put the games on the kitchen table and blew out a breath. "Hell."

"Look, if it's something personal, like you have a health problem and had to go back to take your meds, you should just say so instead of making me resort to using my imagination. For all I know, you have another woman stashed at your cabin and you had to go make some excuse to *her*. I—"

"I don't have another woman stashed in my cabin, and I don't have any health problems." He reached in his pocket. "I went back for these."

He pulled out a box of Trojans and she stared at it, not sure how a girl was supposed to react to *that*.

He tucked the box back in his pocket. "I couldn't think of a way to broach the subject that wouldn't be awkward…and then I messed it up anyway. Look, I'm very attracted to you, and I think you might be attracted to me. When we started talking about sex, I…didn't want to presume, but…I just thought these were good to have on hand."

He was just too cute for words. Cute, and yummy, and adorably trustworthy. Heat unfurled within her already aroused body. But she still wasn't sure what to say that wouldn't make her sound like a woman who could hardly wait to jump into bed with him.

"But don't think I brought these over because I expect anything, because I don't. I'm not making assumptions, and I wasn't even going to mention them unless…well, unless…"

"We needed one?" As juicy as she was feeling right now, she'd lay odds that they would.

"Yeah."

"So the board games were your cover story." She'd never encountered such an endearing combination of uncertainty and confidence in a man.

"A damn lame one, at that. I'd forgotten about the games cupboard." He gazed at her. "Obviously I've screwed this up royally, and if you'd like me to head on back to my cabin, I wouldn't blame you."

"I don't want you to head back."

"Then let's just forget you ever saw that box, okay?"

She smiled. "No chance."

"You never know. Once you're into a hot game of Sorry!, you could block out everything else."

She looked more closely at the boxes on the table. "You brought Sorry!? I used to love that game. Haven't played it in years."

"Great! We'll definitely play it, then." He seemed relieved at the change in topic. "I brought checkers and chess so you wouldn't think I'm an intellectual lightweight, but I'd really rather play Sorry!. It's way more relaxing."

"At the risk of having you think *I'm* an intellectual lightweight, I'd much rather play Sorry!, myself. Chess gives me a headache."

"Me, too." He took off his coat and draped it over a kitchen chair.

She considered suggesting he hang it on one of the hooks by the door beside hers, but any discussion involving the coat would be loaded with subtext because of what the pocket contained. She decided it could stay right on the back of a chair. Handy.

"The pizza smells good."

"I'm afraid it's not very warm anymore. I'll turn the oven on again for a few minutes." She started toward the stove.

"Hey, don't bother." He caught her arm as she walked past him.

She glanced up at him the same moment he touched her, and she came to an instant and complete stop. She even held her breath as she met his gaze and focused on the sensation of those strong fingers gripping her upper arm.

His fingers felt cold, even through her sweatshirt.

Of course they would be. He'd been outside and hadn't worn gloves. But there was nothing cold about the look in his eyes.

He let go of her almost immediately, but his breathing wasn't quite as steady as it had been before. "I... uh, often eat cold pizza."

"So do I, but this time we don't have to." She paused. "Unless you're in a rush?"

"No." He took a deep breath. "No. I think we should take our time."

Her heart rate kicked up a notch. He wasn't talking about the pizza, and they both knew it. "I'll turn on the oven and open another bottle of wine if you'll see to the fire."

"Be happy to."

Moments later they were sitting on the couch, each on their respective ends, but neither of them hugged the corners the way they had an hour ago. Beth decided to take it a step further. She pulled off her monkey slippers and curled her feet under her before picking up her wineglass.

"Great slippers."

"Thanks. I could have bought a zip-up sock-monkey sleeper with feet, but I wasn't ready to regress that far into my childhood."

Mac laughed. "But you thought about getting it, didn't you?"

"For about ten seconds, yes, I did. It looked cozy."

"Speaking of cozy, this sure is." He cradled his

wineglass in one large hand and let out his breath in a contented sigh.

She smiled. "Yes…I can't remember the last time I just…sat. We probably both work too hard. I hardly ever slow down enough to relax in front of a fire and talk." She sipped her wine.

Talking was good. It could lead to other things. Kissing would be good, too. She couldn't help stealing glances at his mouth and wondered what kissing him would be like.

"Turns out there's something specific we need to talk about, though."

"Like what?" Uneasiness pricked her bubble of contentment. She should have known this was all too good to be true.

"Do you know why Ken and Jillian bought this place?"

She glanced over at him. "If you're about to tell me it's haunted, I don't want to hear it. I'm a real wuss when it comes to scary stuff."

Mac swallowed a mouthful of wine and shook his head. "Nothing like that. They bought it because they rented it for a weekend and it put their marriage back on track."

"Aw. Now, that's sweet. I'm happy for them. But what does that have to do with us?"

He looked at her. "It seems that when they began leasing it out for the winter holidays, renters left notes saying they, too, had discovered or rediscovered love in this cabin."

"How nice."

"Yeah, except *everyone* left a note like that."

"Everyone?" Beth scooted around and rested her back against the arm of the couch, so she was sitting cross-legged, facing him. "That's quite a coincidence."

"I know. So now Ken and Jillian, being sociologists, are collecting data so they can study the phenomenon." He paused to take another sip.

"Are you saying we're part of a sociology experiment?"

"I'm afraid so." Angling his knee across the cushion, he shifted so that he was facing her, too. "Did you have a question on your rental agreement asking why you wanted to stay here?"

"Yes."

"They added that to collect more data. What did you say?"

"That I wanted to spend the weekend letting go of any pressure to find a husband and joyfully embrace being single." Her breath caught. "We're a test, aren't we? A test of the cabin's influence!"

"I think we are." He gazed at her. "So how do you feel about that?"

"It's ridiculous. Until a couple of hours ago, you and I had never laid eyes on each other. If they think we're going to meet and instantly fall in love in a couple of days, they're delusional. And for the record, I don't buy the magic-cabin angle."

"Neither do I."

"You know, they probably don't buy it, either.

They're scientists. They're not trying to prove the cabin is magic. They're trying to prove it *isn't* by throwing together two people who are perfectly happy being single."

"Could be."

Beth relaxed against the plump arm of the couch. "Okay, I feel better now that I've figured that out. I admire them both, and I'd hate to think that they've gone loony tunes since I was in Jillian's class eleven years ago."

"So that's the connection. I wondered."

"She and I really clicked, and so I've kept in touch with her over the years. Nothing elaborate, just a phone call once in a while. I'm sure other students have, too. She was that kind of teacher. But we weren't close enough that she'd confide a marital problem."

"Yeah, I didn't find that out until I'd known them for a while. Ken told me after we'd each had a couple of beers." He drained his wineglass. "I think the world of them, too. I just never figured on being part of an experiment."

She leaned forward. "And how do *you* feel about the situation?"

"At first I was irritated." He turned the glass slowly in his hand and watched as it caught the reflection of the fire. "Jillian knows how I feel about my mom fixing me up all the time, so I thought she had a lot of nerve to do it herself. But then..." He looked up and smiled at her. "Then I realized that I'd be an idiot not to take all the time I could get with such a beautiful woman, set up or not."

"Thank you." That smile of his packed a punch. She felt the light brush of panic as she realized how easily she *could* fall for him, magic cabin or not. Better nip that in the bud right now. "Luckily there's no danger that either of us will consider this the first step toward getting engaged."

An unreadable emotion flickered in his eyes. "That would be crazy, wouldn't it?" He set his wineglass on the table and shifted his position on the couch, effectively bringing him closer to her.

"Yep, crazy." But not all that unappealing. Yes, she'd have to be very careful. "For the first time in I don't know how long, I can just relax and enjoy being with a man. And that's special."

"It's special for me, too." He smiled as he leaned toward her.

She mirrored his movements. He was almost within kissing range. She was about to close her eyes in preparation for being kissed when the smoke alarm went off.

They broke apart and she jumped up to discover the kitchen was rapidly filling with smoke from the oven. "That would be our pizza burned to a crisp."

Moving quickly, she switched off the oven and pulled out the charred remains of the pizza while Mac opened the kitchen window and waved the smoke away from the alarm mounted on the wall.

"Stand back." She carried the smoking pizza to the front door. "I'm putting this out in the snow."

"Not in your bare feet." He deftly removed the pan, pot holders and all, from her grip. "While I take this out, you can close the window."

She hurried to do that as the smoke alarm sputtered into silence.

In seconds he was back, rubbing his arms and shivering. "News flash, it's very cold out there."

"I'm sorry, Mac." She stepped closer, wondering if they'd progressed to the stage where she could hug him and warm him up. "That was our dinner, and now it's ruined."

"No worries." He answered her unspoken question by drawing her slowly into his arms. "Here's another news flash—I'm not really here for the food, anyway."

CHAPTER FOUR

ALL THROUGH THEIR CONVERSATION on the couch, Mac had been thinking his reaction to Beth was only growing more intense the longer they were together. Meanwhile, she kept reminding him that it wouldn't lead to anything significant.

He'd decided he'd be a better judge of that after he kissed her. Leaning across a large couch wasn't the most graceful way to make a move, though. If either of them had lost their balance, the kiss could have gotten ugly fast.

Then the smoke alarm had screeched—a blessing in disguise because now they were upright, giving him the chance to gather her close and align his body with hers. He vastly preferred kissing a woman while employing full-on body contact.

God, she felt good, and she smelled even better; the cinnamon he'd noticed earlier blended with a scent that made his blood race. He gazed into her soft green eyes and brushed his thumbs lightly over her cheeks, which had a light dusting of freckles.

Her eyelashes fluttered and then she closed her eyes with a tiny sigh, drawing his attention to her full mouth. She wore no lipstick, but the natural pale rose of her lips turned him on far more than if she'd been wearing the kind of bright color he'd seen in commercials, the kind that was supposed to drive men wild.

Personally, he'd never agreed with that. Unadorned mouths were sexier, especially when they parted in a subtle invitation every red-blooded man understood.

His groin tightened. He wanted to press his mouth against hers, wanted to grant her unspoken wish that he slide his tongue between her lips and discover her secrets. And yet…

Her stand on commitment was clear—she was through seeking it. Only, whenever he looked at her, he saw his future. The belief was irrational and foolish, and he knew it would only set him up for heartbreak. He'd never allowed himself to be so vulnerable to a woman, to need someone who might not need him back.

Then she took the decision away from him. Gripping the back of his head in both hands, she pulled him down into…paradise.

As his protective shields slipped away, he wondered if he'd live to regret this moment. He'd take that chance. Submerging his doubts, he surrendered to the absolute perfection of her kiss.

Their mouths seemed made for each other. His brain stalled out but his instincts took over, guiding him through this wonderland of sensations. She tasted of wine and desire, freedom and adventure. Her kiss hinted at exotic delights that could be his in the warm haven of her arms.

His body responded with hot urgency. He'd intended the kiss to be a gentle exploration of the possibilities between them. Instead, she'd plunged him into a world drenched in passion, leaving him breathless and dazed.

With a soft moan, she wriggled free and stepped back, gulping for air. "You wanted...to go...slow."

"To hell with that." He pulled her into his arms again and recaptured her mouth. They could go slow the next round. For now, he needed her with a desperation that he hadn't experienced in a long time. And that felt good, damn good.

He was so eager that he briefly considered backing her up to the kitchen table. He didn't think he'd get any objection from her. She'd already started unbuttoning his shirt.

But that soft covering on the king-size bed called to him. Fortunately, the bedroom opened right off the kitchen.

He stopped kissing her long enough to reach into his coat pocket and grab the box of condoms.

Handing her the box, he swooped her up in his arms, carried her into the darkened bedroom and deposited her crossways on the bed. She lay in a shaft of light coming from the kitchen, her chest heaving. He took the box from her and tossed it aside, and then he followed her down.

He should stop long enough to take off his work boots, but he couldn't seem to get enough of her mouth, so he made sure his feet stayed on the floor.

She kissed like no other woman he'd known, as if nothing else mattered but that sweet connection.

If her mouth tasted this good, the rest of her must be even better. Between kisses, he began working her out of her clothes. Once her sweatshirt and bra were gone, he set out on a journey of discovery that took him from her lips to the fullness of her breasts.

She whimpered and arched her back as he drew her nipple into his mouth. He cupped her other breast, loving the way she fit perfectly into his hand. He reveled in the silky texture of her skin and the heady aroma of cinnamon and aroused woman.

Touching her was as natural as breathing. She was exotic and new, yet familiar, as if they'd danced this dance before and knew each other's moves. When she moaned softly, he understood without words what she wanted. Sliding his hand inside her panties, he caressed her slick heat.

She gasped and began to quiver.

He continued to stroke her as he slowly kissed his way up from her breasts to recapture her mouth. She returned the kiss with unrestrained hunger, and when he lifted his head, she tried to draw him back down.

He resisted. "Open your eyes," he murmured.

Her lashes fluttered upward, revealing eyes that had grown dark and stormy with need. She said his name on a sigh. "Mac…"

"I'm here." He thrust two fingers in deeper.

"Oh, Mac…it's so good."

"That's the idea." He stroked her with a slow,

steady rhythm and watched color bloom on her cheeks. Pressure built within him, pressure that would have to be dealt with soon, but he wanted to give her this first. He circled her clit with his thumb.

She moaned and lifted her hips, a silent plea in her eyes.

That was his cue to increase the pace. Her soft cries grew louder as he propelled her ever closer toward the brink. Holding her gaze, he paid special attention to her trigger point, and she arched off the bed with a wild cry of release.

As she lay trembling beside him, he leaned down and feathered kisses over her cheeks and mouth. "Happy Thanksgiving."

Her breathless laughter seemed to fill the room with sunshine. "I do like the way you celebrate, Mc-Farland."

"That's only the beginning." Easing away from her, he sat on the edge of the bed and unlaced his work boots.

"Mighty fine beginning."

He glanced over his shoulder and caught her smiling at him in a lazy, sensual way. "Thanks. It's easy with someone as enthusiastic as you are."

"I don't want to give you a big ego, but I'm not always so…enthusiastic."

"No?" He dropped one boot on the floor, pulled off his sock and started on the laces of the second boot. "That's flattering."

"That's the truth. You're one sexy guy."

He paused for a moment. "Some women I know wouldn't agree with you." He dropped the other boot and stood to take off his shirt and jeans.

"Why in the world not?"

"For one thing, I don't own a tux. I've heard women prefer seeing a guy in one of those monkey suits. I guess it's a James Bond thing." He finished stripping down.

"Their loss. Any woman who bases her opinion on your wardrobe isn't worthy of you."

Her compliment soothed a part of him he hadn't realized needed it. "That's nice to hear." He started to join her on the bed.

She held up her hand. "Could you just stand there a second? It's not every day a girl gets to ogle a man like you."

"Now you're being silly." He wasn't used to posing for anyone, and he felt a little self-conscious. "There's nothing special about me."

"That's *so* not true. For one thing, you're gorgeous, and for another thing, you're a responsible guy who takes pride in his work. It's a special combination."

He felt his face grow warm. "I wasn't fishing for—"

"You wouldn't, but I wanted you to know that I feel lucky to be here with you." Her gaze roamed over him and focused on his erect penis. She smiled. "Very lucky."

His self-consciousness disappeared as he laughed.

"That reaction is entirely your fault. You're the sexiest woman I've met in ages."

"Some men I know wouldn't agree with you," she said, echoing his phrase.

"I doubt that."

"Just like women prefer monkey suits, there are men who want their woman to parade around in fishnet stockings and bustiers, and I'm not willing to jump through those hoops just because some guy has a hooker fantasy."

"I've never understood that kind of thing. Who needs the hassle?"

"And that stuff is horribly uncomfortable."

"I'll bet. Personally, I prefer a woman in sweats. They come off really fast." Leaning down, he demonstrated that by divested her of sweatpants and panties in one smooth motion.

She whooped with delight. "Nice move. Very superhero-like."

"Now you're teasing me."

"No." Her smile faded. "I would never tease you about your childhood dreams. No matter what you think, you've achieved them. You're about as super a hero as I've ever run across, braving a blizzard to bring back condoms."

He climbed onto the mattress. "And it's time to open that box."

"I'll do it." Rolling away from him, she reached for the box. "I want you to lie on this incredibly erotic bedspread and let me tend to your needs."

"Aren't you cold? We could get under the—"

"I'm not even slightly cold." She pulled a condom out of the box and ripped the package open. "And if you are, you won't be for long. Lie back."

He stretched out on the bedspread, and lying naked on the soft material was as sinfully decadent as he'd imagined. He'd have to exercise a truckload of self-control if she was planning to— He twitched as she touched his rock-hard penis.

"Take it easy, big boy." She began rolling the condom on. "This will be over in a second."

"That's what I'm worried about." She'd called him a superhero, and he'd always imagined those guys could control their climaxes as easily as they changed the rotation of the earth. Nobody ever talked about a superhero in terms of sex, but Mac had his own ideas about the subject.

"I would love to play a little with this lovely package of yours, but from the way you're clenching your jaw, I think I'd better not."

"Good call."

He sounded frantic but couldn't help it. He was very close to detonating, and watching her put on the condom, her breasts quivering as she worked, her fingers caressing his already overstimulated penis, was almost more than he could take.

"We'll play the next round."

Until she'd said that, it hadn't quite penetrated his brain that he had the whole night to enjoy this woman.

And if the night went well, he'd have tomorrow, too. That was quite a lot to be thankful for.

Then she straddled him and eased slowly down on his aching Johnson, and *thankful* became a sea of gratitude. She took him up to the hilt, and he grabbed two handfuls of the bedspread as he battled the urge to come. She was…perfect.

She leaned forward, her gaze meeting his as she braced her hands on either side of his shoulders. "Cold?"

He struggled to breathe normally. "Not at all."

"Good. Comfy?"

"I'm a little…tense."

"I can tell."

"Don't move yet." Her breasts tantalized him, but if he touched her, he'd go off like a rocket, so he contented himself with admiration.

The light from the kitchen outlined her in gold, giving her an angelic glow. Her face was in shadow, but he caught a lustful gleam in her eyes that hinted she was no angel. He was grateful for that, too.

She held still as he'd requested, although her breasts trembled from her rapid breathing. She might be a little tense, herself. He hoped so. He wanted to make her come again before he lost control.

She cleared her throat. "Sitting by the fire is nice, but this…is nicer."

"Uh-huh."

"Maybe next time we can do both."

"Both?" His brain wasn't functioning at all.

"Sex by the fire."

"Oh. I'd like that." Now, *there* was the understatement of the century. He desperately wanted to touch her. Focusing all his energy on not coming, he bracketed her hips with both hands and groaned at how soft her skin felt beneath his fingertips. "You're beautiful."

"Can I move now?"

"In a minute." Sliding his hands over her hips to her waist, he stroked upward to cup her breasts. His climax hovered nearer as he brushed his thumbs over her nipples. "So beautiful."

Her smooth channel contracted, squeezing his cock, and he gasped.

"Couldn't stop myself." She leaned closer, pushing her breasts into his palms as she dropped a featherlight kiss on his lips. "I can't hold back anymore. I have to move."

His heartbeat thundered in his ears. "Go for it."

She began slowly, lifting and lowering her hips in a gentle rhythm, her breath warm on his face. He felt his control slipping as he rose to meet her next stroke and the soft bedspread moved sensuously beneath him. She moaned and increased the pace, her sleek bottom slapping his thighs in a staccato beat guaranteed to send him into orbit.

She cried out, and he abandoned all restraint, surging upward as his orgasm vibrated through him with the force of a jackhammer. The intensity of it consumed him, blocking out everything else.

But as awareness gradually returned, he discovered

Beth snuggled against his chest and his arms wrapped protectively around her. She didn't seem to mind. It was a start.

Beth rubbed her cheek against his chest. "Mmm. Your hair feels good."

"Now, *there's* a compliment I don't get every day."

"And I don't give it every day. Some guys have too much chest hair and some don't have enough. Yours is just right."

He smiled. "That sounds like a line from 'The Three Bears.'"

"You mean the story of Goldilocks, child vandal?" She lifted her head and propped it on her fist so she could look at him.

He laughed. "Guess so."

"Now, I ask you, what sort of message does that send? Hey, kids, it's okay to walk into a house uninvited, eat the food and break up the furniture before crawling into someone else's bed."

He combed her hair back from her face. " I take it you won't be reading that story to your kids?"

"Not without some discussion, I won't. Those bears should have pressed charges for breaking and entering."

He brushed his knuckles over her soft cheek. She was exactly the sort of spirited woman he'd been looking for all his life…and she wanted nothing to do with a permanent relationship. "I certainly see your point. When you put it that way, Goldilocks isn't quite so cute, is she?"

"Definitely not. And while we're on the subject of damaging reading material, what about Hansel and Gretel? Their parents were going to kill them, so they ran away and got caught by a witch who planned to *eat* them. No wonder kids have nightmares!"

"I'm glad your kids won't be exposed to that horrible stuff," he said, partly to see how she'd react.

"That's if I ever have any, which doesn't seem likely. But if I did, I wouldn't read them fairy tales without talking about the subtext."

"Good for you." He pulled her down for a quick kiss. At least she hadn't proclaimed she'd never have kids. "Now, if you'll excuse me, I need to make a quick trip to the bathroom."

"And I'll bet you're hungry."

"Come to think of it, I am." He hadn't realized it until this very minute. "In fact, I'm starving. What have you got that we could cook up in a hurry?"

"Eggs."

"Great—omelets." He left the bed and headed for the bathroom.

"Can you make an omelet?" she called after him.

"No," he called back. "Can you?"

"No. I thought all bachelors could whip up an omelet. They always do that in the movies."

"Well, this isn't a movie."

"No kidding. Guess we'll have to make do with scrambled. But I'm not very good at that, either."

He chuckled. "Meet me in the kitchen in five minutes. We'll figure this out together." Damn, but he was having fun. Beth was good company, both in bed and out of it.

As he washed up and walked into the empty bedroom in search of his clothes, he thought about that. Without the pressure of a potential commitment, Beth was free to be totally herself. She could be as sexual as she wanted, rant about her least favorite fairy tales and admit she couldn't make an omelet.

She was being totally honest with him. He felt a stab of guilt, because he wasn't being totally honest with her. He'd allowed her to go on thinking they were a two-person army battling society's preoccupation with marriage.

And at the moment he was AWOL from that army. Listening to Beth rummaging around in the cupboards, he couldn't imagine anything nicer than sharing kitchen duties with her for the rest of his life.

But if he told her that, he'd risk destroying the easy camaraderie between them. She might even ask him to leave and he'd never see her again. He wasn't sure he'd come away from that in one piece emotionally. What a mess. For now, he'd better keep his damn mouth shut.

CHAPTER FIVE

WRAPPED IN HER FAVORITE white terry bathrobe, her sock-monkey slippers on her feet, Beth pulled out a carton of eggs from the refrigerator. It was also her only carton of eggs. If Mac was starving, most of them would soon be cracked into a frying pan, leaving her short for future breakfasts.

But after a romp like the one they'd just had, who cared? She'd worry about the food supply later. Maybe they'd have chips and dip for breakfast. She'd brought those, too, because she hardly ever allowed herself that kind of snack, and this long weekend had been about indulging her private pleasures. Little had she known…

Sex with Mac had been beyond incredible, the kind of sex she used to dream of having back in the days when she still thought Mr. Right would show up. Maybe that had been the problem. Two people couldn't have great sex if they were both auditioning for a future partner. Because she and Mac were free of those expectations, they could simply enjoy each other.

Opening cupboard doors, which she now appreciated even more knowing Mac's capable hands had done the refinishing, she located a medium-size bowl and a frying pan. The frying pan was stainless steel instead of nonstick, so she was probably already in trouble. In her limited experience, eggs had a nasty habit of sticking to the bottom of frying pans.

Maybe Mac was more skilled than she was in the kitchen. The chances were good, since almost anyone would be more skilled. She'd never been drawn to cooking, and working in hotel management allowed her to eat meals prepared by the chef she'd hired.

Sergei, her current chef, had offered to provide her with precooked food to bring up here. She should have taken him up on it, but in a moment of temporary insanity, she'd told him she wanted to try making a modified Thanksgiving dinner herself. He'd recommended Cornish hen as being simple and easy.

"Smells good." Mac walked out of the bedroom wearing his jeans and shirt. He'd put on his socks, but not his shoes, and his dark hair was rumpled.

She tried not to stare, but he was easily the most gorgeous man she'd ever shared a kitchen with. "I haven't cooked anything yet."

"Then it must be you that smells so delicious." He walked over, drew her into his arms and leaned down to sniff the curve of her neck. "It's you. You smell like apple pie." He nuzzled behind her ear.

She was so easy. One little nuzzle and her body turned into soft wax. She put up a token protest. "We need to cook up these eggs."

"I'm not as interested in the eggs as I thought."

Loosening the tie of her robe, he slipped his hands inside. "Matter of fact, I don't give a damn about the eggs."

As he caressed her, moving his hands over her breasts, her tummy, and finally reaching between her thighs, she couldn't work up much enthusiasm for the eggs, either. "You said you were hungry."

"I am." He backed her against the counter. "But I have a taste for something else." As her robe fell open, he dropped to his knees.

He nudged her thighs apart. "I never could resist a woman wearing sock-monkey slippers." His warm breath touched her very wet curls.

She shivered in anticipation. When his tongue made contact, she lost all inclination to resist. Not only that, but she aided and abetted, tilting her hips forward and tunneling her fingers through his hair to hold him right there…right *there.* He was just as skilled with his mouth as he was with his hands, bringing her to a climax in an embarrassingly short time.

As her world spun crazily, he rose to his feet and kissed her full on the mouth, bringing with him the flavor of unleashed desire. The commanding pressure of that kiss made her dizzy with pleasure.

"I need you again," he murmured.

She thought he might carry her back to the bedroom, but instead he shoved aside the bowl and frying pan, sending the carton of eggs to the floor. "Mac, the eggs. We—"

"Don't care." He hoisted her to the counter and his mouth covered hers. His zipper rasped, a condom packet crinkled, and then he was there, seeking, finding and pushing deep.

His first thrust nearly lifted her off the smooth surface. Still kissing her, he pulled her to the rounded edge of the counter and held her hips as he sought her heat in a steady, relentless rhythm.

She gripped his shoulders as her body tightened. The waves of an orgasm surged closer with each rocking motion of his hips. What a glorious lover he was.

He lifted his mouth from hers, and his breathing grew labored as he continued to pump into her. "Can't…wait."

"Don't stop." Digging her fingers into his muscular shoulders, she tipped her head back and closed her eyes, focusing on the delicious tension, feeling it ratchet higher, and higher yet, until…*yes*. The spasms shook her, sending heat rocketing through from her head to the tips of her toes.

With one last powerful thrust, he came, his big body shuddering in reaction. Breathing hard, he stood braced against her for several seconds. Finally he drew in a long, shaky breath. "That was incredible."

Lifting her head, she looked into his eyes, still dark with passion. "You have a real knack for this."

"You inspire me."

She met his gaze. "That's good." With any other man, this would be the moment for exchanging emotionally charged statements, statements that could ruin their carefree sexual adventure. "Because I'm sure as hell not feeding you very well."

"True." He glanced down at the smashed cartoon of eggs. "I don't think those can be salvaged."

"Uh, no. And it won't be a lot of fun to clean up, either."

"I'll do it when I come back." He eased away from her and headed into the bedroom.

Beth wiggled down from the counter, being careful not to step in the gooey egg mess. Retying her bathrobe, she grabbed a paper towel from a holder on the counter and crouched beside the oozing carton.

She managed to get the carton into the garbage with minimal dripping on the floor. As she started to work on the floor itself, Mac returned.

"Seriously, let me clean it up. I'm the one who shoved them off the counter."

She stood and handed him the paper towel. "It was a very dramatic and exciting move."

"Maybe, but it was also short-sighted…unless you have another carton?"

"Sorry."

"Then we don't have eggs to work with."

"Just as well. I'm no good at cooking them, anyway, and we've already established that you're not one of those bachelors from the movies who can whip up an omelet on a moment's notice."

He laughed. "No, I'm not, but what are we going to eat?"

"I have chips and dip."

"Chips with ridges?"

She walked to the cupboard and pulled out the bag.

"Perfect. Onion dip?"

"Is there any other kind?"

"Not in my book." Mac grinned at her. "Now, if you just had some beer…"

"I don't. But I do have root beer."

"That's probably better." He wiped up a good portion of the runny yellow glop on the floor and stood to throw away the paper towel in the trash can before grabbing another one. "I'll need my wits about me so I can whip your ass at Sorry!."

"Think again, hotshot." There was something endearing about a rugged guy who wanted to play a board game. "I'm the Sorry! champion of the Tierney family."

He glanced up from his work. "Prepare to meet your match."

It was an innocent comment, which she knew he hadn't meant literally, but it caught her off guard and she was temporarily at a loss for words.

"Just an expression," he said softly.

"Oh, yeah." She recovered quickly. "I knew you didn't really mean…well, we've been over that. We've said where we each stand."

"Absolutely." He went back to cleaning the floor. "I love how uninhibited you are. I don't know if you're always so spontaneous, but—"

"Not really." She walked over to the refrigerator and took out a carton of onion dip as casually as if they were discussing the weather. "I'm sure it's because we're in this unique situation where we're confident neither of us is looking for something long-term."

"That's what I thought." He dampened a third paper towel and wiped the last of the egg from the floor.

"It's good to be on the same page." And given the rewards of said page, she'd damn well stay on it.

WHILE BETH GOT THEIR SNACKS organized, Mac picked up the empty log carrier sitting beside the hearth. Then he put on his boots and coat and headed out the back door to get wood from the stash on the porch. The cold air might slap some sense into him.

Beth still thought they were having a no-strings-attached romp. He couldn't argue with the romp part. He'd never sacrificed a carton of eggs because he required counter space for sex.

But he'd been desperate to make love to her again, afraid that if he didn't change her mind about a commitment this weekend, he might never get another chance. Certainly nothing this perfect, where they were isolated from the rest of the world.

Every minute he spent with her strengthened his belief that they shared a future. She was quickly becoming his gold standard, and if they didn't end up together, he wondered if anyone else would measure up.

But how to convince someone who believed just as strongly in no strings? Apparently his instinctive strategy involved lots of good sex in the hope that she wouldn't want to give him up on Sunday. Yet he wanted her to care for *him* and not just the sex they shared. So he should take the heat down a notch—assuming he could. Playing Sorry! was a step in the right direction.

Some snow had blown under the porch roof, but a canvas cover protected the wood rack. Pulling it off, Mac loaded up the log carrier and covered the wood again. A hot tub sat on the other side of the porch, its vinyl lid mounded with snow.

Mac immediately thought of the fun he and Beth could have in that hot tub if the weather cleared tomorrow. The heavily wooded slope behind the cabin afforded a fair amount of privacy. Then he dismissed the idea. He needed *fewer* reasons to have sex with her, not more.

As he started back toward the door, he noticed two pairs of snowshoes hanging on the wall. Now, *that* would be a better idea than the hot tub. He didn't know a single person who'd tried having sex on snowshoes.

Once he was inside again, he carried the wood over to the fire. Beth was crouched in front of it, trying to coax some life out of the dying embers. She still wore the robe and monkey slippers, which meant that only a terry-cloth sash kept him from touching her naked body.

He banished that tempting thought as he set down the log carrier. "I brought reinforcements."

"Bless you." She reached for a log.

"Wait." He caught her arm and hunkered down beside her. If he looked closely, he'd be able to glimpse her creamy breasts through a gap in the front of her robe. He didn't look. "Let me do this. You might get splinters."

"Hey, Mr. Macho Man, you're not wearing gloves, either. You could also get splinters." She smiled at him, but there was definitely a challenge in those green eyes.

"I'm used to it." He picked up a small log and set it on the coals.

"Me, too." She picked up a slightly larger log and set it crossways on top of his. "In case you didn't notice, I had a blazing fire going when you arrived this afternoon."

"I realize that." He added another log, balancing it so it would catch the flames starting to lick at the wood. "That doesn't change the fact that my hands are a lot tougher than yours. See?" He took her hand and held it up beside his. Touching her without pulling her into his arms took discipline, but he did it.

"Yikes, your fingers are ice-cold!"

"And calloused." He kissed her palm. "Yours are soft and tender." He nibbled at her little finger. "Splinter bait."

She burst out laughing. "Splinter bait? Where did you come up with that?"

"I don't know." He smiled at her. "The point is—"

"You want to do your superhero thing." Laughter had erased the challenging light in her eyes.

"Yes."

"Okay, then, if it makes you happy." She stood. "Let me take your coat."

"Thanks." He gave her the coat, and while she walked over to the row of hooks by the front door, he sat on the couch and took off his boots. He was careful not to allow his movements to dislodge the Sorry! game she'd carefully set up on the middle cushion.

She'd found a TV table somewhere and had placed it in front of the couch to hold a wicker basket of chips and the plastic container of onion dip. His root-beer bottle sat on a coaster on the end table next to him. They were ready to party.

"But just so we're being clear." She tightened the sash on her robe as she walked back to the couch and sat on the other side of the game board. "I can take care of myself."

"I'm sure you can, and I wouldn't want you to change." He knew that establishing her independence had been her focus this weekend, and he appreciated that she could still accept small kindnesses offered by a lover.

He hesitated before he spoke again, not wanting to ask the question, but feeling as if he should, anyway, now that they were talking about it. "Am I messing up your plan by being here?"

She looked into his eyes for a moment. "I think you're becoming an extension of my plan."

"Oh?"

"I never wanted to abandon the idea of sex, even

if I abandoned the idea of marriage. Being here with you demonstrates that I don't have to give it up, especially if I find like-minded men who agree with my thinking on the subject."

"I see." He thought of her hooking up with other "like-minded" guys, and wanted to punch something. It fit her view of the future, but it sure as hell didn't fit his.

"Which colors do you want?"

He glanced down at the board. Right. They were going to play Sorry!. "Red and yellow."

"Perfect. That's how I set it up, so I could have green and blue. Draw a card."

He lost the draw and she got to go first. She chortled like a little kid, and right away, he knew this would be fun.

Was she truly blind to how well-matched they were? She might be if she thought they were only getting along this well because they had no expectations of each other. She'd been working up to this conclusion for years, and she seemed proud of her insight and determined to hold on to it no matter what. He sighed, not sure how to change her mind without ticking her off in the process.

Obviously misunderstanding the sigh, she grinned and threw a chip at him. "Get used to it, dude. I warned you I'm awesome at this game."

"Don't get cocky, dudette." He used the chip to

scoop up some onion dip. "I will prevail." Somehow, he would get her to adjust her thinking. She might not be able to see it yet, but they belonged together.

CHAPTER SIX

MAC PLAYED SORRY! LIKE his hair was on fire, but despite that, he lost the first game. Beth watched for any signs of male petulance over that, and found none. Instead, he suggested a rematch.

He wasn't about to give up, but he wasn't crabby about his poor showing, either. She'd known men who couldn't lose without sulking, but Mac didn't appear to be one of them. He won the second game, so she campaigned for one more to break the tie as they let the fire die down.

Toward the end of the third game, she drew the Sorry! card and sent one of his pieces back to its starting point. "Sorry!"

"No, you're not."

She smirked at him and scooped up a handful of crumbs from the bottom of the chip basket.

When he drew the Sorry! card two moves later, he gave an evil laugh as he returned her token to her home base. "Revenge is sweet."

But his revenge didn't last, and in the end, she was the victor. Picking up the cards, she began shuffling them as she chanted and bobbed her head in time to the rhythm. "I won, oh, yeah, I won."

"No gloating, smarty-pants."

"Gloating is part of the fun." She glanced over and discovered him watching her with amusement. "If you win—which won't happen in this lifetime, but let's imagine that it could—then I give you permission to gloat."

"Thanks." He held her gaze a moment longer before turning his attention to the game. "I don't know about you, but I've never enjoyed a snowstorm this much."

"Me, neither. And I haven't thought about work in hours." He'd told her this afternoon that she'd make time in her life for a man if it mattered enough. Apparently, Mac could make her forget all about her job. That was more than a little bit scary.

Mac put the lid on the game box. "This is the point where I should head home, but I don't think I can get my truck out and I'm not crazy about walking back."

She stared at him in confusion. "You were planning to go home?"

"Wouldn't that be the right thing to do?" He rested the box on his knees and looked at her.

"Well, I—" What was going on? They'd had some excellent sex followed by three rowdy games of Sorry!, and she'd just assumed that he'd spend the night in the king-size bed with her. True, she was somewhat worried because she *really* wanted him there, but she'd decided to deal with her growing attachment later, after the weekend was over. "I…just thought you were staying."

He glanced up. "Are you inviting me, then?"

"Of course! I didn't think I needed to. I expected..." She groaned and squeezed her eyes shut. "Oh, boy." She looked at him. "We said no expectations, right?"

"That's what you said." But there was no condemnation in his voice.

"And I meant it, too. I truly did. So forget about what I expected. I'm inviting you to stay, and I hope you will, not just because you're snowed in and have no choice, but because you want to."

He smiled. "Oh, I want to."

"Good." Her heart beat faster. "That's good."

"But I'm not taking anything for granted."

"I won't, either. Is it okay to leave the fire, do you think?"

"I'm sure it's fine." He stood up, the game box in one hand.

"Then I guess we should..."

"Go to bed?"

"Yes." She picked up the empty dip container and the chip basket. She must still have expectations, because she kept thinking he'd sweep her into his arms and take her there. But he didn't. He seemed to be waiting for her to direct the action.

So she did. "You go ahead. I'll get the lights out here."

"All right."

"You're sure you want to stay?"

His hot gaze left no doubt. "Absolutely."

So kiss me! Ravish me! "Then I'll be there in a sec."

"Great." He walked into the bedroom, depositing the game on the kitchen table on his way past it.

The dynamic between them had changed, and she felt off balance. In fact, she was shaky, as if she'd had too much caffeine. How silly. She'd already had wild sex with this guy twice, and the prospect of climbing into bed with him again shouldn't feel like cliff diving. So why did his sudden distance matter?

As she checked the front-door lock and switched off all the lights, she figured it out. They'd had fantastic sex, but it had essentially been mindless, at least on her part. His eagerness hadn't left her any time to think.

He still seemed eager, but not quite so impulsive. It was almost as if he *wanted* to give her time to think… to feel.

Or not. She blew out a breath, impatient with herself for trying to read meaning into everything. He was probably just tired. She walked into the bedroom and discovered he'd turned down the covers and switched on a bedside lamp.

Coming toward her, he slid the bathrobe from her shoulders. "Thanks for asking me to stay."

"Thanks for staying." She was warmed by the heat in his eyes.

"I love looking at you." He stepped back, his gaze traveling slowly downward and stopping at her feet, still encased in sock-monkey slippers. "Want to keep those on?"

"Please don't tell me you have a slipper fetish."

"Nope. Just don't want your feet to get cold."

She sat on the bed and nudged them off. "Guess you'll just have to keep my feet warm." Then she remembered. She'd put that on her list of things she didn't need a man to provide. She shook off the thought. Asking a man to keep her feet warm for one night wasn't the same as needing him to do it on a regular basis.

"I promise to keep them toasty." He began stripping off his clothes.

Stretching out on the cool sheet, she pulled the blankets around her and propped her head on her hand so she could watch the unveiling of Mac McFarland. From his broad shoulders to his muscled chest, from his six-pack to his erect penis, he was one fine specimen. Her body hummed in readiness, her urgency increasing with every second.

His breathing grew rougher as he took a condom packet from the box and had to work hard to tear it open. "Damn things."

"Lovely things." A delicious shiver of anticipation ran through her. "We'd be severely restricted without them."

He finally opened the packet and rolled on the condom. "That's true." He drew back the covers and slid in beside her. "I just get impatient." Capturing her mouth in a deep kiss, he rolled her under him and in one smooth motion buried his cock to the hilt.

Her heart hammered as she absorbed the sensation of being locked so tightly together she couldn't tell where she left off and he began. They fit perfectly, her body molding to his as if they were meant to join this way. She'd never felt so connected to a man before.

Lifting his mouth from hers, he kissed her cheeks, her eyelids and the tip of her nose. "This is heaven."

"Mmm." She cupped his face and pulled him back to her lips, wanting another sinfully deep kiss with lots of tongue.

But instead of the wild and lusty kiss she'd expected, his mouth gentled over hers. He kissed her tenderly, as if cherishing this bond between them. When he initiated a slow, steady rhythm, her response was instinctive. She lifted into his kiss and opened like a flower beneath him. At the same moment, her womb relaxed, inviting him deeper.

Responding to her total surrender, he groaned and rocked forward, as if he longed to touch her essence. Something was happening between them, something she hadn't intended. The barriers were coming down.

Angling his mouth over hers, molding the kiss until it became two halves of a whole, he began to pump into her in easy, measured strokes. Each time he drove home, the protective shell around her heart cracked a little more. She was defenseless against this tender wooing, helpless to guard her heart.

The insistent, steady thrust, so different from the wild rides they'd enjoyed before, stirred her response as surely and effortlessly as the approaching tide. She didn't strain toward her climax. It simply arrived in a surge of joy.

As she arched upward, Mac lifted his head, gazed into her eyes and continued the easy motion of his hips. "Beth."

The force of her orgasm took her breath away.

"Beth." He said her name again as his eyes darkened. With a gasp, he shoved deep one last time, his body quivering, his cock pulsing within her.

She had never felt so close to a man in her life, yet she'd known him only a matter of hours. The depth of her feelings made no logical sense, but she shouldn't be trying to think in the afterglow of such a powerful climax.

"Beth, I—"

She laid her fingers over his mouth. "Let's not spoil it."

He nodded. "Right."

But even though she'd stopped him from saying anything they might both regret, she couldn't pretend that they'd been enjoying sex for its own sake.

He'd made love to her.

Exactly the thing she'd planned to avoid, and yet she still felt the warmth of it down to her toes.

She wouldn't try to sort it out tonight. Mac left the bed to take care of the condom, but when he returned, he curled his big body around hers and gathered her close. She snuggled against him and fell asleep.

MAC WOKE UP FEELING GREAT. With Beth snuggled in his arms, all was right with his world. Weak light filtered through the wooden blinds, but she was still asleep, her bottom pressed against his morning wood. Sweet agony.

He was so tempted to try to reach the condom box without waking her. He savored the possibility of making love when she was still drowsy and relaxed. But he would put that idea on hold.

If he planned to spend the day with her—and he most certainly did—then he needed a shower, a shave and a toothbrush. Which meant going home again. He hadn't thought of a razor and a toothbrush when he'd grabbed the condoms. Even if he had, he wouldn't have brought them.

The task of wooing Beth was delicate, and he had to take it one step at a time. Easing carefully out of bed, he picked up his clothes from the floor, walked out into the kitchen and closed the door gently behind him. He dressed quietly and listened for any sound to indicate she was waking up. All was silent.

So far, so good. If his plan worked, it could turn out to be a nice surprise. He put on his boots and his coat and made sure his keys were in his pocket. A note might be a good idea, too.

Glancing around the cabin still cloaked mostly in shadow, he spied her yellow legal pad. Bingo. Walking to the end table, he picked it up, along with the pen she'd been using.

He glanced over the list she'd been making of all the reasons she loved living alone. It was a long list, but it demonstrated her self-sufficiency. He prized that quality and considered it the basis of a healthy relationship.

Flipping the top page over, he wrote *"BE BACK SOON"* on the second page and put the legal pad next to the Sorry! box. He listened again, and when he didn't hear her stirring, he unlocked the front door. He closed it behind him and used his own key to relock the door once he was standing on the very cold porch.

The snow had stopped falling during the night, and the pearl-colored sky was clear. Soon the sun would sparkle on the deep layer of snow surrounding the cabin.

It surrounded his truck, too. He could dig it out, but that would take a while, and the road would be treacherous so he'd have to drive slowly. Walking through snow this deep would be even more tedious. Then he remembered the snowshoes hanging on the back porch.

Not wanting to risk going through the house and waking Beth, he plowed his way through the snow and around the cabin. It was tough going, but once he reached the back porch and strapped the snowshoes on his feet, he was golden. He headed cross-country to his cabin.

BETH HEARD SOME NOISE on the back porch and realized Mac wasn't in bed with her anymore. Leaving the warm bed wasn't easy, but she wanted to know what he was up to so early this morning. After putting on her bathrobe, she walked to the window that looked out on the back porch and parted the wooden blinds.

She was just in time to see Mac snowshoeing his way across marshmallow-smooth snow, no doubt returning to his cabin. Shivering, she left the bedroom and spotted her yellow legal pad on the table, the first page turned over. So he'd left a note. That was considerate of him.

He probably had many reasons for going. He likely wanted a shower, a shave and a change of clothes. Spending the night hadn't been a given, so he'd been unprepared, and he might not relish the idea of sharing her razor and toothbrush.

Even so, she was disappointed. She'd hoped they might wake up together, snuggled in that warm bed. Starting the day by making love would have been nice, too.

Who was she kidding? To be more precise, she hadn't *hoped* that would happen. She'd *expected* it after the sweet way he'd treated her last night. Damn. Once again, she'd allowed her expectations to mess with her peace of mind.

She flipped the first page back into place, and there was her list of things she loved about living alone. Sitting on one of the kitchen chairs, she propped her cheek against her hand and read through the list: *control of remote, closet to myself, eat when I want, sleep when I want, bathroom to myself, decorate to my tastes, listen to music I like, enjoy silence.*

It certainly was silent right now. Was she enjoying the silence? No. She missed having Mac around.

She looked over the list again, reminding herself of why she'd come here in the first place—to celebrate being single. Having Mac around wasn't helping.

Apparently she wasn't good at this fling business, at least not yet, and especially not with a guy like Mac, who was so…appealing. She'd never been with a man who literally wiped all her priorities from her mind.

It was easy to turn down a marriage proposal from a jerk who openly admitted he wanted to derail her dreams in favor of his. But Mac would never say something like that, would never consciously expect it, either. But in the end, would he unintentionally woo her away from her responsibilities, from the job she loved?

After all, he had that whole superhero thing going on. Superheroes didn't rescue self-sufficient people. They rescued the weak and needy. Without meaning to, Mac might tempt her into surrendering her personal freedom in exchange for his protection. And she refused to surrender.

She groaned, dreading the pain that she knew was coming, for both of them. But for her own good and his, she had to send him away.

CHAPTER SEVEN

SHOWERED AND SHAVED, with supplies in his backpack, Mac strapped on the snowshoes and headed for the Vickers' cabin. Sunshine had transformed the snow into a field of diamonds so bright he needed goggles, and overhead the sky was superhero blue. Mac could hardly wait to see Beth again. What a glorious Thanksgiving Day this was turning out to be.

Smoke drifted from the cabin's chimney and he took a deep breath of crisp air scented with wood smoke. So she was up. He hadn't planned it this way, but by going home he'd allowed her to have the bathroom to herself. He knew from her list that she preferred that.

He decided to leave the snowshoes on the front porch to use later on. He imagined snowshoeing with Beth while the Cornish game hens roasted, then returning to a warm fire and a celebratory meal. Or maybe they'd snowshoe this morning and make love while the hens roasted.

Inserting his key in the lock, he realized it was already open. She must have done it, anticipating his return. Good sign. Inside, he was greeted by the scent of coffee and his heart warmed at the sight of

Beth curled up on the couch sipping a cup in front of the fire.

She'd put on a soft green sweat suit that perfectly matched her eyes, and unless he was mistaken, she'd washed and styled her hair. Another good sign.

"Hi." He smiled at her as he slipped the pack from his shoulders, mindful of the contents.

"Hi."

His smile faded. She wasn't smiling back. "I borrowed the snowshoes because my truck's socked in."

"I know. I saw you leave."

Still no smile. "Are you upset because I left without saying goodbye?"

"No."

He was having a hard time reading her expression, so he barreled on. "I wanted to let you sleep. I brought the eggs I had in my refrigerator, plus some bread for toast because I couldn't remember if you had that, and—" he reached in the front pocket of the backpack "—a cookbook! I'm going to attempt to make omelets." He waited, expecting her to laugh because they'd joked about it last night.

Instead, she stood and put her coffee mug on the end table. "Mac, this isn't working out."

He felt the words like a blow to the stomach and he sucked in a breath. *Steady. Don't panic.* He did his best to sound calm. "Oh? What's the problem?"

She picked up the legal pad that she'd apparently brought over to the couch while he was gone. "I came here to celebrate being single."

"I know you did." He'd realized on some level they'd have this conversation eventually. He just didn't want to have it so soon. "And I think it's a worthwhile idea. Nobody should assume they have to marry in order to be happy."

She nodded. "We agreed on that from the beginning. But the thing is—"

"Listen, could we talk about this while I start cooking? I don't know about you, but I'm starving to death." He was, and he didn't want to face this discussion on an empty stomach. That wasn't his only reason for starting the omelets, though. He needed to break through this barrier she'd apparently put up while he was gone.

She gazed at him as if trying to decide how to handle that suggestion. "Okay, I guess. I'm sure you are hungry after not getting much food last night and then snowshoeing between our two cabins."

"It's beautiful out there, though." He took off his coat and hung it on a hook by the door before picking up the backpack and carrying it over to the kitchen. Setting it on a chair, he took out the carton of eggs and checked to make sure none of them had broken.

"It looks pretty out the window."

"The snowshoes worked great. There's another set hanging on the back-porch wall." He laid the cookbook on the counter and thumbed through it until he found a recipe for omelets.

"Mac, don't be planning on any activities involving me, okay? That's what I'm trying to tell you."

He glanced at her with a smile, as if she hadn't just threatened to nuke his whole future, the one he'd been planning ever since last night. "Okay. I won't. Do we have a small frying pan?"

"I think so." She gave him a puzzled look, as if she'd expected more of a reaction to her statement.

But he wasn't planning to react yet. In fact, he wanted to stall this discussion for as long as possible.

After going through the cupboards, she came up with a small pan. "How about this?"

"Perfect." He continued to study the recipe. "Now I just need a bowl. I think we'd better make this simple and only add cheese. I know you have some of that."

She set a mixing bowl on the counter next to him, followed by a block of cheese she took out of the refrigerator. She considered the cheese. "I think it needs to be grated. That's what they use at those omelet stations in restaurants."

"Good idea. That'll be your job." He cracked three eggs into the bowl, all the while trying not to worry about her change of attitude. The recipe said to use a whisk, but he grabbed a fork out of the silverware drawer and used that. "Making an omelet is probably just like making scrambled eggs, except you end up with something that looks like a flat rock instead of a handful of pebbles."

That produced the tiniest of smiles. Then she glanced away and took a deep breath. "Here's the deal. I woke up this morning, and you were already on your way home."

"I probably made too much noise on the back porch. Sorry about that."

"I didn't mind waking up. But suddenly I was alone."

"Oh." He was beginning to think leaving had been a really bad idea. If he'd stayed, they wouldn't have had eggs for breakfast, but whatever relationship glue had been working last night would have had time to set. He'd pulled away from her too soon. And now everything rested on omelets. He turned on the burner under the pan. "Do you have any butter?"

"Yes." She opened the refrigerator, took out a wrapped stick of butter and handed it to him. "And I *felt* alone. That's the problem."

"You missed me?"

"Unfortunately."

He stood holding the butter and stared at her. He didn't see that as unfortunate. In fact, he was overjoyed to hear it. "Is that so bad?"

"Yes! I'm here to declare my independence from men, and in less than twelve hours, I miss you when you leave!"

He put down the butter and turned off the stove. This was great news. Maybe the glue had set, after all. "You didn't want to miss me, did you?"

"No." Her gaze was pleading. "But I did, and that means I have more work to do if I'm truly going to be happy with my single life. I need you to leave so I can do that work and get stronger, more self-reliant."

He tried not to show any anxiety over her plan to

kick him out, but his heart was pounding. "Do you mind if we eat breakfast before I go?" He held his breath.

She swallowed. "I suppose not. You went to all this trouble to bring eggs and a cookbook." Then she sighed. "Only that's part of the problem, too. You like coming to the rescue. That's a very considerate trait, but I can't allow a man to rescue me on a regular basis."

"I understand that." He thought she was overreacting to what was only a nice gesture, but he didn't want to fight with her. He switched on the burner again and put some butter in the pan. "If you wouldn't mind locating the grater and grating up some cheese, I'd really appreciate it."

"Oh. Right, that was my job. I'm a little distracted." She opened drawers, found a grater and started energetically shredding cheese onto a plate.

"I glanced at that list of yours." The butter was sizzling, so he dumped the egg mixture in the pan. The cookbook was a little vague on technique, but this looked similar to the way omelet-station chefs operated.

"I've done more than glance at it. After I got cleaned up and made some coffee, I practically memorized it. If I knew how to cross-stitch, I'd make a wall hanging of that list so I'd remember and quit being such a dependent wuss when a nice guy shows up."

He noticed that she had a mound of cheese about

nine inches high and at least that wide. "I think that's enough cheese."

She stopped grating and looked at what she'd done. Then she glanced over at him, and back at the mountain of cheese. "Are you sure?" A ripple of laughter ran through her question.

"Not really. Seems to me you can never have too much grated cheese."

Her eyes sparkled and her lips twitched before she turned away from him. "It would help me immensely if you'd try to be less charming."

"No can do. Charming is my factory setting. If you don't believe me, ask my mom." He reached for a handful of cheese and sprinkled it on top of the eggs.

"That remark is exactly what I'm talking about."

"I tried being nasty once, back in fourth grade." Something was burning, so he grabbed a spatula. "It didn't work out for me." He dug under the egg mixture, and sure enough, it was scorched on the bottom and still runny on the top. "Houston, we have a problem. The bottom's overdone and the top is underdone."

"Let's try this." She held out the pizza pan that was still sitting on the counter from last night. "If you can scoop it on here, I'll stick it in the oven to bake."

"Might work." He made somewhat of a mess, but most of the omelet ended up on the pizza pan. While she slid that in the oven, he turned down the heat and melted more butter. "I'll eat that one. This second try should be better."

"We'll split each one. That's fair, especially since you're doing most of the work."

"You made the coffee."

"Right! I need to pour us each a cup. How about some toast?"

"Absolutely." He noticed that she'd stopped discussing his imminent departure and fallen in with the breakfast plan. Cooperation and compromise could be a beautiful thing. He wondered if she could see how well they achieved it.

She took a second mug from the cupboard. "Do you want to eat at the table or over by the fire?"

"I think we should move the table so we can sit there and still enjoy the fire." He was beginning to hope that if he didn't bring up the subject of lists and the joys of being single, she might drop it completely and they could go back to their regularly scheduled program of having fun together.

"Good idea." She picked up a kitchen chair and carried it into the living room.

He helped her with the table, which they set up behind the couch, and then she stoked the fire. The toast popped about the time the second omelet was done. He couldn't brag about the presentation of the eggs, which looked somewhat mangled on the plate, but at least they had food.

She buttered the toast, poured the coffee and gave them each a fork and a paper napkin. He made sure the burner and oven were off and then hurried over to pull out her chair.

"Why, thank you, Mac."

"You're welcome." He noticed that her legal pad was also on the table beside her plate. Damn, she wasn't going to drop the subject. "Look, I know we need to talk, but let's eat first."

"I won't argue with that. I'm dying of hunger."

"In that case, it won't matter if it's any good or not." But to his surprise, the omelets were okay. The one from the oven tasted a little burned on the bottom, but the second one was decent. Not restaurant quality, but decent.

"Fabulous," Beth said between bites.

"I think the secret is to starve yourself first." But he was pleased with the result. And maybe, just maybe, having a full tummy would mellow her out.

Their plates were empty in record time. Mac sat back with a sigh of satisfaction and picked up his coffee mug.

"Mac, I want to thank you for going to all that trouble. The food was great."

"It wasn't bad." He took note of her resolute expression. She was about to give him the ax. He might buy a little more time by offering to do the dishes, but clearly the stall tactic wasn't working. He might as well face the music. "Look, I'll leave if you want, but first, can I say something?"

Her green eyes grew wary. "Okay."

"Relax. I'm not going to refute your argument. I like the idea that you're self-sufficient. As a handyman, I've met a fair number of women who aren't. I wish they had your self-confidence."

"Apparently I'm not as self-sufficient as I thought, judging from my behavior this weekend."

Mac rested his arms on the table and leaned forward, seeking a connection. "You think you lost focus, don't you?"

She leaned forward, too, but she looked ready for battle, not connection. "I know I did!"

"That's where I disagree. Your focus simply shifted for a while. You could get it back any time you need to. You've already proven you can survive just fine on your own. You've already been doing it."

The determined light of battle intensified in her eyes. "Yes, but I can see myself putting work, or friends or family on the back burner because I'd rather spend time with you. And like I said, you have that superhero thing going on. You have to rescue people. Before you know it, I'll be totally dependent on you for…for everything."

He shook his head. "No, you won't. I'd never encourage that. I've seen what happens when dependent people lose the one they've counted on for all their needs. It's not pretty."

"I don't want to be that kind of person."

"But don't you see, Beth? You couldn't possibly be. You like to rescue people as much as I do!"

She frowned. "I don't think so."

"I do. What's a hotel? It offers shelter for weary

travelers. You rescue them from temporary homelessness."

"Well..."

Sensing he was gaining the advantage, he charged onward. "And what about when you have emergencies there? Don't you get an adrenaline rush when you can solve the problem and save the day?"

"I suppose so, but—"

"Then there's how you reacted to me. You wanted to save me from another awkward dinner at my parents' house. You invited me here, to rescue me from that."

She studied him, obviously intrigued by something she hadn't considered before.

He took a deep breath. "No one can make you forget who you are or change how you want to live your life. I know that for a fact."

The tension drained from her body, and in her eyes he saw a glimmer of hope, as if she wanted to believe him, but wasn't sure that she could.

He had one more thing to say, and it was huge. He swallowed. "You're a strong woman, Beth. But...in your plans, have you left any room for..." His chest tightened. He was far more invested than he realized.

Her gaze held his, and gradually the challenge in her eyes faded to be replaced by something warmer. "For what?" she said softly.

He swallowed. "For falling in love."

She went very still.

Reaching for her hands, he held them tight as his

heart threatened to race out of control. "We haven't known each other very long, and yesterday I would have said this is impossible. Today I know it's not. I'm falling in love with you, Beth."

She trembled but didn't look away.

"And what if...what if you missed me this morning because you're starting to fall in love with me?"

She gripped his hands tighter.

"Does that scare you?"

Her answer was a whisper. "Yes."

But she hadn't denied the possibility that she'd come to care for him as much as he cared for her. Hope bloomed. "You don't have to be scared. I don't want a dependent woman in my life. Don't ever think you have to be weak so I'll feel strong. We can be strong together. Just love me, Beth."

The little sound she made told him it was time to leave the damn table and hold her. Still holding on to her, he stood, knocking over his chair, and drew her out of hers, which also toppled over. Her gaze never left his as he guided her into his arms.

"Spend today with me," he murmured. "Give yourself time to absorb the idea that maybe, just maybe, we belong together, the union of two superheroes."

Tears sparkled in her eyes. "All right."

"Thank you." His mouth captured hers, and he poured all the wonder and gratitude he felt into that kiss. From the way she kissed him back, he thought he had a shot.

When he finally came up for air, he gazed into her

eyes and decided he *definitely* had a shot. She'd never looked at him quite this way before, and he could tell she was thinking about him in a whole new way.

She cupped his face and smiled up at him. "So what next?"

He started to make a suggestion and caught himself. "Your cabin, your call."

Her smile widened. "Good answer."

"So what next?" He didn't care, so long as he'd be with her, although he had a couple of priorities.

"Can I interest you in making love by the fire?"

He loved it when their priorities matched up so well. "You certainly could." And when he kissed her this time, he knew for sure that it would be a very good Thanksgiving, indeed.

EPILOGUE

BETH HAD KNOWN, DEEP DOWN, that she was falling for
Mac from the moment he'd stepped through her door
Wednesday night, but by Sunday morning, she had
no doubts that he was right and this was love with a
capital L. They lay together in the king-size bed planning how they'd arrange their schedules to maximize
time spent together.

He'd also been right when he'd told her that there
was room in her life for a relationship if it was important enough to her. It never had been before, but
with Mac, it was. For now, they'd keep the road busy
between here and Reno, but eventually she hoped to
get a job managing one of the Tahoe hotels.

They'd spent the weekend attempting to cook, with
limited success, and making love with much greater
success. They'd concluded they'd rather make love
than cook. Once she and Mac had dug his truck out
of the snow, they'd indulged in a several-course hotel
meal.

She'd learned his first name was actually Conneach
and had promised not to call him that. They'd compared their taste in books and movies and had even
discussed the hot-button issues of religion and politics.

They didn't agree on everything, and that was okay. She'd finally found a man who was comfortable with differences of opinion.

As the time sped by, Beth became more convinced that they could make a life together. Yet neither of them had mentioned marriage, even though they'd tentatively planned to meet each other's parents within the next couple of weeks.

She'd certainly thought about the idea of a permanent commitment and figured he had, too. But they'd known each other such a short time. All things considered, it was a subject that could wait.

But as she lay beside him gazing into his blue eyes, she remembered a subject that couldn't wait. She couldn't believe she hadn't asked him already. "When's your mother's birthday?"

He blinked. "Not for months. Why?"

"Humor me. When is it, exactly?"

"July nineteenth, which leaves you plenty of time to buy her a present. We should probably get the meet and greet out of the way before you start shopping, though."

"You're absolutely sure about the date, right?"

"Of course I'm sure. Come to think of it, we haven't talked birthdays at all. When's yours?"

"February twelfth."

He nodded. "Okay. Got it."

"You say that as if it's now memorized."

"Which it is. And no, I won't just roll your birthday into Valentine's Day. We'll do each one separate."

"I appreciate that." She gazed at him. "Does that mean you know your dad's and sister's birthdays, too?"

"April sixteenth and September thirtieth. Oh, and by the way, although you didn't ask, mine is October fourth, which gives you almost a whole year to shop."

"Excellent. Thanks for the info." There was so much to look forward to—Christmas, New Year's, Valentine's Day, celebrating Mac's birthday with him for the first time. Happiness filled her heart.

"Why the birthday questions all of a sudden?"

"I once told myself that any guy who could reel off his family's birthdays without a cheat sheet would make me sit up and take notice."

"Wow. I didn't know it was a test. What if I'd failed?"

She stroked his cheek. "I would still love you to pieces."

"But I passed. I should get extra points."

"Oh, you do." She sighed happily. A girl didn't run into a guy like Mac every day of the week and she would be a fool to let him get away. "You most certainly do."

He pulled her closer. "I think I'll collect on them right now."

She nestled against him, her body responding eagerly to the heat in his eyes. "No complaints here, but pretty soon I have to start packing up my stuff."

He nuzzled behind her ear. "And we have to write a note to Ken and Jillian."

"You know they'll think it was the cabin."

He raised his head to look into her eyes. "Do you think it was the cabin?"

"I'm not sure. Do you?"

He shrugged. "Who cares?" He dropped a soft kiss on her lips. "I'm just grateful I found you. I love you, Beth."

"And I love you." As she lost herself in his kiss, she knew she would give thanks for this special weekend for the rest of her life.

* * * * *

THE CHRISTMAS SET-UP

New York Times and *USA TODAY*
Bestselling Author
Jill Shalvis

CHAPTER ONE

"MERRY CHRISTMAS, SIR!" yelled the hot-dog vendor with a wide grin after Jason Monroe gestured for him to keep the change. The kid couldn't have been more than twelve, hustling hot dogs and churros on the street.

Merry Christmas.

It was December 10, and all of San Francisco had been decorated for the holidays since before Thanksgiving. Jason wasn't Scrooge, not exactly, but he sure as hell could do without the tinsel, the faux-wrapped boxes, the sappy music, the blinding, blinking lights.

By the time he entered Steele Architecture and Design where he worked as an associate architect, he'd finished his two loaded hot dogs and was working on the churro as he headed directly toward the boardroom for the weekly staff meeting. Most everyone was already there and Jason eyed his brother at the end of the long conference table. Mike was a draftsman for Steele, which meant he was basically an entry-level developing architect. At that moment he was hunched over some paperwork, laughing with some other draftsmen. They abruptly broke off at the sight of Jason.

Jason narrowed his eyes but everyone was suddenly a flurry of motion, busying themselves with their iPads, iPhones, laptops—

Everyone except Mike. He smiled at Jason innocently, and Jason shook his head. Mike was younger than Jason by five years, which put him at twenty-five going on twelve. He was the only person on earth who could pull Jason's strings and get away with it.

For the past ten years, since their parents' death, Jason had worked his ass off to keep Mike on the straight and narrow. He'd been moderately successful, but it had cost him—literally. When their parents died there'd been medical bills, a bad mortgage and no savings, leaving Jason and Mike with less than nothing. The debt had only racked up further with Jason's college bills, followed by his brother's. And yet somehow Jason couldn't bring himself to sell his parents' house, and every month he scraped up as much as he could to pay the mortgage and taxes. So in ten years, he hadn't even been able to make a dent to his debtload, something he was acutely reminded of every holiday season when it felt as if all he was doing was whipping out his credit card. And then there was his brother, who didn't seem to understand that the "minimum payment" wasn't the credit card company's version of an early Christmas present.

But that wasn't what was bothering him now—it was Mike's expression, that innocence. Mike didn't have an innocent bone in his body. In fact, the last time he'd worn that expression, he'd just glued the caps on all the cylinders holding Jason's building plans, including the ones he'd taken into a city council meeting.

This was what happened when your kid brother was a classic underachieving genius who lived to torture his older brother. But before Jason could find out what Mike was up to this time, Stan Steele, the head of their architecture firm, walked in to the boardroom. Just behind him was Zoe Anders, another associate architect like Jason.

Only, she was nothing like Jason. Zoe was a tall, stacked redhead, a woman who was an enigmatic mix of sweet warmth and sharp ambition.

And she was Jason's only competition for the sole available promotion to principal architect.

Stan waited until Zoe sat…in the only free spot, next to Jason. She crossed her mile-long legs, and though he was sure the sound of smooth skin rubbing against smooth skin was all in his head, Jason was hit with a punch of awareness. An awareness he always felt around her, which actually felt more like…being shot with a stun gun.

He wasn't sure what it was about her. There were other women in the company, some even prettier.

But the only one who stirred him was Zoe. Every single time.

Their gazes met. She audibly sucked in some air and then promptly dropped her portfolio. When she bent to grab it, she spilled her to-go mug of coffee. "Dammit," he heard her mutter, and it made him smile. For the first time he had proof that he wasn't alone in feeling the jolt of awareness between them. He hunkered down to help her gather her things.

"Thanks," she said when he handed her the portfolio. They were both crouched low, face-to-face. Her gaze dropped to his mouth, then jerked away. "I've got it."

Yeah. She did. She definitely had it, whatever "it" was, and it drove him crazy. It had for the entire year they'd both worked here at Steele.

"Okay, everyone," Steele said, tossing a memory stick to each of his eight associate architects. "We're making this fast today, I'm late for a meeting across town. As reported last week, the city's landmark Weller Building is being torn down. Richard D. Weller III is auditioning firms to design the replacement building which will house a new city library, courthouse and family center." Stan stared down first Jason and then Zoe, whom everyone knew were the two hottest up-and-coming architects in the company. "Everyone has to come up with something amazing. Did I say amazing? Make that spectacular. I want Steele Architects to win the bid. It'd be our biggest job since the economy took a shit, and we need it. We need it so bad I'm hanging the principal-architect promotion on it. Understood?"

Zoe held Steele's gaze evenly, coolly, then flashed the smile that could melt the Arctic. "Absolutely, sir."

Jason looked away from the smile so as not to get sucked into what he thought of as the Zoe-Vortex. If he looked into it too long, he'd fall in and never be able to get out. And right now he couldn't afford that kind of lapse.

He nodded to Steele. It didn't matter what anyone's success had been over the past year, this project was now the only one that counted. He was okay with that. He needed something to occupy him during the "merry" season, and this would be it.

"You have one month," Steele said. He glared at the pack of draftsmen, including Mike. "And you. You all have work. Go. For the love of God, go impress me."

Zoe gathered her file, smiled at everyone but Jason and left the room behind Steele.

Jason watched her go. Okay, so he watched her ass go, but it was one hell of a sweet ass...

He turned to Mike, who raised his brows.

"No pressure or anything, huh?" Mike said.

Jason shrugged. "It'll be fine."

"I don't know, man. You're in your holiday funk. Zoe could totally kick your ass if she wants to."

Jason was of the never-let-'em-see-you-sweat school, so he gathered his things and stood. "It'll be fine," he repeated.

He hadn't had any problems rising to the top before. He'd finish this year off in the same vein, secure the promotion and maybe find his damn happy while he was at it.

"Maybe you should combine forces," Mike said in a careful voice that had Jason taking a second look at him.

Mike blinked once, slow as an owl, which meant only one thing—he was up to no good. Again. "Combine forces?"

"Yeah," Mike said. "Work with the hot girl instead of against her. Combine your talents, win the bid and then let your past record up the ante in your favor for the principal-architect position. Win-win."

"I can win on my own merit."

"Okay, whatever… If you're sure."

He was. Besides, he and Zoe wouldn't work well together. All they ever did when they were in the same room was raise the temperature. Jason shook his head and left the conference room.

One month. He had one month to create the project of his life, get the promotion and start to earn enough money to get out from the debt threatening to drag him under.

And hope like hell in the doing so that it made him feel something, *anything*, again.

THE MINUTE JASON LEFT the boardroom, Mike turned to Alicia, Kent and Tucker, his fellow cohorts in the Trouble Department. "Okay, so where were we?"

They were using Alicia's iPad to fill out an agreement on a Lake Tahoe rental cabin. Her idea, as she was the romantic of the group. The cabin was owned by Ken and Jillian Vickers, who'd been two of Mike's favorite college professors. The Vickers had fallen in love for the second time in their cabin and enjoyed nothing more than renting it out to couples—or potential couples in this case.

Jason had seemed really down lately, and Mike wanted to remind his brother that life was about much more than just work. Alicia was helping him execute the reminder.

The thing was, Jason was smart and incredibly intuitive. Which meant Mike's plan had to be sneaky—not a problem, since Mike had majored in Sneak.

Jason wasn't going to know what hit him. Mike grinned at the thought.

"Smile now," Alicia said. "Because later, when he finds out what you've done, he's going to kill you." She turned her iPad to him, Kent and Tucker and revealed their progress. "We're on the last question: why is Jason choosing to vacation at the cabin."

Well, Jason wasn't *choosing* to vacation there. Not exactly. Mike was choosing it for him. "Say that he hopes the place will bring him luck in love."

"What?" Kent said. "Jason would never say that. He doesn't even know what love is."

"He used to," Mike said. "I'm only trying to remind him of it. And it's not like I can just come right out and say 'I'm trying to get the two most high-profile, ambitious, fast-tracked architects in the city laid,' can I? It'd sound crass."

"As opposed to actually *being* crass," Alicia said dryly.

"My intentions are completely altruistic," Mike said to her. "Look, just write up some romantic, fluffy paragraph about how much the mountains mean to both of them."

"Zoe's afraid of spiders and bears, and she doesn't even know she's going to the mountains," Alicia said.

"Yeah, leave that part out," Mike said.

"Can we put down how anal she is?" Tucker asked.

Alicia rolled her eyes.

"Oh!" Kent said, lighting up like the Christmas lights already strung on the wall behind him. "Make sure to add that she's a quick drunk. Can't hold her liquor. One glass of champagne at last year's office party and she was all up in Santa's grill—"

Alicia smacked him. "She was *dating* Santa at the time."

"I'm just saying, you might want to make sure the liquor cabinet's stocked," Kent pointed out.

"I don't think I'm comfortable with this," Alicia said.

"It's for the greater good of the entire office," Mike told her. "Those two have been sniffing around each other for months. And Jason's grumpy as hell. This'll put a smile back on his face."

"Maybe they're already sleeping together," Kent said.

"If they were sleeping together, they wouldn't still have all that sexual tension," Alicia said. "Did you see what happened when he looked at her during the meeting? She dropped her portfolio and coffee. Then they both stared at each other like moon birds."

"What the hell are moon birds?" Kent asked.

Alicia rolled her eyes again. Tucker scratched his jaw. "They do keep staring at each other... Maybe Kent's right. Maybe they're already doing it."

"Trust me," Mike said. "If Jason was getting laid, I'd know it." He turned to Alicia. "Don't think of it as a setup, consider it my early Christmas present to my dear brother. Write something mushy on the application and send it."

CHAPTER TWO

TWO WEEKS LATER, ZOE caught herself staring at her cute little miniature Christmas tree instead of her computer screen...and the blank page on her drawing program. Behind that were all the Weller specs, just waiting for the glorious design that she hadn't come up with yet. She had some ideas and notes on the memory stick currently plugged into her laptop, and the design was in her head, or at least she was beginning to think so, but she hadn't quite been able to get it on the screen. She had a lot going on in her head.

For one thing, it was already Christmas Eve day. She was leaving here by noon to get to her family gathering up north, but she had told herself she wasn't going anywhere until she accomplished *something*.

Jason walked by her office in his usual long-legged, effortless stride. He glanced in at her and slapped a big hand on her open door, slowing his forward motion. There was a beat of...whatever there always was between them. Uncomfortable awareness, she supposed, and braced for its inevitable follow-up—a rush of adrenaline. Yep, there it was now.

She tried to attribute the feeling to a surge of competition, but she knew better than that. He was effortlessly sexy, and while Zoe was a lot of things, she wasn't immune to effortlessly sexy. Or at least his particular brand of it.

"You finished yet?" he asked.

"Finished what?" she volleyed back, even though she knew exactly what he was fishing for.

Not fooled, Jason smiled. He had a killer smile, and he knew it. He was six foot two, built like the mountain biker he was on the weekends, yet, in an oddly attractive contrast, he dressed like a sexy nerd. Today that meant dark blue khakis and a dark blue button-down shirt with the top button undone behind a loosely knotted, hipster-cool tie. There were hiking boots on his big feet.

That, combined with the full head of unruly dark chestnut hair that fell to his loose collar, equaled a devastatingly handsome combination that he seemed utterly oblivious to. He was also oblivious to her go-away glare.

"Having problems?" he said.

Yes! She was careful not to look at her blank screen. "Of course not."

"We've only got two weeks left before we have to present our concepts to Steele."

"I realize that, thank you."

Jason's brows raised as he studied her, his sharp green eyes missing nothing—not the fact that she was wearing her lucky suit for the second time that week (she'd been hoping it would inspire her), or that she was having a bad hair day, or that her eyes were lined with exhaustion because she couldn't sleep.

He took this all in, and though she expected him to flash another grin, maybe with some taunting in it—or at the very least teasing—he didn't.

"You okay?" he asked instead.

Surprised, she was momentarily caught off guard. They didn't do this, the personal thing. They were much better at competition, and had been since they'd first met, constantly trying to one-up each other on the ladder rungs of ambition.

Zoe knew that everyone talked about her and Jason behind their backs, speculating about the tension between them, wondering if they were sleeping together.

They weren't.

For one thing, she refused to sleep with anyone who routinely went toe-to-toe with her and often won—she got enough of that with her overly ambitious sisters—no matter how gorgeous he was.

And he *was* gorgeous. But her secret crush on him was going to stay secret. Forever. Because the second reason she'd never sleep with Jason was that he was fond of petite blondes, and Zoe wasn't petite or blonde.

"I'm fine. Busy."

"Want help?" he asked, coming into her office with the transparent intent to look at her screen.

Which was blank, thank you very much—something she absolutely did not want him to know. She practically flew out of her chair and around her desk toward him to stop his progress, tripping over her own heels. He caught her against him and she braced herself, hands on his chest, realizing two things. He was even bigger up close and personal than she'd thought. And, even more disconcerting, beneath the office clothes, he was solid with muscle.

She wasn't a small woman. She'd gotten her height from her six-foot-four father. She was the shortest Anders in the bunch at five-nine, and she liked heels. In them, she was just at six feet tall, but she still she had to tip her head up a few inches to see into Jason's eyes.

"Nice diversion technique," he said, his big hands on her hips, holding her upright with a grip that suggested mountain biking did a body good.

"Diversion?" She batted him away, but he didn't go far.

Because he was very busy trying to look over her shoulder at her screen. "Yeah," he said. "But you're going to have to do better than a hug to distract me."

"I was not trying to hug you! And you are *not* getting even a glimpse at my screen." Hell, no. Embarrassing herself was not the plan for today. She pushed him again, ignoring the fact that her fingers were tingling from the feel they'd gotten of him, or the way his scent was invading her senses.

Or how she hadn't budged him at all.

"If you're having trouble," he said, "I could help."

She laughed. "You're going to help me?"

"Sure."

"You've never offered such a thing before."

"You've never given me the time of day before."

"I'm not giving it to you now."

He smiled, slightly lopsided and sexy as hell. The appetizer on his smile menu. "We could combine our efforts," he said.

"I'm *not* having trouble." She narrowed her eyes. "Are *you?*"

He laughed as if that was the most ridiculous thing he'd ever heard, and she had to smile that she'd even suggested it. Jason was a designer genius. He never had trouble. With anything. Or if he did, he kept it deep inside. "Go away, Jason."

He was still close, too close. In her near tumble, a strand of her long hair had caught on the day-old stubble of his jaw. She reached up to tug it free and another of those bolts of sensation went through her.

Not annoyance.

Not adrenaline.

Lust.

His eyes darkened, the only sign that he felt it, too. That, and the way his hands tightened on her hips. There was another beat, and for a minute she thought he was going to kiss her.

"Zoe?" Susan, her assistant, called from her desk out front, making Zoe jump.

Susan was one of a handful of office-support staff. "I've got the reference books you requested," she yelled.

Zoe shut her laptop and brushed past Jason without looking at him again. She accepted the reference material from Susan, and then was waylaid by Steele for a few minutes, exchanging pleasantries. Steele's personality matched his name. He was respectful of women but not especially modern enough to fully believe in one. Zoe intended to change that.

By the time she got back to her office, Jason was gone.

Which was good. Perfect, really.

Letting out a breath, she turned away from her laptop and stared out her office window. San Francisco had definitely dressed up for the holidays this year and was lit up like a Christmas snow globe, even in full daylight.

It was beautiful.

But she couldn't enjoy it. Not when she hadn't settled on anything close to a design worthy of the Weller project. And, as Jason had so thoughtfully pointed out, she had only two weeks left.

Sighing, she scrubbed her hands over her face. Her mind wasn't on the project, but the promotion, which she wanted with all her ambitious heart. It would give her a welcome leg up in the rivalry between her and her siblings. Her three older sisters had a head start. Cindy, Leanne and Valerie were a brain surgeon, a rocket scientist and a district attorney, respectively. Cindy and Leanne had married professional white-collar guys and were raising kids. Valerie had a significant other and was expected to reveal a diamond at some point over the Christmas holidays.

All three practical, logical, smart-as-hell, right-side-of-the-brain, classic overachievers. Zoe used the other side of her brain, the "artist" side, and was an associate architect in a troubled field that traditionally had never been all that kind to women.

Tonight she'd be smack in the center of the Anders' family annual Christmas getaway, in their mountain cabin out in the middle of the Sierras, surrounded by nothing but snow and woods and more than one considerable ego. This time, Zoe wanted to be able to hold her head high and tell her sisters that she was finally on her way in her career. This time *she* was special.

Except that without an architectural plan for the Weller Center, she wasn't.

She turned back to her desk and opened her laptop to eject the memory stick and pack up to leave.

But the memory stick wasn't there. She searched the desk, the floor, everywhere.

It was gone. And so were all her notes and ideas.

She whirled to the door and nearly growled.

Jason.

Grinding her back teeth together, she headed down the hall toward his office. The lights were off, so she hit the switch. His desk was clear of anything, including his laptop. The room was cool and quiet, and it took her a minute to realize what made it feel so stark. She hadn't noticed before, probably because she'd always avoided his space, but unlike the rest of the entire floor, Jason's office was utterly devoid of Christmas decorations.

She turned back the way she'd come and stopped at Susan's desk. "Have you seen Jason?"

"He's gone."

"Gone where?"

"Left. In fact, you just missed him."

Zoe stared at her. "But he was just here."

"Yep. And now he's gone. He's heading out of town, I believe, and not expected in the office again until next week." Susan smiled. "It's Christmas Eve, Zoe. We're all gone, or close to it," she added cheerfully, grabbing her things.

Zoe marched straight to Mike's cubicle, which was the virtual opposite of his brother's office. Every corner was decorated and lit for the holidays to within an inch of its life, including the naughty Mrs. Santa calendar hanging on the corkboard behind his desk.

Mike was on his feet, pulling on a jacket. "Hey," he said with a smile. "Just caught me."

"Where's your brother?"

"Jason?"

"Do you have another obnoxious, sneaky, desperately competitive brother who steals files in order to gain the upper hand because they know they're going to lose?"

Mike laughed. "Ah… You caught him."

Zoe narrowed her eyes. "Are you telling me he really did it, he stole my flash drive?"

He hesitated. "I'm telling you to never underestimate my brother when it comes to getting what he wants," Mike said with a cryptic smile. "Not that he'd admit that."

"Where is he?" Zoe managed to say with what she felt was remarkable calm. "Susan mentioned something about him getting out of town?"

"Yep. He's probably halfway to Lake Tahoe by now." Mike scooped up his portfolio and laptop.

"Lake Tahoe?"

"Yeah, I rented a cabin for my girlfriend and I, but she has to stay in town to do a family thing so we're staying at mine and Jason's place instead. Jason took the cabin to give us some privacy."

Zoe sighed. It could be worse. Lake Tahoe was four hours away but only about an hour and a half out of her way to her family's Christmas gathering in Quincy. Not that it mattered. She wanted her files back. She also wanted to wring Jason's neck. "I need the address."

Mike rubbed his jaw as he looked at her ruefully.

"Mike."

"He specifically said he wanted to be alone."

Uh-huh. She just bet.

"And there's a storm coming," Mike said. "You might get stuck there."

"I have all-wheel drive, I'll be fine." Besides, she'd checked the weather. She had until tomorrow morning before the heavy snow hit, and by then she'd be in Quincy with her family. "I'll owe you a favor."

Mike's eyes lit. "Yeah?"

"Yeah."

Balancing his laptop and portfolio, he scribbled an address down on a piece of paper for her. "I'll deny giving you this."

"I wouldn't expect anything less."

MIKE WATCHED HER WALK AWAY, his smile spreading as he sent out a three-way text:

Operation Getting Jason and Zoe Laid is in progress.

CHAPTER THREE

JASON STOOD STARING at the cabin's empty woodstove. Outside it was pitch-black in the way only the Sierras could be at night. There were no city lights, nothing but a tiny sliver of the moon peeking out from the long fingers of silvery clouds spreading across the sky with increasing speed.

The storm was moving in. He was going to get a white Christmas. Woo hoo.

He didn't waste his breath cursing his brother, the reason he was here. But wasn't it just like Mike to book a nonrefundable weekend at a cabin with the bills mounting and the creditors circling.

It was maybe twenty degrees outside. Inside wasn't much warmer. The place was a low-frills log cabin, beautiful in its simplicity.

And damn cold.

But it was a blissful Christmas-free zone, and a welcome change from the house he shared with Mike in San Francisco. He loved his brother, but even though they'd both suffered the same holiday shock when they lost their parents ten years ago the week before Christmas to a drunk driver, only Jason had seemed to retain his resentment of the season.

Mike had gone the opposite route, probably out of sheer orneriness. Whatever, it didn't matter to Jason as long as his brother was happy. And by all accounts, he seemed to be. He was dating Cara, and if anything, Cara was even more into Christmas than Mike.

A match made in heaven.

On his way to the cabin, he'd stopped at a small mom-and-pop grocery store down the road. The pretty clerk had offered to make up some meals from the deli and deliver them in about an hour, which worked for him. He wasn't much of a cook. Takeout was his specialty, but he doubted there was any takeout within miles of the cabin. So he'd prepaid for the meals and gone on his way.

When he'd entered the cabin, Jason had dropped his duffel bag on the one and only bed in the place and had immediately gone in search of heat.

There was a sticky note on the woodstove telling him that the wood was stacked on the back deck if he wanted to start a fire.

He craned his neck and eyed the thermostat hanging in the window… Yep, twenty degrees, so hell yes he wanted to start a fire. He'd do that then get down to business on the Weller project.

He'd been slaving at it for days now and was having a hell of a time. He had the outline in his mind, knew what he wanted to accomplish, but couldn't make the building itself reflect his vision, and it was driving him nuts.

Peace and quiet was all he needed.

He got to work, loading wood from outside. On his fifth trek from the back deck, a strong gust of wind hit and then a loud crack. He looked up just in time to see a large branch from a two-hundred-foot pine begin to fall. Instinct propelled him backward, the wood flying out of his arms.

The branch hit just outside the deck, a good ten feet away. Jason would have laughed at himself…except his quick movement with his arms full of wood had sent a shaft of pain through his shoulder and neck, making it impossible to laugh, much less move.

Shit. Last year he'd had a spectacular crash on a mountain bike and he'd pinched a nerve in his neck. Given the fire ripping along his nerves, he'd just re-aggravated it.

Grating his teeth, he managed to get inside the cabin, but it cost him. Pain from the spasm was licking along his entire body now.

From experience, he knew there were only two things that would give him relief. Good drugs and heat. Since he had neither, a hot shower would have to do. Only when he made his way to the bathroom, he saw that there was only an old-fashioned, freestanding claw-foot bathtub.

This just got better and better. He needed a trip to the chiropractor, a heat pack and a bottle of Vicodin—none of which was within his reach at the moment. Driving the three and a half hours home just might do him in, so, moving like an old man, he filled the tub, turning the water on with his toes when he couldn't bend over. He managed to strip down, barely, as even the slightest movement provoked pain like a stab with a hot poker. Getting into the tub was an exercise in torture itself, but he managed.

Just as he settled into the hot water, he heard a knock at the door. He was two hundred miles from home and no one but Mike knew he was here. The nearest neighbor was a good quarter of a mile away. Jason eyed his naked bod, then his clothes lying on the floor, damp now from the water that had sloshed over the side of the tub. He looked at the open bathroom door and calculated the additional pain it would cause him to get out of the tub, get dressed and to the front door.

Not going to happen.

The knock came again, less patient this time. "Go away."

Blissfully, whoever it was did just that. When no further sound came, Jason sank back and did his best to relax, purposely not thinking about how he was going to get out of the tub when the water got cold.

WHEN NO ONE ANSWERED her knock, Zoe hugged herself and stomped her feet. She couldn't feel her toes. Each breath crystallized in front of her face, reminding her that she should have changed from her work clothes to something with layers. Lots of layers.

But she'd been in a hurry to get here. The night was dark, but she could see Jason's truck in the driveway. Damn him. There was a light on inside the cabin. He was in there, possibly reading her files and also quite probably laughing at her.

Furious, she glanced at her watch. She hadn't gotten out of the office as fast as she'd hoped, and it was already seven o'clock. If she got the memory stick from him in the next few minutes, she could maybe be at her family's cabin by ten. That wasn't too bad.

But Jason wasn't answering.

The ratfink bastard. She walked around to the back. To her surprise, the sliding glass door off the deck was open. At her feet were a bunch of logs, haphazardly scattered as if they'd been dropped. Uncertain, she stepped to the open door. "Hello? Jason?"

There was a single beat of silence, then a low but deeply heartfelt oath uttered in a familiar baritone.

Jason.

Was he trying to sneak out the front door? With steam coming out her ears—which, by the way, were nearly frozen solid—Zoe let herself in. Unlike Jason, she shut the door—not that it mattered. It was as cold inside as out. She followed the string of swearwords, leading her to the open bathroom door. She stared in shock.

Jason lay sprawled in the bathtub. Steam was rising from the water, fogging the room, but not enough. "You're...*naked!*"

"Yes, that's how I usually bathe," he muttered. "And if it's such a traumatic sight, stop staring. What the hell are you even doing here?"

"I'm—" So help her, she tried to stop staring but her eyes wouldn't behave.

"Either strip down and join me or get out of my bathroom," he told her.

She tried to tear her gaze off his body, but there wasn't a red-blooded woman alive who could have resisted looking. So she slapped a hand over her eyes. "I'm so mad at you."

When he didn't respond to this open invitation to war, Zoe scissored open her fingers and took a peek at him. His big, leanly muscled body was still quite naked. Naked and wet and gleaming and...

Magnificent.

So much so that it took her a shamefully long beat to realize that something was wrong, seriously wrong. His big hands were gripping the sides of the tub, his face a mask of agony.

"What is it?" she asked, dropping her purse. "What's happened?" Kneeling before the tub, she set her hand on his arm, which was hard as a rock and bunched with tension. "Jason?"

"Go away." He spoke through clenched teeth, sweat beading on his temples.

"I can't," she said. "Because someone in this bathroom is an infantile moron and stole my files, which I'm not leaving without. Now, tell me what's wrong." She'd already seen everything he had, so she didn't bother to cover her eyes now. In fact, she ran her gaze over him, this time looking for blood or an obvious injury. But all she saw were two long, powerful legs, a chest and a set of abs carved to absolute perfection, and—

"That's not where I'm hurt," he said dryly.

Right. It wasn't his legs, either, though they were shifting restlessly. His hands were white-knuckled, his arms like rocks. That left his shoulders and neck, or possibly a migraine, but he didn't seem light sensitive so she leaned over him and ran her hands up both impressive biceps. His right shoulder was unnaturally bunched, and when she got to the back of his neck, he let out a low sound, nearly a growl.

"Don't," he said, his voice so low it was almost inaudible, but the warning was plain. He didn't want to be touched.

Maybe it was because she'd been the baby of a bunch of siblings. Or maybe because she herself always found herself scrapping and fighting for every ounce of success she'd ever had. For *anything* she'd ever had. But she couldn't stand to see anything in pain, even her arch nemesis.

So she ignored his warnings, and the fact that his wet, silky hair brushed her fingertips as she moved behind him and began massaging the terrible knot she found between his shoulder and neck. His skin was warm to the touch and smooth, taut over hard muscle.

"So is this the only way you could win this promotion," she asked, trying to lighten the mood. "Steal my files and then hurt yourself so I'll feel too sympathetic to strangle you?"

He groaned, and the sound snaked through her and

made her belly quiver. "I don't know what you're talking about. I didn't steal your files," he said roughly, eyes closing as he very carefully shifted to give her more room to work on his neck.

"I don't believe you for one second, of course." He'd really done a number on himself. She could feel the muscle spasming, so she worked him harder, digging her fingers into the spot. He jerked and grunted in pain, and she had to steel herself against the stab of sympathy. "Since when are you so weak that you have to steal *and* lie?"

"I didn't—" His face twisted and he gasped, the sound pure agony. "Right there—"

"I've got it. Now tell me you took my memory stick and where it is so I can take it and go before the storm hits." And hopefully before he'd had a chance to look at the material and realize that she'd gotten absolutely *nowhere* on her design.

With a softer groan, he shifted again. "Look, despite the fact that you're crazy, I'll say whatever you want me to say. I'll do anything you want, just don't stop doing whatever it is you're doing."

Letting out a breath, she kneaded the knots ruthlessly hard for long minutes. His eyes were closed, the muscles in his jaw bunching with every touch. "Relax," she suggested.

His barely audible "trying" was accompanied by "oh, Christ" when she dug in particularly deep.

"Why would I steal anything from you, much less your files?" he said eventually through gritted teeth.

"Especially when I have my own design, the one that's going to win?"

She went still, the zinger surprisingly hitting a bull's-eye.

When she didn't immediately rally with a reply, he opened his eyes. "Hey, you're supposed to hit back. It's what we do."

She forced herself to breathe. "I can win."

He stared at her. "Well, yeah. Of course you can. Zoe...I was just being a jerk because usually we—" He broke off at the sound of footsteps on the hardwood floor, walking up to the bathroom door.

The woman who appeared in the doorway was either directly from Santa's workshop or heading to a Maxim photo shoot. She was in her early twenties; a tiny, curvy little blonde with a bright white smile and a skimpy red sweater, emphasis on the skimpy.

"Who are you?" Zoe asked.

"Santa's Helper. From the deli." The woman's eyes were on Jason. "No one answered the front door, but there were two cars so I walked around. The back door was unlocked. You should be more careful about that, you're going to get bears." Her eyes were locked on Jason's gorgeous anatomy. "Oh, my..."

Jason reached out for the washcloth hanging off the soap rack and dropped it over his lap. "I didn't answer for a good reason."

The woman went into a full pout, quite the feat with her thick frosted gloss. "I brought your groceries. And some eggnog. I sorta thought we might—"

"Sorry, you got the wrong idea," Jason said. He closed his eyes, jaw bunching. "Thanks for the groceries but I'm not fit for company."

"Hmph." She slid Zoe a hard look. "Who's she?"

Zoe opened her mouth to say "none of your business," but Jason answered before she could. "Homecare nurse."

Zoe narrowed her eyes as the woman took in Zoe's navy business suit—modestly cut, since Zoe hated when men at work didn't meet her eyes because they were too busy looking about eight inches south.

"Whatever. Your loss, dude," the woman finally said, and tossed her hair. She gave Jason's washcloth one more slow appraisal and sighed in disappointment. "Is someone going to tip me, or what?"

Zoe saw Jason's helpless grimace and with a sigh, she reached into her purse and grabbed a five, slapping it into the woman's hand. Five seconds later, the front door slammed shut behind her.

"Three things," Zoe said to Jason. "One, you're a pig. And two, you owe me five bucks."

Jason's eyes were closed again. He looked like the epitome of a Hollywood actor sprawled out on a movie set—except for the gray pallor of his complexion.

"What's the third thing?" he asked.

"Your washcloth isn't big enough."

CHAPTER FOUR

SHE HAD TO HELP HIM OUT of the tub. Jason was sure those minutes were burned into his memory, having Zoe's hands all over his naked, wet body.

And her washcloth comment hadn't helped any, either.

The moment he was standing on the tile floor, she tossed him a towel and ran out of the bathroom as if there was a fire on her ass.

He moved slowly, cautiously, but the hot water and her massage had helped considerably. He wrapped the towel around his hips and followed her, dripping water.

She was ahead of him, moving through the living room straight into the small kitchen, looking around.

"What are you doing?" he asked.

She whirled to face him. "Where is it?"

"What?"

"The memory stick!" She had her hands on her hips now. "Give it to me and I'll be out of here, and we never have to discuss this evening ever again."

She was still dressed as she'd been at work, in her usual business suit that he was certain she thought said: *power.* But what it really said was that she'd bought the suit off the rack a size too big to hide her smoking-hot bod so that the guys in the office wouldn't stare at her.

They still stared, they just did it behind her back. No one could help it. She was tall and her body had curves, *real* curves, the kind a man dreamed about when alone in his bed at night. When she took her blazer off at work, every man in the vicinity lost brain cells.

But even with that rocking body, it was her eyes that held Jason. They slayed him every single time she directed them on him. Right now those sharp green eyes were saying "bring it, bitch," and he couldn't help it, he smiled.

She didn't return it. Her hair was aflame beneath the kitchen lights, held out of her face by a clip, though there were a few stubborn strands that had found their freedom and lay along her temples and jawline. He started to drop his head a little and stop staring at her, but at the movement, pain slashed through him, making him hiss in a breath.

"Oh, no. No, no, no," she said. "That isn't going to work." She poked him in the bare chest with her finger. "I'm not going to feel sorry for you." With a sound of annoyance, she was on the move again, this time toward the front door.

"You're leaving?"

"You're not going to admit what you did, fine. I'm out. I still have a two-hour drive ahead of me to meet up with my family at their Quincy cabin."

Quincy was at *least* a two-hour drive, up a narrow two-lane highway that wasn't exactly a walk in the park, especially at night.

Not your problem... But he followed her to the door, oddly reluctant to let her go. "What if my neck goes into spasm again? I might drown in the tub."

"Be sure to leave me the memory stick in your will."

She was already at the door and he felt a surge of adrenaline hit him as he tried to figure out a way to get her to stay. Which meant that he was crazy.

In the end he went with the only way he knew how to get her attention—by goading her. "Know what I think?" he asked her stiff spine. "I think you don't really believe I stole your file. That's just your excuse to see me."

She whipped around. "Listen, pal. I saw *way* more of you than I planned on."

"A bonus."

She stared at him in disbelief. "You cost me away time with my family."

"Your sisters," he said, pulling out that little tidbit from conversations he'd overheard at some point or another. "Three of them, right? That's a lot of estrogen in one place."

"Yeah," she admitted with what might have been a very tiny smile on her mouth. "So much so that my dad chops the wood with an ax instead of the brand-new logger he purchased because it takes about ten times as long."

"Then you should be thanking me. Like you said, you killed some time here."

She rolled her eyes and once again turned to the door, and he felt his gut sink to his very cold toes. "Wait." Moving carefully, he spun her around to face him.

She took in his bare chest and his towel, and swallowed hard.

Just that little involuntary movement made him forget being hurt and cold. In fact, it made him something else entirely, not a great thing while wearing only a towel.

Clearing his throat, he said, "Why don't we work together on this thing. We—"

Suddenly she frowned, her eyes focusing behind him.

"What?" Moving like a turtle, hoping to God that whatever she was seeing wasn't a bear, he looked behind him.

"There's no Christmas decorations," she said.

He blinked. "It's a rental cabin."

"Yes, but you're staying here alone? Through Christmas?"

"Yes…"

"Without a single holiday decoration?"

Turning, he headed straight to the small bar between the kitchen area and living room. It was past time for a drink of something, preferably something hard that would make him forget why he wanted her to stay. Halfway there, his towel began to slip and in the name of any modesty he might have left, he grabbed it at the last second, receiving another stab of pain for his effort. He stifled his reaction and poured a healthy shot of scotch.

"Thought your neck hurt," she said, and he could tell by her voice that she'd moved somewhere between the door and where he stood.

"Kills," he said without even attempting to face her. He did however manage to *very* slightly tilt his head and toss back the whole shot. And then a second one. Oh, look at that, he was over her already.

"You're supposed to ask your guest if she wants any."

"You're driving. And you're not my guest. You let yourself in to yell at me and got a peep show in the process." The hell with this. "Look, either stay and join forces with me on this project or go. Your choice."

She stared at him, and he couldn't blame her. Working together was not only a rash idea, it was a stupid one. And given the way she was gaping at him, she knew it.

Whatever. She could let herself out, he didn't care. He needed some clothes and food and sleep, and he'd take them in any order he could get. Setting the shot glass down, he left her alone to figure her shit out and headed toward the bedroom for his duffel bag, holding on to the towel with one hand and using the other to rub at the back of his aching neck and shoulder. It was starting to seize again, and he paused in the hallway, undecided as to whether to get back into the tub or just pass out on the bed and hope he woke up feeling better.

Pass out, he decided, and very carefully sprawled out on the bed facedown, head carefully turned to the one side that didn't hurt. He was cold, but to get under the covers meant moving. And he was done moving, so he closed his eyes.

WORK TOGETHER? WAS HE insane?

Dammit, Zoe thought, watching him walk out of the living room. Not crazy. He was moving with such careful purpose that she knew he wasn't faking the pain.

She couldn't leave him like that, not without making sure he was going to be okay. And then there was the little matter of the flash drive. Not to mention the fact that she wouldn't mind getting a peek at his design.

The bathroom was lit but empty. She pulled the plug on the drain but drew the line at picking up his clothes. Then she peered into the bedroom. The bathroom light slanted in, revealing one big and still very naked man on the bed. His shoulders were wide, his back sleek and delineated with strength. The towel was low enough on his hips that she could see the line where his tan faded to pale skin. His butt was… bitable.

The only sound in the room was her own accelerated breathing and…a rumbling stomach.

Not hers. "Jason?"

"Either shoot me or go away." His stomach rumbled again, and the sound created the oddest reaction in her—tenderness. Now *she* was the crazy one. "You're hungry."

That he didn't respond was answer enough. She walked into the room and tried to dislodge the blanket beneath him. No go. He was a solid, unmovable log. And when her hand brushed his shoulder, his skin was icy cold. A solid, unmovable *frozen* log. She tried again to get at the blanket beneath him, except this time the only thing that happened was that his towel loosened.

"You're determined to see my bare ass again, aren't you?" he muttered, but didn't budge an inch.

"Shut up." Turning, she spied a throw blanket over a chair in the corner and tossed that over him. "Better?"

"Perfect."

"Do you have anything for the pain?"

"I don't need anything."

"Jason."

"No, I don't have anything. I'm fine."

She nodded even though he couldn't see her, and headed to the door, taking one last look back. "You're going to be okay, right?"

"Perfect," he repeated, still not moving.

Once again, he was full of shit. She really needed to get the hell out, but she couldn't get past one thing. He was going to be here, alone on Christmas, without even a single bough of holly.

Or an ounce of Christmas spirit.

Shaking her head, she returned to the kitchen. He was hungry, and clearly unable to get up and about. She'd just bring him something to eat and be gone.

The refrigerator was empty, and so was the freezer. Then she remembered "Santa's Helper." She found the two bags of groceries still on the floor in the entryway. Chips, cheese, crackers, deli meat, containers of potato salad, chickens wings, apples, a loaf of French bread and beer, along with several candy bars and the local newspaper. Leaving Jason the wings and salad for tomorrow, she sliced up some of the bread and made a sandwich with the cheese and meat. She cut up an apple and completed the meal with a side of the chips. Then she rifled through her purse for aspirin, but found only extra-strength Midol. She brought the plate into the bedroom. "Jason?"

"Are you wearing the Santa's Helper costume?"

"No."

"*Could* you wear the Santa's Helper costume?"

"Only in your dreams." She set the sandwich down on the nightstand. "I brought food."

There was surprise in the ensuing silence and then, with a groan, Jason started for the lamp and groaned again.

Zoe leaned over him and turned it on.

With the slow precision of the inebriated or someone in great pain, he rolled over.

His hair, dampened by his bath, was a rumpled, tousled mess. If she'd let hers dry like that she'd look ridiculous, but on Jason it gave him a dark edge and was disturbingly sexy.

She helped prop him up with some pillows. He let out a sigh of relief when she'd finished, but Zoe wasn't relieved in the slightest. Sitting at his hip on his bed while he lay naked beneath nothing but a thin blanket and towel was…well, she wasn't sure exactly.

Liar, an inner voice said. *Your nipples are hard. You know exactly what you are—aroused.* "Here." She handed him the two Midol.

"What are they?"

She hesitated. "Feel-happy pills?"

"You carry Vicodin?"

"They're not quite that happy. They're Midol."

He gave her a you-have-got-to-be-kidding look and retracted his hand as if she'd asked him to touch a spitting cobra. *"No."*

"Oh, for God's sake, it's all I have. Take them, it'll help."

"How do I know you're not just going to blackmail me later and threaten to tell the guys you got me to take Midol."

"Trust me, *no one* is going to hear of this little adventure."

He took the pills. "So am I going to get all bitchy and start whining now that I'm swallowing chick pills?"

She actually laughed. "No, it's going to take *away* your bitchiness and whininess. At least if there's a God."

A very small smile curved his lips. "Nice spread," he said, gesturing to the plate with the perfectly made sandwich, carefully cut down the center, the sliced apple and chips, neatly segregated. "I had no idea you had it in you."

"You don't know a lot about me."

"True," he said. "You hide from me at work."

"We're competitors."

"We're coworkers. There's a difference, not that you've ever noticed." He handed her half the sandwich.

"I can't," she said. "It's for you. And I have to go."

"Eat first. You've got a long drive." At her surprise, he lifted his good shoulder. "Quincy, you said, right? To your family thing."

"You actually *do* listen, I had no idea."

"You don't know a lot about me," he said, mirroring her own words at him. "Eat."

It was a command, however softly uttered, and she hated commands. She'd grown up with them, dealt with them at work, tolerated them from her older sisters and...everyone. But then he added the coup de grâce, a softly uttered "please," which sounded more genuine and sincere than anything she'd ever heard from him, and she caved like a cheap suitcase. She took the sandwhich and she ate.

CHAPTER FIVE

THEY SHARED THE SANDWICH and the apple but Zoe flatly refused the chips. "They're barbecue," she told Jason, as if this explained it all.

It didn't. "You don't like barbecue?" he asked.

"Love them." But she was staring down the chips as if they were her mortal enemy.

"I'd shake my head in utter confusion," he said. "If I could move my neck."

"They're fattening."

He stared at her for a beat. "There's maybe twenty chips on this plate. How many calories could your half possibly be?"

"A million. And you wouldn't understand," she said, still staring down at the chips, naked longing on her face.

"Why not?"

"Because look at you." She waved a hand toward his torso. "You're perfect."

He laughed, but she wasn't laughing along with him. He swallowed the last of his half of the sandwich and ran a finger along her temple, then along her earlobe, enjoying that it made her shiver. "You're pretty damn perfect yourself, Zoe."

She closed her eyes. "Don't." Then she belied that statement by leaning into him.

His fingers slid into her hair, drawing her closer, then closer still so that she was leaning over him, hands braced on the bed on either side of his hips. "You are," he breathed against her lips.

Her gaze dropped to his mouth. "At the office—"

"We're not at the office."

"No kidding," she whispered. Their lips brushed together, and she let out a shaky breath, her eyes soft as her chest settled against his. Her body heat was seeping into him, warming the core of him. She was a strong woman, one of the strongest he'd ever met, and having her melt all over him was the most rewarding thing he'd ever felt.

"Jason?"

He tightened his hold on her, frustrated that he couldn't move when what he wanted to do was roll her beneath him and feel her body wrap around his. "Yeah?"

"I still don't like you."

Somehow, though he was both in pain and aroused as hell, he still had room to laugh.

"But you smell like chips," she said, close enough that their lips were still nearly touching. "And I like chips. A lot. Goddammit, you're going to taste good." She was breathless, and so was he.

Her voice was low and sexy, but somehow surprised and curious. Then her tongue outlined his lower lip and *he* was the surprised one. "Christ, Zoe."

"I know." She pulled back and covered her face with her hands. "God. I'm sorry." She dropped her hands and pointed at him. "But this is all your fault."

He laughed again. He couldn't remember the last time he'd wanted to strangle a woman at the same moment he'd wanted to strip her naked and bury himself inside her. "My fault?"

"Yes! I mean, you're lying there, hurt and in pain, and I...I can't stand it when someone's hurting or in pain. And then there's the chips. The irresistible *barbecue* chips, Jason. I mean, why couldn't it have been plain chips? Plain, I could have resisted—" She started to get up, but he managed to snake his fingers around her wrist.

One little tug and she was back on the bed. Another tug and he put her off balance so that she fell over him.

He threaded his fingers in her hair, tilted her head so he didn't have to tilt his and kissed her, long and slow and deep. He knew she was right there with him when she moaned low in her throat and pressed up against him, her hands running restlessly over whatever she could reach, making a sound of frustration when she was thwarted by the blanket between them. She tugged, reminding him he was bare-ass naked beneath it. "Zoe," he said in warning.

"Not done tasting the chips," she murmured, and brought his mouth back to hers.

Not one to argue with a woman—not when her hands were on the move southward and heading toward home base—Jason gave in, nipping her jaw, running his tongue over the hollow of her throat.

"This is crazy," she gasped, even as she arched against him, moaning with pleasure. Her suit jacket was in his way, so he nudged it from her shoulders. She never took her mouth off him as she shimmied out of it.

"Crazy," he agreed, pulling her so that she was now straddling his hips.

"I mean, I could totally resist you if I wanted."

"Good." His hands went straight to her blouse, flicking the buttons open as she wriggled on him and made his eyes cross with lust. Her skirt had risen up past her thighs so that the only thing separating them was the thin blanket and what looked like a very sexy pair of silky pale blue panties.

She got busy sucking on his tongue. Not wanting to disturb that, Jason spread her blouse wide and tugged the cups of her bra down.

Her fingernails dug into his shoulders, slid quickly down his chest to his abs and back up, as if she couldn't get enough of him. He urged her even closer so that he could suck her nipple between his tongue and the roof of his mouth. The sweet sounds she made in response wreaked havoc on any control he had left. She was writhing on him, her eyes closed, mouth open, skin dewy and flushed.

She was his every fantasy.

"I want you," he said hoarsely. "Zoe, I want—"

"Yes. God, yes," she said with a shudder as he

lifted her enough to rip away the blanket and then the towel from between them.

"Oh," she murmured huskily in soft pleasure as she stared down at the part of him that was the most happy to be there. She wrapped her fingers around him, making him thrust up into her hand. But the movement jarred his neck and he sucked in a breath as the pain slapped him.

"Oh, God," she said shakily, still holding him in her hands. "Are you okay? Should we stop?"

"Only if you want to see a grown man cry," he managed to say, gripping her ass in one hand, rolling her nipple between his fingers with his other. He hadn't chosen to be here, certainly hadn't planned on this, but now there was nowhere else he wanted to be. He wanted to stay like this, exactly like this, with her. And even though he told himself there was no sense in craving things he couldn't have, he continued to tease and coax her body into needing his.

"Don't move," she demanded. "You hear me? I'll do it."

He'd never been much for following directions, and he'd certainly never lay pliant in bed before, but there was something about letting her be in control, letting her have her way with him that excited him.

"Condom?" she whispered.

He stared at her, gobsmacked. Never in his life had he forgotten a condom. "I don't—" *Shit*. "I didn't expect—"

"I'm on the pill," she murmured. "And I haven't had sex in two years."

"Two years—"

"You?"

"I've never had sex without a condom. But—"

The words backed up in his throat when she scraped her panties to one side and guided him home.

Oh, God. The feel of her silky wet heat... She'd told him not to move, but he couldn't help it. He reached down and rubbed his thumb over her until she gasped.

"There." Her fingers dug into his biceps. "Oh, God, Jason. There."

Which he took to mean "don't stop." He didn't, and she gasped again, and then she cried out and came. Watching her, hearing her, did him in. He wasn't going to last. He gripped her hips, desperate to hold it together.

"Jason. God, Jason."

"I know." He wanted to slow down, wanted to build the pleasure for her again, but the way she was looking down at him, the bewildered arousal, the tight need, how she'd given herself to him after not being with anyone in so long, was seriously testing his control. "Come here," he whispered. She leaned over him, sucking his lower lip into her mouth.

His control slipped yet another notch and he rocked his hips into hers, holding there, sucking in air as she grinded on him. He closed his eyes. *"Zoe."*

"Mmm," was all she seemed to be able to get out. He slid a hand between their bodies and stroked, watching as she quivered, loving the way her head fell back on her shoulders, how she cried out and shuddered and came all over him. It was the most erotic, gorgeous sight he'd ever seen, and far too much for his already shaky control. Unable to hold back, he followed her over.

CHAPTER SIX

WHEN ZOE CAUGHT HER BREATH, she realized she was plastered up against Jason, arms and legs wrapped around him like a monkey, her face pressed hard to his throat.

Way to resist him, Zoe. She pulled free and got off the bed.

"Zoe?" His voice was low, husky. One hundred percent sated male.

Because just the sound of him softened her resistance, she turned her back to him so she could straighten her panties and fix the cups of her bra. She was bending for her jacket when she heard the low groan.

It wasn't a pleasure-filled groan, either. And she now knew the difference. Grimacing at her weakness, she whirled around to find him struggling to his feet.

And he *was* struggling, pain etched in every line of his face.

With a sigh, she moved back to the bed, putting her hands on his bare chest. "Stop. You're going to make it worse."

Ignoring her, he slowly and cautiously straightened. "Jason, stop. Stay in bed."

Swearing, he started to reach for the blanket and went pale. She grabbed the thing and wrapped it around him, her fingers brushing his perfect torso as much as possible.

"Say the word and the blanket is gone," he said.

Her gaze flew to his. "You're hurting. How could you possibly want round two?"

"Testosterone," he said simply. "Testosterone would follow a woman with an ass as sweet as yours straight into the depths of hell." He paused. "And you should talk. You just totally felt me up while you were wrapping the blanket around me. You want round two just as bad as me."

"Two years," she repeated.

"Why so long?" he asked softly.

Since that was a question that she didn't want to face, she bent and searched for her heels, locating them just under the bed. Jamming her feet into them, she headed out of the bedroom. "We aren't going to speak of this to anyone."

He was following her, but said nothing. She decided to take his silence as agreement but made the fatal mistake of looking back at him.

His hair was more rumpled than ever, and still dead sexy. He hadn't shaved this morning, maybe not yesterday, either. And she knew firsthand what that dark scruff felt like on her skin. She had the whisker burns on her breasts and throat to prove it. He was holding his head at a funny angle, assuring her that however much she wanted to be gone, he was still absolutely hurting. "Are you going to be okay?" she asked.

He arched a brow. "If I said no, would you jump my bones again?"

She felt the blush spread across her cheeks. Good. He was still an ass. That made resisting him easier. "I need my files."

"I told you, I don't have them. It was supposed to start snowing tonight. Has it started?"

She peeked outside. Tiny little flakes were coming down. "Just, the roads should still be okay." As for the missing memory stick, she'd live. It would involve embarrassing herself in front of her boss, but she'd email him and admit to needing another copy of the specs, and she remembered most of her notes and ideas. "I meant what I said. Promise me that this stays between us."

"Which? The fact that I gave you two orgasms, or that you lost your own files?"

"You were counting?"

"Not necessary. Each time you came, you dug your nails into my back." His expression was pure smug male. "Well worth it, of course."

She narrowed her eyes, trying to ignore the fact that despite his best efforts, the blanket was slipping. She knew damn well he had to be freezing. Not that she cared. She huffed out a breath. "Look, we're not teenagers. It's happened, it's done, we deal with it. All I'm saying is that we don't ever have to discuss it."

"It?"

"Our...nakedness," she clarified.

"And the orgasms."

"Yes, those, too," she said with what she felt was remarkable calm.

"And the cuddling afterward?" he asked. "Is that off limits as well, the way you curled into me all soft and warm and purring like a well-fed kitten?"

"I did not—" She grated her teeth. Okay, so she had. "Are you saying you *want* everyone to know about this?"

Instead of answering, he turned and walked into the kitchen, still moving in a way that gave away his pain. She let out a breath, torn. Torn by him, dammit. How could it be that she didn't want to go? "Jason."

He didn't answer, but she could hear a cell phone going off. His, she decided by the ringtone. Then she heard him swear, and then the sound of glass shattering.

Zoe ran into the kitchen and found Jason standing barefoot amongst shards of glass on the floor. "Did you cut yourself?" she asked.

"I'm not a complete moron."

"Don't move."

"I won't," he bit out. "I can't."

She could see that was true. He was very still, probably because he couldn't move without pain. Since she had her heels on, she walked right up to him and crouched, scooping up pieces of glass. "What happened?"

"I got a text from Mike and I dropped my glass."

The glass had broken in six or seven pieces. She carefully picked them up one at a time, trying not to notice his bare feet. A man's feet shouldn't be sexy, and yet there they were. Being sexy. "Must have been some text," she said.

"Mike has your damn file. He sent you up here thinking he was playing matchmaker because he didn't want me to be alone on Christmas."

Still kneeling at his feet, Zoe went still, then tipped her head back to look at him. "What?"

"Yeah," Jason said grimly. "That's my brother, always the helpful one. Look, I'm sorry, he's an asshole. Although you thought *I* stole the damn file, so that means you were sure I was the asshole, so…"

She shook her head, unable to process anything past the roar of the blood in her own ears. "We were had by your brother?"

"Seems like it."

"Oh, my God." She rose to her feet, fists clenched. "He wanted us to—"

"Which we did," he pointed out.

She stared at him. *"Ohmigod,"* she repeated.

That sexy muscle in his jaw bunched again. "I'll apologize for my idiot of a brother, Zoe. But no one forced us to—"

"Don't say it," she warned, pointing at him, shaking with anger. Or maybe that was just humiliation. *All your own fault,* she reminded herself, suddenly painfully aware of their conflicting ambitions and how much was at stake here if word got out of what had happened between them. "We *aren't* discussing it, remember? *Ever.*" She let out a breath and shook her head. "You didn't text him back, right? You didn't tell him that we—"

"Christ, no. Although I might kill him. You don't mind that, right?"

"I'll hold him down for you," she said grimly.

A ghost of a smile crossed his lips.

She searched out the trash can, dumped the glass in it and found a little hand broom, using it carefully so he wouldn't have trouble after she was gone, hating that she even cared. "I saw a bear box for the trash outside when I came in. I'm going to go dump this there and then be on my way."

"Wait." He vanished for a minute and then came back and handed something to her. A memory stick. His.

"Jason, I can't—"

"My design isn't on there, but all the specs are, so at least you can get something done before you get yours back from Mike. If you want."

"What will you do?"

"I'll figure it out."

She stared down at the stick, not sure how to reconcile all her feelings. She'd been so mad, so hurt… and then naked.

And now he had to go and be such a good guy.

It was quite the offer. She knew how ambitious he was, and his talent backed up that ambition. He wanted to win this design, this promotion, every bit as much as she did, maybe more.

She curled her fingers around the stick. Maybe her best bet was to work with him. They could submit their plan to Steele together and then their boss could decide based on their past work who'd get the promotion...

No. It was crazy. It was.

"Promise me, Jason, that this whole sex thing is as good as forgotten."

Something flickered in his eyes, coming and going so fast she couldn't put her finger on the emotion. "I promise," he said softly.

A victory.

But for some reason it felt hollow as she walked out the back and into the night.

JASON GOT HIMSELF BACK TO BED, carefully lowered his body to it, then did his best to get comfortable, which turned out to be an impossible task. At least the Midol Zoe had given him made him sleepy.

Or maybe that had been the mind-blowing orgasm.

In either case, his neck hurt like hell and his feet were cold, but there was nothing he could do about either so he made himself relax.

Promise me, Jason, Zoe had said, *that this whole sex thing is as good as forgotten.*

Her words bounced around in his head. His last thought as he drifted off to sleep was that she'd extracted a promise from him that he should have been happy to make, but he hadn't, not at all. Nope, against his better judgment, he didn't want to forget a single minute of it. In fact, he wanted more.

ZOE GOT ABOUT A MILE DOWN the road on the very narrow, very curvy two-lane highway when she realized she was leaving for the wrong reason. So she'd been manipulated by Mike, so what. Yeah, it was all a big joke and she'd gotten caught up in it and slept with Jason.

It was nothing.

But she couldn't make herself believe it. Mostly because she never got caught up in a man, not like that, not even when she had a silly little crush on the guy—which she'd had.

Had. Past tense, she assured herself. Crush over.

Fingers tight on the wheel, she made a sharp turn and slid a little bit on some ice. Her heart was in her throat when she steered out of it. She slowed way down but there were no city lights, no streetlights and no other cars. The only thing relieving the relentless dark was the white of the heavy snow and the two inconsequential beams of her headlights.

When she slid again, she pulled over. Mother Nature was trying to tell her something, the same something her gut was trying to tell her. Her cell vibrated an incoming text, and she read the message from her oldest sister.

The roads are iced over up here. If you haven't left SF yet, don't. Wait until daylight.

Zoe stared out her windshield for a long moment. She could go a few miles, where she'd come to a small mining town with a few inns. Or she could turn around and go back to Tahoe where there was a man in nothing but a blanket and enough testosterone and pheromones to keep her warm until morning…

It was really no contest. She turned around and drove back to the cabin. She knocked, a sense of déjà vu coming over her when Jason didn't answer.

Once again, she let herself in, but this time she found Jason asleep on the bed.

Feeling like Goldilocks, she tiptoed out of the bedroom. She couldn't bring herself to wake him up, and she certainly couldn't crawl into bed with him. So she went out to her car for her bag.

As she hauled her bag out of the trunk, her gaze landed on the Christmas decorations she'd promised her mom that she'd bring to the cabin.

She grabbed them along with her other things. What the hell. If she wasn't going to spend the evening with her family decorating, she could do it here.

Inside the cabin, she lit a fire, proud of her ability to do so even if it took almost a full box of matches until she got the thing crackling with heat.

By now the snow was coming down, casting a beautiful blanket of white over everything.

She'd made the right decision. So why was she feeling so…discombobulated? She glanced toward the bedroom.

Because you're playing Goldilocks…

She nibbled on her lower lip, not sleepy. If she had made it to Quincy, she'd be in the midst of her family right now, arguing and bickering and being reminded that no matter what she did she was still the baby of the family and could never catch up to her siblings' accomplishments. She sent them all a text, then strung pretty little white lights along the small bar and fireplace. There was a potted pothos plant in one corner, nearly as tall as she was. She turned it into a Christmas tree, hanging small red and gold balls from the branches. The boughs of holly she spread on the mantel and on the windowsills. She went a little bit crazy with the tinsel, but the flashes of silver and gold felt cheery. The whole place felt cheery. And cozy. And warm.

She'd told herself she'd done it only for her own enjoyment, so she wouldn't get sad about not getting to Quincy. But when she was finished and standing in the center of the living room, enjoying the ambience, she realized she hadn't done it for herself at all.

She'd done it for Jason.

So who was the liar now?

God. She scrubbed a hand over her eyes and tried to clear her mind, but it wouldn't clear. Instead, it was stuck replaying those few moments hours ago, when she'd been in Jason's arms. She was staring into the flickering flames, but all she could see was the look on his face as he'd emptied himself into her, his head thrown back, the muscles corded in his throat, groaning her name.

Confused and aroused and angry at herself all over again, she got her bag and pulled out her laptop. She plugged in Jason's memory stick, brought up her design program and went to work. And for the first time in two weeks, her brain kicked into gear. Probably because the alternative activity—climbing into bed with Jason—was an even more terrifying prospect than not having a design for the Weller project.

CHAPTER SEVEN

JASON WOKE AT SOME POINT just past dawn and lay perfectly still, taking stock of his situation. The bedroom was warm, which was strange since he'd never gotten around to starting a fire. His neck and shoulder weren't sending a stab of pain through him with each heartbeat, which he took as a good sign. He tested himself by carefully shifting.

An ache answered. And a twinge. But compared to the stabbing pain of the night before, he was ready to go. Maybe not mountain biking, but he could probably put on his own socks today, so that was a bonus.

The hot bath the night before had helped.

So had Zoe's massage.

And the orgasm…that had been a very unexpected bonus. The image of Zoe riding him to her own pleasure was one he wouldn't be forgetting any time soon. In fact, just thinking about it made him wish she was still here.

And not just for sex, although he wouldn't turn it down. The truth was, he'd enjoyed her company.

A lot.

Who'd have thought that the woman who'd been dogging his tail at the firm, chasing his dream, even beating him at his own game was not just a challenge but someone he wouldn't mind getting to know better.

Groggy as hell, he staggered into the bathroom and took a shower. Not a morning person, he used all the hot water in the hopes it'd wake him up, but it didn't happen. The only thing that could possibly save him was coffee. He'd give his left nut for coffee.

Which he'd forgotten to bring or buy.

Still in the bathroom, he pulled up the protective shades on the small window. "Holy shit," he said, stunned to find that a foot of snow had fallen overnight. His car was covered.

As was a second car, next to his. What the hell? He left the bathroom and entered the living room, stopping in shock in the doorway.

There were lights. Lots of lights, blinking in bright colors. And were those...*balls* hanging from the rafters? Yes. Yes, those were indeed balls, in red and gold. And the tinsel. Christ, the tinsel would take him hours, if not *days,* to get rid of.

His gaze slid to the couch and the woman slowly sitting up.

"Hi," Zoe said, voice morning thick. She didn't quite meet his eyes as she attempted to pat down her hair.

It'd broken free of its clip and appeared to have rioted, floating around her face and shoulders like a fiery red cloud. He could have told her not to bother trying to control it. He happened to like the way it caught the lights and glimmered under them, but knew if she glimpsed herself in the mirror, she wasn't going to feel the same way.

But none of her crazy and utterly unintentional sexiness could take away from the fact that she'd *decorated.*

"Do you ever wear clothes?" she asked.

He looked down at himself. Once again he was wearing only a towel. "Wait right there." He vanished into the bedroom, where he rifled through his duffel bag and came up with a pair of Levi's and a long-sleeved Henley. His feet were still bare, but his neck was giving him twinges again and he wasn't going to move more than necessary. He left the bedroom and went straight to the couch, which was now empty of one Zoe Anders.

Turning in a circle, he saw she'd gone into the bathroom. He could hear the shower running, and went to warn her that he'd just used all the hot water. He lifted his hand to knock, but suddenly there was a feminine screech of shock and outrage.

With a grin, he let his hand fall to his side. Served her right, Ms. Decorating Queen. He was still staring at the living room, the sparkling, twinkling living room, when she came out of the bathroom.

She was wearing a bright red hoodie, trimmed in white with two tassels that bumped against her gorgeous breasts, and a zipper that went right between. His first thought was to take the tab of the zipper between his teeth and tug down. But that might have been his early-morning erection doing his thinking for him. Her black leggings were nice, too, emphasizing those mile-long legs that he wouldn't mind having wrapped around him again. But the fantasy was hard to put together with all the blinking lights.

"I didn't get far on the road," she said. "It was snowing really hard and my tires—"

He tore his eyes away from the lights. "Are you okay? Did you spin out?"

"No, nothing like that." She grimaced. "Okay, that was a lie. I slipped once or twice, got scared and came back." She grimaced again. "Okay, that was another lie. I came back because I wanted to." She nibbled on her lower lip as her gaze took him in from head to toe and then back again, lingering at the bulge just behind his button fly. When her tongue darted out and ran over her bitten lower lip, that bulge twitched. "But then when I got here, I didn't think waking you up was wise," she murmured.

Truer words had never been spoken. "But decorating was?"

"You like it?" she asked, eyeing the place with unmistakable pride. "No one should celebrate the season without a little cheer, so…um, happy cheer."

He opened his mouth to tell her how he felt about the over-the-top, gaudy decorations and the stupid holiday, but she was smiling. A real smile, too, not her work smile or her I-think-you're-such-a-schmuck smile. It was a genuine show of humor and warmth, directed at him. He actually got dizzy from it. There she stood, looking sweet and adorable and uninten-

tionally sexy as hell. He forced a smile. "It's...bright."
He angled away to give himself a moment, and that's
when he saw it. She'd turned the plant in the corner
into a Christmas tree.

A Charlie Brown Christmas tree...

She came up at his side, still smiling. "Isn't it cute?
And look." She pointed to the fireplace, which had
been burdened with both flickering lights *and* tinsel.
"There's no doubt it's Christmas morning now, right?"

Something in his chest tightened. It was Christmas morning and she'd planned to be with her family,
celebrating. Instead, she was here with him, stuck. It
wasn't his fault, at least not directly, but he felt like
the Grinch who'd stolen her Christmas. "I'm sorry,"
he said. "Sorry you're stuck here."

She turned to him. Unlike most of the women he'd
had in his life, she came up past his shoulder. If he
bent only the slightest bit, he could kiss her.

"It's not your fault," she said. "I'll get to Quincy
soon enough. Do you like the decorations, Jason?"

Quandary. Did he lie his ass off, or go with honesty? Either was tricky, but if he knew one thing, it
was that women didn't usually really want the truth.
"They're...great."

She stared at him for a beat. "You don't like them."

"No, I—"

"Tell me the truth."

He let out a breath. "I came up here to be alone and
not celebrate Christmas."

She was silent for a single heartbeat, then headed

around the couch, scooping up an empty bag. She then moved to the kitchen and began shoving the holly lining the counter back into the bag.

Jason let out a breath. "Wait. Zoe…"

She turned to face him. Her face was devoid of makeup, which made her look impossibly young and fresh and…good. Far too good for the likes of him.

"I'm sorry," she said. "I was wrong to intrude." She went back to undecorating, her actions uncharacteristically jerky. She was embarrassed, which he hated.

"Zoe, stop. Just leave it."

He scrubbed a hand over his face and looked around for a diversion. His gaze landed on her opened laptop on the coffee table, and the drawing pad next to it. The pad held the bare-bones sketch of a complex that he knew instantly was her version of the Weller courthouse and library. He hit a key on the laptop and brought it back to life, and yeah, as he'd figured, her drawing program was up, mirroring what she'd sketched. The lines were clean, bold and somehow both modern and classic at the same time. She was good, really good.

"I was working," she said. "Last night, before I fell asleep. I'm stuck, to be honest. I can't figure the rest out."

He shook his head and hunted up his laptop, bringing up the design that had been driving him insane for two weeks now. He had the family center—also bare bones—but the library had been eluding him.

She stared at it, then him. "Do you see what we did?" she whispered.

"You mean that we each designed the parts of the complex that the other is missing? And that they complement each other in a very spooky way? Yeah." He shook his head. "Imagine what would happen if we combined forces instead of competing with each other," he said softly, thinking that at least if they worked together, he wouldn't get shut out of the promotion.

She just stared at him. Apparently the idea hadn't become any more palatable since he'd last brought it up.

Fine. This was his deal and he could nab it on his own, even if he was beginning to question whether his need for the promotion was any greater than hers. "I need caffeine," he said, his only defense.

"I have coffee beans in my bag. There's a coffeemaker on the counter. Do you want—"

"Yes," he said firmly. She moved to the kitchen and within a few minutes the scent of the brewing coffee was filtering through his brain and chasing away some of the morning fog.

Combine forces.

They'd certainly combined forces pretty damn fine last night. But to do so in bed was one thing. Work was another entirely.

Wasn't it?

CHAPTER EIGHT

JASON FOUND TWO MUGS in the cabinet. Zoe poured. He took a big gulp and sighed as the caffeine hit his system and began to fuel his brain.

They moved back into the living room and sat by the big picture window, watching as the morning chased away the dawn.

It was still just lightly snowing, but it was gathering speed now.

Zoe stared at the lump of white that was her car. "It's probably not a good idea to go driving in that."

It wasn't really a question, but rather a genuine statement of fact. She didn't let much show in her voice, but when he looked at her, took in her profile as she gazed outside, he could feel her sadness. That stubborn strand of hair was in her eyes again and he found himself sweeping it aside, stroking her temple, tucking the hair behind her ear and then lingering. "You wanted to be with your family."

"It's Christmas," she said as if that explained it all. "Don't you and Mike celebrate with your family?"

"Mike's celebrating with his girlfriend this year."

"So he said. Won't you miss him?"

"We live together *and* work together. We see each other every day."

"I don't see my family much, just a couple of times a year," she said. "They're all so busy."

There was a wistful tone to her voice that he fully understood. If he could have his parents back, he'd sure as hell want to spend time with them. "Are you close?"

"If by close you mean constantly competing and trying to be the best and one-up each other, then yes." She lifted a shoulder. "We gather in Quincy every year, away from everyone's jobs and responsibilities. My dad makes eggnog. My mom cooks a feast. My sisters regress to teenagers in spite of having their own families, spending the holiday arguing and trading clothes and hair products. Oh, and we decorate. And we *always* fight over whose turn it is to put the star on the tree. Somehow it's never my turn, which is really annoying. That's what happens when your sisters are a brain surgeon, a rocket scientist and a district attorney, respectively."

"Holy shit," he said.

"Yeah, it's a lot to live up to."

"You're an architect," he pointed out. "What's that, chopped liver?"

"Well, becoming one didn't require a Ph.D or being elected, did it?"

"You try to prove yourself to them."

She sighed. "It's stupid, really. I don't know why

I try, but the promotion at work…I want it so bad. I want to be someone in their eyes, you know?"

"I meant what I said before," he said quietly. "About doing the design together."

"You'd really share the credit." Her voice was doubtful. Not that he could blame her, he wasn't exactly known for wanting to share anything. "Yeah. I think we'd make a hell of a team."

She looked at him for a long time. "This isn't like you. You want that promotion, too."

He did. And it would fix everything for him. The extra money would help him get out of debt, keep his brother out of trouble—and keep his parents' house out of the hands of the bank. And yet…

His parents' house had only been a home because of the love they'd filled it with. What was the point of keeping it if he spent all his time at work? And if it came at the expense of Zoe's happiness, would it be worth it?

"What would Steele think?" she asked. "You know he's all about pitting us against each other to keep the sense of competition ramped up."

"Maybe it's time to shake up his expectations," he said.

She frowned and sipped her coffee. "I used to try to live up to expectations. Now I'm just trying to own who and what I am."

He smiled. "And who and what are you?"

"A sister, a daughter, a friend." She smiled back. "A really great architect, and…"

"And?"

She turned then and met his gaze, her own green eyes unusually soft and revealing. "Last night, for a little while at least, I was a lover."

"Yeah," he said, voice going low at the memory. "And trust me when I say this, Zoe. You're amazing at everything you do. And I mean everything."

"Except decorating."

He grimaced, and set down first his coffee and then hers. "It's not you," he said.

"Oh, God. Okay, wait," she said. "Let me brace myself for the it's-not-you-it's-me speech." She shifted a bit and then nodded. "Okay, ready. Let me have it."

"It really isn't you. I haven't celebrated the holidays since my parents died the week before Christmas ten years ago."

CHAPTER NINE

At Jason's words, Zoe's heart caught in her throat. "Jason, God. I...I had no idea they were gone. I'm so sorry."

"It's been a long time." He lifted his head to meet her eyes. "They died in a car accident when a drunk driver hit them head-on."

Zoe's breath left her in a whoosh at the shock. She couldn't even begin to imagine how he and Mike had suffered. "How old were you?"

"Twenty. Mike was fifteen." He shrugged as if his young age had been of no consequence. Devastation was devastation. "Ever since then, I've done my best to be gone or too busy to bother with Christmas. Mike does the opposite. He goes overboard. Crazy overboard."

Zoe winced and eyed the decorations. "Like putting up all sorts of festive stuff?"

"Last year he rented a snow machine and blasted the entire front yard of our house. Six inches. We had every kid for miles out there having snowball fights."

Her gut squeezed. "And you hated it?"

"No." He shook his head, his eyes back on the view out the window, as if he was seeing another time, another place. "I just missed having my parents there. It's always been easier to just not celebrate."

There was a lump in her throat that she couldn't swallow. "You have no other family?"

"No. It's just me and Mike." He shrugged. "And actually, living with Mike is like living with an entire frat house, so it's not as if we've been alone."

"You're alone this weekend," she said softly.

"Not anymore."

"No." She put her hand over his. It was the first time since last night that she'd touched him. She wasn't sure how he would take it. He could be difficult to read, especially when he had his game face on. But right now his eyes were warm and open, and he entwined his fingers in hers. His other hand slid to the nape of her neck and drew her closer, then closer still, so that they were sharing air. "So are we going to do this?" he asked. "Cocreate the design?"

She waited for the nerves to hit but they didn't. The only thing that did hit her was a certainty that she could trust him, and that combining forces was a great idea. "Yes," she said. "Let's do it."

His smile was slow and sexy. Everything he did was slow and sexy, including, she discovered, watching him work.

They did just that for several hours, stopping to eat, then getting back to it, working until their two separate ideas had become one project. One really great project.

"What now?" she asked as the light of the day was

waning. "Shovel my car out? Undecorate the rest of the cabin? Scrounge for food?"

"None of the above. There's something else I've been wanting to do all day," he said, his lips ghosting hers with each word. And then there were no more words because he was pulling her into his lap and kissing her, hot and deep. She would have happily stayed there, snuggled up against him, except her cell phone began buzzing from the depths of her purse.

And from somewhere in the cabin came the sound of another cell phone going off, Jason's. The sound reminded her that this wasn't the real world. The real world was her family, who were probably still hoping the storm had abated enough for her to get to them. The real world was a place where she and Jason didn't like each other all that much.

And that real world was calling.

VERY AWARE OF ZOE IN the kitchen talking softly on the phone to what sounded like her mother, Jason went hunting for his own cell phone.

He'd gotten a call from Mike, which he returned.

"Merry Christmas," Mike said. "I got you something that you had no idea you needed but is perfect for you—one tall, gorgeous redhead. You're welcome."

"I ought to kill you, not thank you," Jason said, looking over his shoulder to make sure Zoe couldn't hear him. "But it'll have to wait."

Mike paused then laughed in disbelief. "She's still there? Man, you're better than I thought."

"It's a snowstorm, you dumbass. Because of you, she's stuck here with me instead of being with her family."

"Huh," Mike said.

"Huh what?"

"You're emotionally involved."

"What?" Jason shook his head. "When have I ever been emotionally involved?"

"You just said she was stuck with you instead of being with her family, which means you've had at least one conversation, and a fairly deep conversation at that. And you mentioned her family. You're emotionally involved."

Shit, Jason thought. He was. He was completely and utterly emotionally involved.

"Before you hang up on me," Mike said, the good humor gone from his voice. "We got another letter about the house from the bank. Man, we have to let it go, it's killing you trying to keep it."

He sighed. "Merry Christmas, Mike."

Jason hung up, his anger and annoyance at his brother's meddling, nosy, manipulative ways drained. He no longer was certain of his own motivations for anything. Now that he'd realized he had feelings for Zoe, real feelings, how could he compete with her for the promotion, when she wanted it as badly as he did? Needed it just as much? But if he didn't get the promotion and the raise, how could he keep up with their debt, stave off the bank's foreclosure for one more month?

Tired of himself, he powered the phone off and tossed it aside, turning to face Zoe as she came back into the living room.

"Everything okay?" she asked.

"Other than my brother owes you big-time?" He smiled, feeling surprisingly okay. "Yeah. Everything's good. You?"

"My mother's upset with me for missing the driving window to get up there. She says that without me, my older sisters are turning on each other instead of ganging up on me." She smiled. "And my dad has already locked himself in the den with the remote. Estrogen overload."

"I'm sorry you're missing it."

She shook her head. "It's okay." She paused. "I also checked my messages. I just got an offer from an L.A. architectural firm. Same position as where I'm at now with Steele, but there're better opportunities for me there."

He went still. "You're moving?"

"Maybe. If I don't get the promotion."

He tried to imagine what it would be like at Steele without her, but couldn't. He tried to imagine his life without her, but couldn't.

"Jason—"

He wasn't sure who moved first, but suddenly they met in the middle of the room and were kissing hard, bodies smashed up against each other.

"I still don't know what this is," she said when they broke apart to breathe.

Jason knew what this was. Lust, pure and simple.

Zoe's hands fisted in his shirt, holding him close, as if she wanted to make sure he couldn't escape. "Yesterday I said I didn't like you," she said. "I didn't mean it. I was mad and out of my comfort zone. And then after we…"

When she trailed off, he lifted a brow, purposely not helping her out, enjoying the blush that crossed her cheeks.

"After we had sex," she finished unsteadily, "I planned to just forget the whole thing."

He let out a low laugh, and she seemed to relax a little, smiling ruefully. "Yeah, I might as well have tried to forget my own name." She shook her head. "Being with you was…"

"Pretty damn amazing."

"Yes." She sighed with remembered pleasure, her eyes glazing over a little. "You made me feel pretty. Sexy. Wanted. And it'd been a long time since I'd felt that way with a guy."

It was the same for him, he realized. He'd nearly forgotten what it was like to have his heart skip a beat when a woman, the right woman, smiled at him. Or how his stomach could tighten at just the sight of her. And how the way she looked at him never failed to send lust and hunger and need surging and colliding through him. "You make me feel things, too, Zoe. More than I'd counted on."

She laughed and backed away, turning from him. "Let me guess—annoyed and frustrated, right?"

His eyes were on her sweet ass as she bent to shut the laptop. "Actually, my feelings are more base than that."

When she straightened, her cheeks went even redder, but her eyes never left his. "Something else we have in common."

"Is that right?"

She nodded. "I know that I made you promise not to discuss what happened here, but I want you to understand that I'm not ashamed of what we did. Not with our design, or…or in there." She pointed to the bedroom. "I just—" She broke off, looking as if she could use some help out of the hole she'd just jumped into.

Jason stepped closer to her and brought her mouth back to his. "We don't have to do this, Zoe. We don't have to put words to what happened here."

She looked at him for a moment. "Like a Christmas pass, or something?"

"It can be anything you want," he said. "So what do you want?"

CHAPTER TEN

ZOE STARED AT JASON. This could be anything she wanted? "That's a lot of power."

"Do your worst," he said, and backed her to the door, his hands on either side of her face as he leaned in, pressing her between the hard wood and his even harder body.

It was arousing as hell. So was how his mouth was exploring the sweet spot beneath her ear, making her not care that he didn't have the answers.

"I don't know what we're doing," she whispered. "Or where it could go." God, his mouth. She shifted, giving him better access.

"Me neither," he said. "But I do know that it's been a damn long time since I wanted to spend the holidays with anyone. I'm glad you're here, Zoe."

Her bones dissolved as her fingers slid into his hair, rocking into him. "I can feel that."

He smiled. "Yeah?"

"Yeah. How's your neck?"

"Let's find out." Grabbing her hand, he tugged her into the bedroom. He reached for her sweater, but she was already unzipping it and peeling it away from her body.

He let out a breath and ran a finger over the lace edging of her bra. "Pretty." Then he flicked open the front hook and tossed it aside as her breasts spilled free. "I dreamed about you last night." He cupped her breasts, his thumbs gliding over her nipples.

Her eyes drifted shut as desire rolled over her. She kicked off her boots and pushed down her leggings, backing up to the bed. "What did you dream about?"

"How you taste." He nudged her flat on her back so that her legs were still hanging off the bed, and dropped to his knees. When he winced, some of the erotic haze cleared and she came up on her elbows, concerned.

"I'm fine." Then he proved it by hooking his long fingers into her panties, drawing them down her legs.

This left her in quite the vulnerable position, but before she could give that too much thought, he pressed his mouth to first one inner thigh, then the other, and then...God, and then...in between.

"This," he murmured against her wet flesh. "I dreamed about doing this."

She was so primed and ready, she came in minutes under his tongue and fingers, shuddering as he held her down and made her come yet again. When he dropped at her side on the bed, she crawled up his still fully clothed body, straddling him. "This is new," she said, still breathless. "Usually it's you who's naked."

"I couldn't take off my shirt," he said, voice rough and tight. Beneath her, she could feel him vibrating with tension. Sexual tension, not pain.

"I've got it," she said, and pushed his shirt off his shoulders, kissing everything she exposed: his collarbone, a pec. When she ran her tongue over his nipple, he hissed in a breath. "You're okay, right?" she asked.

Instead of answering, he reached down and unbuttoned and unzipped his jeans, then thrust up into her. The moan escaped before she could stop herself.

"Come here," he said—demanded—and then without waiting for her, he tugged so that she fell over him, her hair falling around them like a curtain.

"Careful," she gasped as his lips nestled along her throat, her jaw, his hands going to her ass to rock into her, burying himself so deep inside her she could nearly taste him. "I don't want to hurt you."

"You're killing me," he murmured, tightening his grip. "Don't stop now."

Her eyes fell closed as his warm, strong hands slid up her back into her hair, holding her for a deliciously slow, deep kiss.

"I can feel you tighten on me," he said, his voice low and serrated.

She opened her eyes to find his face only inches below her. Deep, dark hungry orbs stared back at her, and if she hadn't known it was impossible, she'd have sworn that there was real emotion in them, not just lust.

Need. Hunger. Even affection. And maybe even more. But she wouldn't be fooled by that—this was sex, nothing more than sex. She closed her eyes again.

"Zoe." His voice was rough. "Zoe, look at me."

Not wanting to because she wouldn't be able to hold back, she shook her head.

"Please."

She'd already proven that she couldn't resist a "please" from him. So she opened her eyes. He smiled, and taking her hands in his, locked their fingers together.

Slowly he pulled them up over his head so that she was stretched taut over his entire length, their mouths a breath apart. Even though he was beneath her and she had all the power, she felt pinned by him. Pinned by his hands, his body, his gaze, and the feeling was like falling into a chasm. Her breath lodged in her throat because the expression on his face and in his eyes had none of the cool detachment she'd come to expect from him. There was nothing guarded, shielded or protected about him. He was showing her everything.

All of him.

It terrified her because she knew he'd want the same from her. Proving it, he let his lips graze her forehead, her eyes, her cheeks, her nose, her jaw. He dipped his tongue into the hollow at the base of her throat and smiled at the shiver that racked her frame. He was playing havoc with her senses, with her heart. "Jason—"

"Give me all you have, Zoe. Give me all of you."

Done, she thought as they began to move, as she arched into his touch, and she did give him everything she had.

"God, Zoe," he murmured, voice rough and shaky. "You feel so good. Don't stop."

She didn't. She kept the pace, and in spite of his neck and shoulder, he kept up with her, the muscles in his arms chording with the effort. He was filling her up, her body and her senses, and the wave crashed over her. Lost in it, drowning in the wondrous sensuousness of it, of *him,* she fell forward. He caught her, pulling her in even as he was still shuddering with his own release.

JASON SAT UP VERY CAREFULLY. Zoe was curled at his side, fast asleep. In her sleep she reached out for him. He ran a finger over her shoulder, across her collarbone, and then, because she was soft and warm and *his,* he cupped her breast. Her nipple hardened for him and stirred his blood.

He'd just had her and it still wasn't enough.

He was afraid it never would be. He wanted to unwrap her like an exquisitely wrapped gift, one layer at a time, until he had every single inch of her.

For keeps.

He knew that if this weekend hadn't happened, he'd have missed out on this, on her, the best thing to happen to him in…ever. And as surely as he knew that, he also knew that he had to make certain she got the Weller project. She damn well deserved it. She needed it.

And he needed her. Even though he'd be giving up the promotion, no amount of money was equal to what Zoe was worth to him. He could sell his parents' house. He'd force Mike to kick up his own game and help with the debts. Whatever he had to do, because he wanted Zoe in his life.

"You okay?" she murmured, and opened her eyes, her mouth curving at the sight of him.

"I don't know."

Her smile faded and she sat up, reaching to him. "Your neck or shoulder—"

He caught her hands. "I want to partner with you."

"I believe we just did that."

"I meant us," he said. "I want to see where this goes."

"We know where we go. Straight to bed." She flashed an unsure smile. "Twice now."

He laughed softly. "Yeah, and that's nice. But it's more than that."

A light came in her eyes that he read as hope. It gave him a surge of that very same emotion. "I feel things for you, Zoe. I know I promised that we wouldn't tell anyone, and we don't have to. I don't give a shit about the office or what anyone thinks, but this is real, this thing between us. I want it to be real."

She was quiet so long he was certain he'd blown it. When she got up to her knees he thought she was going to leave the bed, and he was sure he'd blown it. But she didn't go anywhere. She crawled into his lap and pressed her lips to his jaw, then one corner of his mouth, and then the other.

"I have to be honest with you, Jason."

Oh, Christ. His hands tightened on her hips, his mind already formulating a plan on how to talk her out of walking away from him.

"I could really fall for you," she said softly. "So I need you to be careful what you tell me."

His head came up and he met her eyes, which were shimmering brilliantly. Warmth and emotion, so much emotion, rushed his chest so that he couldn't draw air back in. "I've been falling for you for a damn long time, Zoe. Being with you here made me feel…alive. *You* make me feel alive, Zoe. You always have."

"You never let on," she whispered. "Not a single word."

"Well, you weren't exactly an open book, either," he reminded her with a smile. "I never knew how you felt about me. I'm still not sure."

"Should I tell you?" She let her hands slide down his chest, over his abs, and then lower, making him suck in a breath. "Or maybe I should show you…"

He slid his fingers into her hair, stopping her from sliding down his body to show him with her mouth. Which he wanted. Bad. But first he needed to say it. "We're going to do this," he said. "We're going to make this work."

"Do you want a contract?"

Hell, yes. He wanted her to promise not to go to L.A., but he wasn't that big a bastard to ask that of her. He'd take whatever she could give him. He ran his thumb over her lower lip. "A verbal agreement," he said. "Sealed with a kiss."

She wrapped her arms around him. "We're going to give this a shot," she said. "You and me. Together. In the office, and out of the office. In bed, and out of it. Wherever you'll have me, I'll be there."

"Everywhere," he said fiercely. "I want you everywhere."

"Done. Now shut up and kiss me, Jason."

He did, and her answering kiss, given with her entire heart and soul, was the ultimate Christmas gift and everything he ever wanted. He had no idea how he'd gotten so damn lucky, but he knew one thing for sure. He wasn't going to let it get away from him.

EPILOGUE

Two WEEKS LATER the entire office was seated around the huge conference table. Steele was standing at the head. "The Weller project has been awarded," he said.

Everyone straightened and waited.

Zoe glanced across the table and met Jason's eyes. After their stay at the Tahoe cabin, Zoe had finally gotten up to visit her family for a few days. The following Friday night, when they'd both been back in the city, Jason had taken her out. They'd ended up at his place and she hadn't gone home until Sunday night.

The week had been busy—too busy to get together—but the following weekend they'd changed things up and spent it at her place.

Now it was Monday and she was still glowing from the two orgasms she'd had that morning, courtesy of the sexiest man she'd ever been with.

A week ago Jason had submitted their design, and she knew they'd given it their best shot. Steele hadn't said one word about the two of them collaborating, or what it would mean for the promotion. She'd taken another call from the L.A. firm, but she'd put them off, suddenly not in a huge hurry to go anywhere.

"The design picked was one of ours," Steele said.

All eyes swiveled first to Jason, and then to Zoe. Zoe was good under pressure. She smiled evenly, even as her heart kicked hard. No one knew about them.

Yet.

They'd agreed they wanted to keep their relationship to themselves until they knew exactly what they were doing. But she now knew what she was doing—she was falling in love. In fact, she'd fallen, hard.

Jason's mouth was serious, his eyes lit with the same emotion that had been making her life heaven on earth for two weeks now.

"The winning design was done by..." Steele paused for dramatic effect. Then he smiled. "Zoe Anders. The Weller people called it—and I quote—'groundbreaking, amazing, *perfect*.' So let me also announce our newest principal architect, Zoe Anders."

Her jaw dropped. Her heart stopped, too, and she stared at Jason.

He was still looking at her, something new in his eyes that she hadn't seen before.

Steele hit a button on the remote in his hand and the design came up on the large flat screen behind him, the design that had been created only thanks to Jason.

It was Jason's *and* hers, merged together, but he'd taken his name off the project. For her. That's what was in his eyes. Before she could fully process this, she was surrounded by her coworkers. Someone popped a bottle of champagne, and everyone wanted to shake her hand. She scanned the crowd for Jason, but he was gone. She headed for Steele. "Can I have a moment?"

"After what you've done, you can have five," he quipped.

"That project was both mine and Jason's. Together."

Steele's brows went up. "Is that right?"

"That's right. He deserves the credit, too."

"You want to share the spotlight?"

"We're a team," she said, and meant that in every sense of the word.

A few minutes later she finally found Jason outside on the balcony overlooking the lights of San Francisco far below. "What was that?" she asked.

He turned and faced her, pulling her into him. His mouth sought hers, his tongue tracing her bottom lip, seeking entrance, which she gave. With a groan, his hand came up to cradle her head, tilting her face so he could deepen the kiss, apparently not caring who saw them. His tongue plundered her mouth, taking possession, demanding a response, which she freely gave. Finally, she tore free and smacked his chest. "You took your name off the design."

"We both know it was mostly your design. Your work. I wanted you to get the credit."

"So you just gave away your shot at the promotion?" she asked, afraid of what that meant for him. Would he resent her? Pull away? Pretend what they'd shared hadn't happened? "Why?"

"Why?"

"Yes, *why* did you do it? To make sure I kept sleeping with you on the weekends? Because you should know, I plan to keep doing that anyway. I don't need you to feel sorry for me, or humor me."

"First of all," he said, eyes flashing, "this wasn't about sympathy, or humoring you, or ensuring a booty call on the weekends. You're good, Zoe. So damn good. Too good for Steele, to be honest." A muscle jumped in his jaw and he reached for her. "I admire your work, I always have. You deserve this. You deserve a hell of a lot more. You deserve L.A. if you want to go."

Her breath caught. "You said first of all. What was the second of all?"

He stared into her eyes. "Second of all, I want to be with you. And I don't give a shit who knows it. This is far more than weekend fun. I love you."

"You...love me?"

"Yes. And I'll love you from six hundred miles away in L.A. if I have to—I just hope not to have to."

"I love you, too, Jason."

With a smile, he bent his head toward her, but she put her hand on his chest. "So...you got me the promotion to keep me here?" she asked.

"No, *you* got the promotion."

She laughed. "I just spilled your beans to Steele."

He didn't look all that surprised, which made her heart beat even harder for him. He knew her. He got her.

"What now, Zoe?"

"Do we need a new deal?" she asked, her throat tight with emotion. Good emotion. Heart-deep emotion.

"Yes," he said. "The terms are that there are no terms. No competition, no race. You give me all you can of yourself, always, and I will do the same."

"Always?"

"Always," he said firmly.

"For how long?"

"As long as you'll have me."

Her breath caught. "That might be a damn long time."

"Counting on it," he said, and pulled her in hard and kissed her to seal the deal.

* * * * *

THE NEW YEAR'S DEAL

USA TODAY Bestselling Author
Julie Kenner

PROLOGUE

Five Years Ago...

UNTIL THIS MOMENT, Cleo had been certain that the term *broken heart* was only a figure of speech. But it wasn't. Right now, her heart was split wide, and she wasn't sure if she'd be able to survive the bleeding.

And it wasn't just a selfish pain that she was feeling— the loss of Josh and the destruction of all their plans. It was the horrible sense that she was watching *his* dreams go spiraling away, and no matter how much she begged and pleaded, she couldn't convince him to grab tight to them and not let go. She would have given anything to have spared him from the pain, to take back everything that had happened over the last five days. But she couldn't, and the horrible weight of futility bore down on her.

"Josh, please," she said, turning to face him on the couch in his apartment, though she knew that the battle was already lost. "Think about everything you're giving up."

The fact that he gave her a smile then only made her heart break a little bit more. "I have thought about it," he said, leaning across the couch and taking her hands. "I'm giving up my plans—and that's all they were, just plans—in order to save a legacy."

"But—"

"It's my family, Cleo. Do you really think I have a choice?"

"Of course you have a choice! Everyone has a choice." She sounded desperate, and she hated that, but she wanted so badly to make him understand. He had so much to offer the world, and his plans had been so big and so grand. She hated to see him throw them away.

"You're right," he said. "I do have a choice. And this is what I'm choosing. My family. Our business. Our history and, yes, our legacy. I can't let it go. Not like this."

Five days ago, his father—the president of Goodson Mining, the owner and operator of the largest privately held gold mine in Nevada—had suffered a fatal aneurysm. Paramedics had arrived within minutes, but it was too late. Frank Goodson was gone, along with his passion for the art of mining, his metallurgical skills and his deft hand at running one of Nevada's major businesses.

Josh's mother had been too devastated to even be able to call her son. The call had come from Frank's brother. Josh and Cleo—both of whom had finished their final exams at the University of Nevada at Reno and were still on campus waiting for graduation day—had hurried to Carlin, Nevada, to be with

Josh's mother. And now Josh had decided that he had to stay.

Frank's death had saddened Cleo, and she'd known that Josh's reaction would be intense. He and his father had been incredibly close. It had been Frank who had urged Josh to get his undergraduate degree in metallurgical engineering but then pursue a political science postgraduate degree. "I've made the company strong," Frank had said the first year that Cleo had joined them for Thanksgiving. "It will be Josh who takes it multinational." He'd laughed then, and squeezed his wife's waist. "Marion would never let me out of her sight long enough for me to make the trips to investigate other properties." His wife had pecked him affectionately on the cheek, her hands tight on his shoulders. Cleo had assumed that Frank was joking, of course. How could Marion not want the business to expand?

She'd envied Josh that Thanksgiving, though. She had no family—only her mother who ran a small art gallery in Seattle. She adored her mom, and there was no bigger fan of Cleo's than Elizabeth Daire, but since it was just the two of them, Thanksgivings were never big, boisterous affairs. In Josh's world, they were, and she'd loved the noisy chaos of his extended family, cousins and nieces and nephews and all the rest, most of whom worked in some capacity at Goodson Mining.

"He wouldn't want you to do this, Josh," she said, meaning Frank. She fought the tears that were determined to flow. "He wanted you to go to Harvard." *He wanted you to go there with me, to be with me*, she thought, though she didn't say it. That was pure self-ishness, and she was trying very hard to be pragmatic, even though she wanted to be as selfish as a toddler.

"He wanted me to be prepared for the politics of growing the business," Josh said, "and I am." He sat down beside her and held her hand. "Would the connections and friends I'd make in grad school help? Of course. But what it really takes to expand a mining company is production. And that doesn't take political connections. It takes engineering skill and that, I've got. I *can* run this company, Cleo. I've been apprenticed here my entire life, and now I have the formal education to back it up."

The tears she'd been holding in trickled down her cheeks, and he brushed them away. "If I left for grad school, I'd come back with the degree. But the company would be gone. Ruined. I'm certain of it. And the company was the reason I wanted to go away—so that I would come back to it stronger. But it doesn't matter how strong I am if it doesn't exist. Don't you see? I can't abandon the company, because that means abandoning my dreams. Grad school can wait. Harvard's not going anywhere. Do you understand?"

She nodded, because objectively, she did. From the first moment they'd met, he'd shared with her his passion for the company—he'd even spent every summer working at the mines—so had she, for that matter, with Frank giving her temp jobs in the office while

Josh went off and worked in the actual field. She'd seen firsthand how much Josh loved his work. And she'd also seen that although his mother and uncle and half a dozen other members of his family all worked at the mines, none had the mind that Frank had—or that Josh had inherited. Those two men had an inherent sense of where and how to work the mines to best extract the gold, and how to process the ore so that the gold shipped from Goodson Mining was considered the purest in the business. Josh was right—without him, the company would surely go under, and the Goodson family would be destitute.

Josh needed the business, and his family needed Josh.

So, yes, she understood. For that matter, she understood more than she wanted to. After all, she had her own passion. She was going to law school. She'd been accepted to Harvard, and she knew that practicing law was in her blood. It was the one thing she'd wanted more than anything, and though she'd thought that Josh would be moving East with her, the fact that he'd chosen another path wasn't going to stop her. But it saddened her. Oh, how it saddened her.

"I wish things were different."

His simple smile needed no words. Even so, he said, "Me, too."

The next words were the hardest she ever spoke. "We're breaking up, Josh."

He turned sharply to look at her. "What?"

"Would you ask me to stay with you? To go to law

school in Nevada? Or to quit altogether and marry you?"

"I—" She saw the confusion flash on his face, then the determination. "No. I know how much being a lawyer means to you," he said. "And I know what Harvard means to you. Marriage? I'd ask in a heartbeat, but you'd say no, and honestly, I'd want you to, especially if getting married now meant abandoning your dreams. And a long-distance marriage isn't the way to start out. Not for anyone."

She cocked her head. "You want me to follow my dream, but you won't follow yours?"

"I *am,*" he said passionately. "I already told you. Goodson Mining is my dream and my life. Going away now would kill it. I'm following my plan, Cleo, just a bit differently than I'd thought."

"Than *we'd* planned," she said sadly.

"We don't have to break up."

She shook her head. "We do, and you already said why. A long-distance marriage is no way to start out. If we don't break up officially, then we're still together. Not married, but together. And, Josh, that just isn't right." She drew in a breath to bolster her courage, because she knew she was right. "We both have to focus," she said. "We can't be worrying about what's going on across an entire continent."

"And in 1865, I would have seen your point," he said. "But these days, you can get from coast to coast in the same amount of time it takes to have dinner and a movie."

"It's not fair to try to win an argument by making me laugh!"

"I'm not trying to be fair." He knelt down in front of her and took her free hand, the one without the crumpled tissue. "Four years, Cleo. We've been together since the second week of school. And we're just going to blow that off?"

"We're not," she said, determined to be determined. "But from the first moment we met, we've both talked about our careers. It's been the Holy Grail for each of us. And I'm not willing to let either one of us get distracted. You need to focus all your time and energy on putting the pieces of the business back together, and I need to focus on learning the law."

"And after that?"

She cocked her head, hearing something unspoken in his words. "What do you mean?"

"I mean, just because it won't work right now doesn't mean I want to lose you forever."

"Josh, you're making this harder."

"Trust me when I say I'm not trying to make it easier." He moved closer, the smell of his soap tickling her senses.

"Five years," he said. "All I ask is that we meet again in five years. We meet. We reevaluate. We spend a few days together catching up, sharing our adventures. We have a bit of fun. Maybe we'll rekindle something special."

Special. The way he said the word made her entire

body tingle. It was what they'd always believed. That they—Josh and Cleo, the couple—were special.

But she couldn't let herself think about that. Not now. Not when she was going away. Not when they were breaking up. She met his eyes. "Maybe we'll realize that we're destined to just be friends."

He nodded, as self-assured as always. "We might. We owe it to ourselves to find out. And I can't think of a better friend to spend a weekend with. Can you?"

"I'll be a big-shot attorney by then," she hedged. But she was smiling as she said it. "I might be in trial."

"Then we meet on December 30. You won't be in trial over the holidays. We'll spend one night catching up, and the next night celebrating a new year. At the Tahoe Oasis," he added, referring to the little motel he'd taken her to on their six-month anniversary. A dive, but oozing with nostalgia.

"I don't know," she said, but her tone said *absolutely*.

He grinned. He'd caught the tone. He knew her that well.

"Then just don't think about it," he said, a tease in his voice and a spark in his eye. "Don't think at all." He tugged her to him, his lips pressing against hers, pulling her closer, making her wish that she was the kind of girl who could give up law school and Harvard and just stay with him. But she'd known who she was for too long, and she wouldn't be Cleo if she stayed.

"Josh," she whispered when they broke the kiss.

He eased back, shaking his head. "Five years," he said. "Promise me."

"Yes, yes. Five years." She met his eyes. "We'll be different people." She sat up a little straighter, not liking what she was about to say. Not liking the truth of it. "It might be hard to see each other again. A lot can change in five years."

"A lot can," he agreed, taking her hands and pulling her close. "So you'd better come here now and give me something to remember us by."

CHAPTER ONE

Five Years Later...

"I'M BREAKING THE CARDINAL rule against praising young associates," Leon Parker said, leaning back against the rich leather of his desk chair. "But in your case all the partners thought an exception was called for. You're quite an asset to Jameson, Parker and Lowe, Ms. Daire. I want you to know that I take full credit for recruiting you to the firm."

She laughed, hoping that she looked cool and casual, and that her face didn't reveal that she was mentally turning cartwheels around the senior partner's office. "I enjoy my work," she said. "I'm glad it shows."

"You enjoy it, and you're extremely good at it." He turned to his computer monitor and started scrolling through something on the screen. She couldn't see it, but she was certain that he was reviewing the billable-hour reports for all the junior associates. Cleo had joined the firm fresh from Harvard two years ago, and Leon had become both her cheerleader and her mentor. That she'd lived up to his faith in her made her flush with pride—and made her wonder what new responsibility she'd earned.

Don't ask, she told herself. *There may be nothing.* This was the end-of-year review, and associates in their second year did not get handed cases. Not at a major Washington firm. Not so soon.

But maybe taking a deposition? Arguing a motion? Maybe…

Leon stood and walked to his window. The blinds were open, and the view of Capitol Hill was magnificent and awe-inspiring. She was exactly where she wanted to be, and sometimes the wonder of that was so intense it made her feel as if she was as light as air, and she'd fly as high as the sun with joy.

"—Consolidated Mineral?"

She jumped, realizing that she'd missed part of what he'd been saying, and there was no way to cover except the truth. "I'm sorry. I— What did you say?"

He glanced over his shoulder at her, his indulgent smile telling her that he knew exactly where her thoughts had been. "I was asking if you were familiar with Consolidated Mineral Corporation's current litigation."

"Oh." She dug into her memory and found a mention of the litigation in the *Wall Street Journal.* It wasn't a case that the firm was handling. "Well, yeah. Consolidated is suing one of its subcontractors. Breach of contract, negligence, a slew of claims."

"But what makes the case truly intriguing is that the subcontractor is wholly owned by Argentina."

"Really?" Her mind was spinning. "Suing a government entity. That's messy business."

"Very," Leon said. "From both sides. Do you happen to know which firms are handling the litigation?"

"Sure," she said, her eyes narrowing since this entire conversation seemed pointless, and yet Leon didn't make idle conversation. She named off the two firms, both competitors of Jameson, Parker and Lowe.

"As it happens, Gimble and Cleary has asked us to come on as cocounsel. In particular, they want us to focus on the causes of action that address the quality of the ore. Our first task will be to decide if summary judgment is appropriate, and on which claims. After that, we'll take it one step at a time. I don't think I need to tell you how big an opportunity this is for the firm."

"No, sir," she said. Gimble and Cleary represented Argentina. And having a nation among the firm's clients would definitely be a feather in their cap. "Do you want me to start briefing the key issues?"

"I want you as my second chair."

It was a good thing that she was sitting down, because Cleo wasn't certain her legs would have supported her. Second chair was literally the copilot in a trial. And, sure, it was only a section of a bigger litigation, but still. She'd be right there. Sitting at counsel table. Possibly examining the witnesses.

This was far and away the biggest step forward she'd taken in her career.

"Unless you'd like to stay on your current docket?"

"No, no," she said. "I'm good. This is good."

He laughed. "As I mentioned at the start of the meeting, the partners are all very impressed by your work."

"Are the files here? Can I review them?"

"I've already had Ellen copy the key portions of the case file for you. She messengered them to your apartment this afternoon. The package is with your doorman."

"My apartment?"

"Cleo, tomorrow's Christmas. And I believe you're scheduled to be off next week?"

"I am, but—"

"No buts. We're going to get very busy, very fast. Enjoy the time off while you can. Read the file. Learn the case. Spend a couple of hours on the internet and see if you can track down some potential expert witnesses. We'll need both consulting experts and testifying experts in a number of related fields, and be sure to do a Lexis search to see where they've testified before. Is that enough to keep you busy over the holidays?"

She stood up and met his grin. "I think that will do it. And thank you."

"Don't thank me. You're the one who's been working hard."

"Right. Thanks," she said again, because she was flustered, but she knew he'd forgive her. "I'll just go."

He chuckled as she slipped out his door and closed

it behind her. She made it all the way to her office before she shut her own door, clapped her hands over her mouth and screamed with joy.

She was on her way—she was really on her way!

She was pacing her office—more like skipping, actually—her mind going into overdrive as she thought about what she needed to do, to read, to organize—when Perry walked in. As soon as the door closed behind him, she threw herself into his arms. His arms tightened around her automatically, but they didn't stay that way long. He released her and pushed her back, his eyes taking in her face, his expression curious.

"Good review?" he asked. "Jameson told me I was getting a raise, but other than that it was pretty dry. But he's not as much of a talker as Leon." Perry shrugged. "Then again, he knows that the law's only a stepping stone for me." Perry made no secret of his political ambitions, and it had been that single-mindedness that had first attracted her to him, though their romantic relationship hadn't lasted.

Cleo stepped away and leaned against her desk. "It *was* a good review, but it was also much more than that." She knew she had to look ridiculous—like a balloon about to explode with good news. She'd dated Perry for almost a year, and they were still friends, though he wanted to be more. With all that between them, she should want to blurt it out to him, but somehow the words weren't quite coming.

"Well, go on. Don't leave me in suspense."

That was enough to open the floodgates, and she told him everything Leon had shared with her about the case. She didn't tell him what it could mean for her career—he was a second-year associate just as she was; he knew. "The workload is going to be incredible," she said. "But the legal issues at the core are fascinating." And, of course, there was the faith in her that Leon was demonstrating. The kind of faith that made all her hard work over the years worth it.

"Sounds great," he said. "See if you can assign me to it, too. An international case like that? Can you imagine the political connections I could make?"

"I can imagine," she said, hoping that she'd kept the dryness out of her voice. She'd been drawn initially to the fact that he was so focused on his political dreams. But as she watched him, she'd realized that she was frustrated by how he intended to get there. He seemed more interested in furthering the career he didn't yet have than focusing on the one that he did. A shame, too, because as far as the law went, he was brilliant. But his eyes were set on politics, for reasons he'd never been able to articulate to her.

At first, she'd thought he had a calling to help the world, but over time, she'd realized that he simply wanted to be where the action was. It hadn't been an easy realization to stomach, and it had triggered their breakup.

She shook her head, dispelling the thoughts. Now really wasn't the time. "I hardly have a say on who's assigned to the case."

"Sure you do. That's what the lead associate does, right? And second chair puts you in the hot seat."

He was right, but she knew right then she wasn't going to assign him to the case—not when his motive was something other than the work. But, again, she wasn't going to get into it now. "I'm not even thinking about it until next year. Leon said to chill, rest and relax until we return after the holidays, and I intend to take his advice."

"You're off to Seattle tonight?" he asked.

"Four days with Mom, then I'm back here."

"And we're on for Jameson's New Year's Eve party?" he asked, referring to the big bash the senior partner threw every year. He stepped close to her when he said it, and pulled her into a lazy dance move.

She laughed as he dipped her. "We're on," she said. For one brief moment when the party was announced, she'd considered not going. She was five years out of college now—and that meant that this was the year that she and Josh had planned to meet in Tahoe.

But she hadn't heard a word from Josh in almost a year—not an email, not a letter, nothing. And she could hardly fly to Tahoe to see an old college boyfriend when she'd promised Perry he had dibs on her for New Year's. As friends only, of course. And though she was certain that Perry hoped to make it more, she'd made her position perfectly clear. A true politician, Perry swore he'd change her mind.

"Good," Perry said, still holding her. "Because Jameson mentioned that Senator Ellis is going to be there. I want to make a good impression with the most gorgeous woman I know on my arm."

It was a genuine compliment, and he meant it, but something about the way he said it—as if her looks were a check mark on his political scorecard—irritated her. Another reminder of why they didn't click.

She eased out of his arms. "I better get home. I still have to pack."

"Have a good Christmas," he said. "I can't wait for New Year's Eve."

"I'm looking forward to it, too," she said. But when she slipped out of the office, it wasn't Perry she was thinking of, it was Josh.

Her dreams were starting to come true. And she hoped with all her heart that his were, as well.

"I DON'T KNOW WHAT you're upset about, Josh," Marion Goodson said as she carried a stack of dishes from the dining table to the kitchen. "She's a perfectly lovely girl."

"She seems very nice," Josh said, reminding himself that he shouldn't raise his voice to his mother, that she only wanted what was best for him, and that the fact that she had pretty much just sent his entire Christmas weekend spiraling down into an uncomfortable, awkward mire was no reason to disown his family. "But I'm not interested in her, Ma."

"But why not? She's smart, she's pretty. You think she's pretty, right?"

He glanced out the dining room window to where

the woman in question—their new neighbor, Selina Perez—was sipping coffee with his aunt. "Sure. She's pretty. But I'm not interested in being fixed up by my mother. Especially not at Christmas. I thought I was going to relax. Spend some time with you and the rest of the family."

"And that's what you're doing." She came over and gave him a hug. "Don't you think Selina fits into the family? And if you settle down—get married, have kids—maybe you won't keep pushing this nonsense about expanding the company."

"Mom, we've been over this. Expansion is good."

"Not if it takes you away from where you're needed. You're the lifeblood of this company, sweetheart, and you know it. Besides, with your father gone, I want you here."

She took his hand, and he melted just a little bit. She could be a pain, all right. But she was still his mother.

But that didn't mean she had carte blanche over his personal life, and a wife and kids wasn't the kind of expansion he wanted right now.

Except, of course, that wasn't true. He didn't want that with Selina. But if Marion had invited Cleo to dinner…

But better not to go there. Those days were long past, and he was no longer the wide-eyed kid fresh out of college. Besides, he'd seen Cleo's picture on her Facebook page, and she looked more than happy on the arm of some other attorney named Perry. He winced. *Perry.* He'd lost the woman he'd loved to a guy named Perry.

"I just think you need to start considering these things. Who'll keep the company going after you're gone? You need a wife. Children."

"Mom."

She looked at him, all smiles and innocence. He sighed, then gestured toward the back door. Everyone was gathered on the sunporch, the kids playing in the yard. "You go," he said. "I'll clear the dishes."

"Oh, no—"

"My Christmas gift to you." He pressed a kiss to her cheek. "You work too hard, Ma."

She squeezed his hand and called him a good boy and took her coffee out the back door. Josh smiled. He may not have learned a lot in his twenty-seven years, but at least he'd learned how to work his mother.

He was loading the dishwasher the way she liked it—rear to front—when Selina came in. "I told them I was going to warm up my coffee."

He nodded toward the carafe. "Help yourself."

"Right." She filled her cup. "Look, I don't really want coffee. I came in to apologize."

He looked up from the dishes he'd been stacking. "For?"

"I swear I had no idea this was a setup, and if I had, I never would have—I mean, I live next door. Slightly awkward, right?"

"Just slightly." He grabbed a towel and dried his hands, then poured a cup for himself. "Sorry about my mom. They don't warn you that women have biological *grand*children clocks and my lack of dating has been a source of frustration for her. I've been focusing on the company. She's concerned about grandkids."

"Moms can be like that. But she's proud of what you've done with the business. She's said as much to me at least a dozen times."

"Thanks," he said, and meant it. He leaned against the counter and took a sip of coffee. "There's a lot more I could do with it." He waved a hand, as if he could wipe the conversation out of the air. He did have big plans for the company, but it wasn't entirely his decision. The board had to approve any plans for expansion, and his mother and relatives made up the board. He understood their fears about weakening the fundamental structure of the business, but at the same time he was certain that it wasn't fear that was keeping his mother from endorsing his expansion plans—it was love. She knew that if the company grew, that would mean a branch office and he would spend more time away. And Marion Goodson wasn't happy with distance or change. She'd been bedridden for a month after Josh's dad passed away, and Cleo's departure on top of that had just about wiped her out.

"The truth is, I think she expected that the house would be full of grandkids by now," he said.

"Why?"

He shrugged. "I had a girlfriend, and Mom saw how good we were together."

Selina's head cocked to the side. "What happened? Bad breakup?"

"No," he said, because as much as it had hurt, it hadn't been bad. "Just…life."

"She left you for someone else?"

"I think she's dating someone else now, but no. She left me for law school."

Selina's brows rose. "And so it's over? Law school doesn't last forever. Now, *my* breakup…" She trailed off with a shudder. "We were engaged, I caught him in bed with a skank from his office and that was the end of that."

"Prick."

She laughed. "You're being too kind to him, but yeah. Honestly, I'm glad it happened before we got married. But it's still hard around the holidays. No date for New Year's Eve and all that. But you—why can't you start it up again?"

Why not, indeed? "New Year's Eve," he whispered, not realizing he was speaking aloud. Was it possible that Cleo…

"Oh, I'm so sorry," Selina said. "I didn't mean that at all. Really."

Josh frowned, confused. "Mean what?"

"I saw your face. I promise I wasn't hitting you up for a date."

He hurried to correct her. "No, no. I wasn't thinking you had. It's just…I wonder if I already have one." He slipped his hand into his pocket. It wasn't there, of course. For years he'd kept the pocket watch with him always. A beautiful gold antique that Cleo had given him for his twentieth birthday. She'd had it inscribed with the word *Forever*.

For months after she left, he'd carried it in his pocket, and he could still imagine the way it felt in his hands, the cool metal, the raised design. He'd forced himself to quit carrying it three years ago. Josh might be sentimental about some things, especially Cleo, but he wasn't stupid.

"How can you not be sure you have one?"

He considered blowing off the question. He didn't really know Selina, and it was a ridiculous thought, anyway. Of course Cleo wasn't going to show. She was in Washington now, and that was almost two thousand miles from Tahoe. And while there'd once been a time when he hadn't believed it would be possible, she was now a hell of a lot further than two thousand miles from Josh. She was a lifetime away, and then some.

But Selina was looking at him with genuine interest, and so he told her about the deal he and Cleo had made to reunite in five years. And instead of saying he was an idiot to even still entertain the memory of that promise, much less hold out any hope that Cleo would actually show, she plunked her coffee down on the counter, grabbed his hands and said, "You have to go."

"She's dating a guy named Perry."

"Do you want her back?"

"More than anything," he said, and realized as he

spoke that the words were true. He more than missed her. He wanted her. Hell, he needed her.

"Then go. If you don't, you'll always wonder if she showed up." Her grin was both mischievous and understanding. "You know I'm right."

The back door opened and Marion paused in the entrance, her eyes fixed on their still-joined hands. "And how's it going in here?" she asked with a mother's forced casualness.

Josh met Selina's eyes, saw her wink and laughed. "It's going great, Ma. We were just planning New Year's Eve."

JOSH STARED AT THE BURNED-OUT shell of a building and told himself that it wasn't an omen. So the Tahoe Oasis had burned. That didn't mean his reunion with Cleo was going to crash and burn, as well.

Except, of course, it did.

They'd said they were going to meet at the small motel. Presumably she'd call to make a reservation, find out the place was gone and blow it off. Or she'd take the plunge and email him, asking for their revised plans.

Except he'd had no email, and surely she would have made travel arrangements by now.

Dammit.

Hell, she'd probably forgotten about their reunion altogether. Or figured that since she was with Perry there really was no point.

Perry. He was really beginning to not like that guy.

He turned in a slow circle, happy to see that the little diner across the street hadn't been affected by the blaze, and he headed in that direction, thinking about breakfast. It was three days after Christmas, and he'd awakened that morning with Selina's advice on his mind. *Keep the date.*

He'd ignored the voice at first—there were things to be done at the office even if he had given the staff the week off. It had been an excellent year for Goodson Mining, but Josh was still determined to convince the board that expansion was the best thing for the company, even if that meant doing a bit of headhunting and finding people he could trust to run point in Washington and around the globe, keeping him free to stay in Nevada and run the show from the center of an expanding web. It wasn't the job he'd dreamed of, but life had taken a sharp turn with his father's death and it was what it was. As his mother repeatedly reminded him, the family needed him in Carlin. They didn't, of course, but he'd never manage to convince his mother—or the board—of that.

He'd stood in his empty office that morning with absolutely no intention of flying to Reno and then making the drive to Tahoe. What would be the point?

But he couldn't escape the fear that she'd show and he wouldn't be there.

And so he'd decided to keep the date. Come to Tahoe. Hang out until New Year's Eve. And maybe, just maybe, when the new year came and Cleo hadn't shown, he'd be finally over her.

Except now that he was here, he was terrified that really would happen. That she wouldn't come. And now that the Oasis was destroyed, that she *couldn't* come.

Well, damn.

"Josh? Josh Goodson?"

He swiveled and found himself looking into a familiar face. "Professor Vickers?" Jillian Vickers was older now, but he would have recognized the smiling face of his favorite sociology professor anywhere.

"Please, it's been what? Five years? Call me Jillian." She gestured to a booth. "Join me? I'm waiting for a to-go order, and I'd love to catch up."

"Sure." Josh signaled to the waitress then followed Jillian to a corner booth with a view of the burned-out Oasis and the mountains rising behind it.

"Such a shame," Jillian said. "The owners were about to start renovating the motel, too. I saw the plans. It was going to be charming. I'm sure they'll rebuild, but it'll take time."

Josh nodded, silently cursing his bad luck. Right then, he didn't much care if the Oasis ever got rebuilt. He needed it to be there now, and that just wasn't possible.

"So where are you going to stay?"

He glanced at Jillian. "I'm sorry?"

"You're staying up here until the new year, aren't you?"

"Oh. No, I—no." Maybe this was an omen. The universe's way of saying that he needed to just let

Cleo go. "I have to get back to work. There's an insane amount to be done."

"To work? But no one works on New Year's Eve! You'd miss all the fun." Her eyes twinkled. "You'd miss Cleo."

It was as if she'd kicked the breath right out of him. "You know?"

"Cleo told me about your deal when she came to the house to say goodbye. Five years." She reached across the booth and squeezed his hands. "Don't you want to be here when she comes?"

"*If* she comes. She's knee deep in a new life now. She even has a boyfriend."

Jillian waved her hand dismissively. "Maybe she's dating, maybe she's not. But you two were in love. Have a little faith in romance, Josh."

He glanced out the window at the charred remains of the motel. "I need more than faith. I need a roof."

This time, her smile was smug. "As it happens, Ken and I can help with that…"

CHAPTER TWO

JILLIAN GLANCED THROUGH THE window to where Josh sat sipping his espresso on the porch in front of a small fire in the chiminea. Despite a blizzard at Thanksgiving and more snow at Christmas, the days leading up to the new year had turned unseasonably warm, and she was looking forward to taking her own coffee and some cookies out on the porch, as well.

Their house in Reno was overflowing with family, and though Jillian loved being surrounded by the kids and grandkids, that morning she and Ken had decided to grab some alone time and drive to the cabin. They'd received two espresso machines for Christmas, and rather than return one, they'd decided to bring it up to Lake Tahoe. Sitting in front of the fire sipping a cappuccino sounded too decadent to pass up.

Once there, Ken had discovered a few odds and ends that needed repairing, and so she'd left him in handyman heaven and headed to the diner to pick up some lunch. Now she was certain that it was fate that had delivered that extra espresso machine. Because if it weren't for that machine, she never would have bumped into Josh Goodson. And that was very fortuitous indeed.

She busied herself putting cookies on a plate, feeling her husband's amused eyes on her.

"All right. Fess up, Jillian. What are you up to?"

She looked up at Ken who was leaning against the counter with a Cheshire cat grin on his wonderful, tanned face.

"Can't I invite a former student to the cabin for coffee without you turning suspicious on me?"

"No," he said. "You really can't."

She playfully whapped him with the kitchen towel. "Don't pretend like you don't remember Josh and Cleo. You were rooting for those kids as much as I was."

Jillian and Ken Vickers both taught at the university in Reno, and Josh and Cleo had each passed through their classrooms at various points throughout their four-year undergrad, and after a small seminar course, the Vickers and the young couple had become close friends. The kids would often come over to Jillian and Ken's house on the weekends for burgers or steaks—Ken was an artist with a grill—and they'd spent long evenings discussing everything from movies to politics to books to food.

Jillian had seen the way those two were with each other—how much they reminded her of herself and Ken back when they were young—and she'd actually cried when she'd learned that Cleo was leaving for law school at Harvard, and that they were breaking up instead of trying to manage a long-distance relationship.

"They aren't us," Ken said, stepping up behind her. He pressed his hands against her shoulders, and she leaned back against him, wishing she could hug Josh and Cleo to her and make them be as happy as she and Ken were.

"I just wish—"

"I know." He kissed the top of her head. "But everyone has to find their own path. Sometimes it's rocky. It was even for us."

He was right. They'd had their hard days as well as their easy ones, and it had been Tahoe and this cabin that had changed everything for them. It had become their special hideaway, the cabin that had rekindled their love, making it grow and change, bonds forged stronger than before. They used to spend all their free time up here, but once their extended family grew too big to fit, they started renting it out. And that turned out to be quite an experience, because it wasn't long before renters would report back that they'd either found or rekindled romance in the cabin.

Being scientists, Ken and Jillian had decided to more formally investigate their hypothesis that something…well, something *romantic* was up with the cabin.

"They're perfect for our study, you know," Jillian said.

Ken scowled, not even pretending that he didn't understand. "In case you didn't notice, only Josh is here."

"Okay, so we let Josh stay here. It's serendipity that

we don't have a renter for New Year's this year, and I'm sure he could use the break."

"And Cleo? You're just going to drop the idea of bringing them together?"

"Do you think I should?"

"If I said yes, would you listen?"

She feigned shock. "Of course I'd listen. And then I'd do exactly what I'd planned."

"Then I guess I might as well get on board." He took the tray from her with a smile. "Besides, they deserve the same shot we had." His eyes narrowed. "So what are you going to do?"

"Me?" she asked innocently. "I'm not going to do anything. Except maybe have a teensy little talk with Josh. After all, he's going to be staying in the cabin for a few days. And he's an inquisitive young man who took a number of sociology courses. I'm sure he'd be fascinated to know the history of the cabin. Its lore. Its secrets."

Ken was fighting a smile when he said, "We agreed not to let the renters know the theory in advance. That would skew the data."

"We did," she agreed. "Good thing Josh isn't one of our renters. He's just a friend who needs a cabin for the holiday. And a nudge," she added. "He just needs an itty-bitty nudge."

Ken could no longer hold back a smile as Jillian walked out to the porch, offered Josh a cookie and said, "I have a crazy idea…"

"I THINK YOU'RE ALL SET," Stephanie Evans said, looking over at Cleo from where she sat on the couch, hunched over a laptop.

Cleo was at the oak desk that dominated her living room, her eyes swimming from reading a series of reports regarding the quality of gold ore produced in one of the Argentine mines. She looked up, grateful for the distraction. "You got all those depositions input?"

Stephanie laughed. "It's not that hard to input them into the system. You stick to practicing law—I'll stick to doing the stuff behind the scenes."

Stephanie worked as a paralegal at the firm, and she and Cleo had become good friends the first week that Cleo had come on board. A friendship that was well proven by the fact that Stephanie had come over in the middle of her holiday to load Cleo's laptop up. "You know you're a saint, right?"

"Ha!" Stephanie said. "If I were a saint I would have done this before you left for your mom's instead of waiting until you got back."

True enough. Cleo had spent Christmas and a couple more days with her mother in Seattle, having a wonderful time hanging out and pretending that she didn't want to be prepping for the case. And, yes, using her mother's internet connection to try to track down a testifying expert witness or two.

But before she could even talk to those witnesses, she needed to understand the science. Which meant she had to get her consulting expert in place first—

he or she would be her guide through the wilds of ore and mining. It was important that a consultant know the business, but also be patient. A teacher. And unfortunately for Cleo, she'd known the best person for the job even before she opened her laptop and started surfing—Josh Goodson.

Awkward much?

"You ought to just call him," Stephanie said, demonstrating just how good a friend she was by, apparently, reading Cleo's mind. She took a sip of wine. "Oh, don't give me that look. You've told me five times that your old boyfriend understands the mining business backward and forward. Give him a call. Ask if he'll consult. What's the big?"

"It just seems so out of the blue. We've barely communicated in years, and then—*poof!*—I'm asking him for a favor?"

"Presumably the firm will pay him," Stephanie said reasonably.

"I think it would be awkward." She didn't tell Stephanie that she and Josh had once planned to meet in just a few days. Five years. New Year's Eve. But that plan had clearly been abandoned. No one just showed up at a Lake Tahoe motel for a date scheduled five years prior without an email or a phone call or a letter. And yet at the same time, that long-ago date was a big elephant in the room. She couldn't ever talk to Josh again without mentioning it. And she certainly couldn't call him this week to ask about mining when that five-year plan was hanging above their heads flashing like a neon sign.

She frowned, suddenly picturing a neon elephant. Maybe she *was* working too hard.

"Cleo?"

She shook her head. "Not happening," she said to Stephanie. "But grab your coat and I'll buy you a drink. We should celebrate."

"Celebrate what?"

"That you got the depositions into the database. That my eyes didn't fall out reading those reports. That it's almost the end of the year. Anything you want."

"When you put it like that…" Stephanie stood. "Want to call Perry and some of the guys?"

"Nah," Cleo said, then shrugged when Stephanie glanced at her sideways. "This can be a girls' night." That sounded reasonable enough, but the truth was, she was thinking of Josh. And she'd rather keep her Josh memories away from her current Perry reality—whatever that reality was.

They headed out the door, thoughts of the case dropped in favor of a serious discussion about what they were wearing to Mr. Jameson's party on New Year's Eve, and where they should go right then for a drink and some appetizers. They were about to push through the double glass doors that fronted Cleo's building when the doorman signaled to her.

"Got a letter for you. Just arrived by courier."

Cleo eyed Stephanie. "Duty calls." Probably something about the case. For the most part, Leon hadn't been bugging her too much—he'd been the one who insisted she not work over the holidays, after all—but he had sent her a few documents, along with some random emails listing various notes and tasks. This time, he'd probably sent her testimony excerpts. She'd mentioned that she wanted to read some deposition testimony given by a few of the experts she had on her preliminary list. No way was she putting someone on the stand who either came off poorly or who had argued the other side of the case in another litigation.

But she knew the moment the doorman handed her the envelope that this wasn't testimony. It was a Federal Express envelope and it felt as if there was nothing in it at all. The return address was from a shipping service, referenced by a client number, so she didn't know who the package had come from. She ripped it open and found a small envelope inside. It simply had her name on it.

Stephanie peered over her shoulder. "Wedding invitation. Or someone's graduation."

"By courier?"

"Maybe they really want you to come to the wedding?"

Cleo slid her finger under the flap of the envelope and tugged on the card. A simple piece of fine, embossed card stock. Stephanie was probably right about the wedding.

But as soon as the card came free, Cleo knew that

she was wrong. An invitation, yes. A wedding, no. It read:

> *Cleo,*
> *It's been five years.*
> *I hope you remember what that means.*
> *Josh*

Beneath the message there was an address, but Cleo barely noticed it. For that matter, Cleo barely noticed anything. Her heart was pounding too loud, and her hand was actually shaking.

"Cleo?" Stephanie frowned at her. "What is it?" She didn't wait for Cleo to answer. She took the card then whistled.

Cleo nodded, as if the whistle had expressed a complete thought. She supposed in a way it had. Steph's sharp note pretty much summed up Cleo's feelings at the moment.

She read the words again, trying to intuit some meaning. They were dry. Not romantic. Not overly friendly. Not sentimental.

She wondered what that meant.

"We said that we'd meet no matter what. Even if we were just catching up. Just two friends seeing where the other had gone in life." She passed Steph the card. "Is that what he—"

"I don't know," Stephanie said. "It's not exactly a love poem, but…"

"But what?"

"Well, it's like an omen, don't you think?"

Cleo squinted, trying to figure out what her friend was talking about.

"I mean, you were just saying you couldn't call him out of the blue and talk about the case. And here he is, contacting you. So it wouldn't be out of the blue. And the card does seem…steady."

"Steady?" Cleo repeated.

"You know. Like he genuinely wants to see you. Wants to catch up. And that's good, right? Because that means you can still work with him."

"Right," Cleo said, but a heavy knot was forming in her stomach at the words *work with him*. But why? Was it because she was nervous about asking him to consult for the case? Or was it because she'd secretly hoped that if they had a reunion, it would be about more than just catching up and sorting out business?

"So what are you going to do?" Stephanie was peering into her face so intently that Cleo felt a bit like one of those bugs in a glass jar.

"I'm going to go to Tahoe," she said before she could talk herself out of it. "Like you said, it's an omen. And I need a witness."

"And you want to see him again," Stephanie prompted.

Cleo hesitated then nodded. "Yeah," she admitted to her best friend. "I do."

OUTSIDE OF THE AIRPORT, Reno was dry and sunny, a nice change from the icy slush she'd left behind in Washington. Because she'd waited until the last minute, she hadn't been able to get an early flight, and she'd arrived in Reno in the late afternoon on December 30. She snagged an SUV from the rental car place, just in case there was snow, and set out toward the mountains. And Josh.

Normally, the drive would be relaxing. The subtle shift from desert to mountain. The evergreens. The smattering of snow that grew to a fluffy white blanket as she climbed higher. It was beautiful—nature at its finest—and while she loved winters in D.C., she'd missed the pure beauty of the mountains while living among towering steel and concrete.

Beautiful, inspirational…and she couldn't enjoy any of it. She was just too darn antsy. Nerves. After all, she hadn't seen him in years. She didn't know what he'd been up to, if they'd still get along, if that spark between them would still be there.

No. She shook her head, dispelling all memories of their college years. There hadn't been the slightest hint of romance in the card he'd sent. And as she'd told Stephanie when her friend had dropped her at the airport, that was a good thing. Because Cleo had a huge case to focus on. And a confusing relationship with Perry. So a romantic New Year's rendezvous with Josh would be one complication too many.

She'd only come because she'd made a promise… and, yes, because she needed a witness. Which meant that this was a *business trip.* Cleo kept repeating that to herself as she wheeled her way up the mountain.

She made exceptional time—probably because her

foot was like a lead weight on the accelerator—and went straight to the Tahoe Oasis. When she saw it had burned down, she realized why Josh had included an address. He'd scoped the place out, found a different location for their rendezvous and had been kind enough to send it. Good on him.

It took Cleo a while to find the nicely secluded cabin, following the twists and turns dictated by the on-board GPS system. By the time she arrived, the sky was orange with the setting sun, and a gentle snow was starting to fall.

Idly she wondered if Josh had thought to bring candles, then immediately banished the idea.

Business. Friendship. Catching up.

That was all good. *That*, she could handle.

She shifted the Jeep into park and took a breath. The cabin looked empty. No car in the driveway, no Welcome Cleo banner strung across the front porch.

She ignored the tiny lump of disappointment in her throat. Instead, she told herself that it was fortunate that Josh wasn't here—it would give her time to look around, to get the feel of the place. To settle in before he came back. Most likely he was at the market, buying cheese and crackers and fruit and chocolate.

She'd go in, make herself at home and surprise him when he returned. He'd be thrilled she was there, right? After all, he was the one who'd invited her.

What was so nerve-racking about that?

Nothing, right? *Right*.

With her mind made up and her nerves battled into submission, she opened the car door and slid out. She grabbed her purse but left her luggage. Time enough for that later.

The front porch was charming and cozy, the two chairs and chiminea giving it a casual, lived-in feel, and for the first time, Cleo wondered if this was Josh's home. The last she'd heard, he was still in Carlin at the mining company. But that was at least a year ago, and a lot of things could change in a year.

She might be expected, but walking straight in seemed too forward, so she rapped on the door. Nobody answered, which wasn't a huge surprise considering she'd already figured he was away running errands. With any luck, he'd hid a key for her or just left the door unlocked.

She tried the knob, certain she couldn't be that lucky, and was surprised when it turned in her hand. She pushed the door open and stepped inside.

Instantly, she knew she'd love staying here. The cabin was cozy, but not tiny. Warm and inviting. A fire burned in the fireplace, and she frowned, wondering what possessed Josh to leave with a fire still burning.

She stepped farther inside and caught the scent of an Italian sauce—tomatoes, oregano, basil. She turned in the direction of the kitchen and gasped when she saw a simple table covered with a red-checkered tablecloth. A candle burned in an empty wine bottle, the wax snaking down. A basket of bread sat on the table, right next to another bottle of wine, this one full and uncorked. Two places were set.

And that's when she noticed the music. Very low, almost inaudible. But oh, so familiar. "That's Amore."

She realized that her hand had crept to her mouth, her pulse had increased and she was holding back tears as her senses went into overdrive—he'd created the tiny restaurant they'd visited on their very first date.

And what a date it had been. She'd had a personal rule never to eat spaghetti on a date—because, really, how can you do it neatly?—but the restaurant was such a dive that they'd had no choice. That was all that was on the menu.

It hadn't mattered, though. It had been perfect. They'd drunk wine and eaten bread and twirled spaghetti on their forks as they'd talked about their lives and their plans.

And it was only after the date that they both realized the similarities to *Lady and the Tramp*—the song, the spaghetti, the tablecloth.

"Hey, Lady."

The soft voice came from behind her, and she twirled without hesitation. "Hey, Tramp."

The words were out of her mouth, easy and comfortable, before she saw where he was standing and what he was wearing—in the bathroom doorway in nothing but a pair of tight, low-slung jeans, giving her a picture-perfect view of his tight abs and broad, glistening shoulders. Suffice it to say that he hadn't let his body go soft after college.

"I was actually planning on being fully dressed when you got here."

"It is the conventional way to greet people," she said. She glanced between him and the tiny kitchen, and all those decadent thoughts that she'd pushed to the back of her mind came right to the front again.

Stop it, Cleo.

She'd come to talk business.

Josh, apparently, had much more romantic ideas.

Which meant that this holiday had taken a very sharp turn toward awkward.

CHAPTER THREE

She'd come.

He realized only then that he'd feared that she wouldn't. That when Jillian had suggested sending her the card with the cabin's address, he'd merely been tilting at windmills.

He'd told himself when he'd sent the courier off that only two results were possible—one, she didn't want any sort of future with him and would fail to show. Or two, that she'd understand that this getaway represented a second chance for the two of them, and by getting on a plane and coming, that she was silently agreeing to take that chance.

Josh hadn't realized just how much he wanted that second chance with Cleo until Jillian had told him the wild story about the cabin. As crazy as it sounded, the little retreat seemed to bring couples together—forging new bonds and repairing worn relationships.

He would have dismissed Jillian's theory out of hand, except that he had too much respect for both Ken and Jillian, and they were both saying the same thing. More than that, they were saying that he could have the cabin for his reunion with Cleo.

He wasn't sure if it was their suggestion to send

the card, or if he'd thought of that on his own. All he knew was that as soon as the idea was in his head, he'd had to do it. All his reservations about not knowing whether she'd have come without a push faded from his mind when he considered the possibility—however wild and crazy—that getting Cleo into this cabin would also mean getting Cleo.

It was a revelation that almost knocked him over with its intensity. Suddenly, there was a goal in his life that he *could* reach. Maybe he'd never convince the board to expand the company, but he could win Cleo back. Their love had a quality and depth to it that made him certain that even the passing of five years—that even the existence of a man named Perry—made failure impossible. If he wanted her, he would win her.

And he did want her. Desperately.

And once he had her, everything else would seem so much less important.

So he'd sent the card. And he'd planned this reunion, all the way down to the tablecloth and the music.

But now, seeing her expression, he wondered if he'd gone too far, too fast. She'd come, and that had to mean that she believed at least in the potential of a reunion. But at the same time right then she looked like a deer in the headlights.

Maybe he had laid it on a bit strong.

"Too much?" he asked, cocking his head toward the faux restaurant.

She looked at him, her mouth open a little, and

then, incongruously, she burst out laughing. "Well, you always did know how to surprise me."

He relaxed. Whatever tension had filled the room between them had faded with her smile. "What's even more surprising is that the food is actually going to be better than it was from that restaurant."

She quirked a brow. "That's not actually surprising," she said, and they both laughed.

She had a point—that first meal had been barely edible. Still, Josh felt he'd outdone himself tonight. He'd spent so much time in the kitchen preparing the sauce, in fact, that he'd gotten into the shower later than he'd planned. Thus the half-naked state, which, he only just realized, was still his state of clothing.

The realization shot another warm burst of satisfaction through him—even after all these years, he was that comfortable with her.

As if she was reading his mind—another good sign in Josh's opinion—she looked him up and down. "Not that the view isn't great, but if you're planning on dishing out hot spaghetti sauce, I think a shirt might be in order. They don't teach many first-aid skills in law school."

"I wouldn't have expected you to be so conventional," he said. "But if you insist."

"I think I'll have to." Her eyes sparkled with amusement, and Josh's heart leaped. Despite a rocky start, this was going well.

"Give me one second," he said then hurried into the bedroom to change. He returned to find her gone. A cold wave of disappointment mixed with fear crashed over him. Disappointment that this reunion had failed. Fear that he'd never get her back. The depth of his emotion didn't surprise him. For five years, he may have subjugated his thoughts and feelings for Cleo. But now that she was back to being front and center in his mind, he knew that he had to have her—or, at the very least, he had to try.

If she'd decided to turn tail and run, then he intended to run after her.

He heard a noise from the kitchen area, and turned in that direction, relieved.

She was standing by the counter, an inscrutable expression on her face. "For a second, I thought you'd gone," he said.

His words seemed to baffle her. She gestured to the stove. "I was going to dive in and stir the sauce, put on water for the spaghetti. Maybe make a salad." She shrugged self-consciously. "Sorry. I guess I'm falling back into old habits."

"I don't mind," he said. "But it's your night to be waited on, remember?"

She shook her head, her expression determined. "Don't be silly. Come on. It'll be fun to do it together."

With an ease that surprised him, she slipped over to the stereo. She stopped the loop he'd set for "That's Amore" and scrolled through the playlist on his iPod. A few minutes later, and Lyle Lovett filled the small kitchen. "There," she said, coming back to him and bumping him with her hip. "Music to cook by."

He couldn't disagree, and as Lyle crooned about his life and loves, Josh and Cleo worked side by side in the kitchen, boiling the pasta, stirring the sauce, making the salad. Deciding to push his luck a little, Josh plucked an olive out of a jar and held it out for Cleo, who was rhythmically stirring the sauce in time with the music. She hesitated, but then her lips parted. He fed her the olive, his fingertips brushing her lip. It was the most erotic sensation he'd experienced in years.

For a second, Cleo held his gaze. Then she blinked, and the moment was over. She turned back to the stove. "I think the pasta's done," she said. Josh had never been so disappointed by food being ready to eat.

Once the table was set, he pulled out her chair for her, and she sat with a flourish. "Thank you, kind sir," she said with a small smile. And although there was nothing wrong with the way she said it, he sensed a distance between them.

He sat opposite and took a sip of wine, and the reason fell into place with a unique clarity. She'd helped him cook. She'd changed the music to something light and not particularly romantic. Without saying a word, she'd shifted the tone of the evening he'd planned to something much more casual, more platonic.

And yet she was still here, sitting across from him, sipping wine and looking relaxed.

Josh had spent the last five years in high-powered negotiations, and he understood what was happening.

He'd moved faster than she'd expected and put her off balance. She was pulling back, creating distance so that she could regain her footing. But she wasn't running. She wasn't saying no.

That was okay by Josh; he wasn't in a hurry. He didn't need to be, because the woman he wanted was only a few feet away. And surely he could span a few feet over the course of a couple of days.

He leaned back in his chair, silently letting her know that if distance was what she needed to feel comfortable, then he was more than willing to give it to her. "So tell me about Washington. About the firm." He grinned. "Have you made partner yet?"

It was small talk, and yet with Cleo it didn't seem like small talk. Especially when her face lit up at the mention of her work. She talked with ease, telling him about the people in the firm, about her boss and mentor, about the excitement of delving into a new case, of prepping for depositions. He stopped her occasionally to ask questions, which she answered in detail, throwing in funny stories about client faux pas or the quirks of the judges she'd met. Her face glowed as she spoke, and seeing it gave him a nostalgic pang, because that was what he'd loved most about her—the intensity with which she loved her world and her work. Everything about her in college had been focused on being an attorney, and now that she'd made it, it was clear how much she loved it. The work, the firm, her friends. Even, please no, a possible boyfriend.

He cleared his throat. "I saw a picture of you on Facebook with someone named Perry." He hesitated then dove straight in, needing the answer. "Are you guys dating?"

"Perry? We did for a while. But now, no." Her words were firm, and Josh was almost knocked over by his relief.

"You look happy," he said, the simple words somehow managing to convey everything he saw in her.

"I am," she said. "And it keeps getting better. In fact, I was just assigned an amazing case. One I think you might be interested in. Our client is actually Argentina."

"No kidding?" He leaned forward. "Just last year I had a proposal before the board to—" He cut himself off. Remembering the way the board—led by his mother—had put an end to his plans to partner with an Argentine mining concern would only put a damper on the evening. *"But Josh,"* she'd said. *"We need you here, not galavanting off to South America."*

He should have pressed the point. He was certain that the venture would have tripled Goodson Mining's net worth. But his mother had fingered the ring she wore on a chain around her neck—his father's wedding ring—and said that she didn't know what she'd do without Josh around. He'd quit pushing for the venture.

"Josh?" Cleo's forehead crinkled. "What is it?"

"Nothing. It just— The deal fell through. It's fair to say I was disappointed."

"I'm sorry to hear that. I know how much getting into the international market means to you."

He brushed it off as if it was nothing. "We're on you now," he said. "So, you got this case...?"

"It's a huge opportunity. I've only been on it for a few days, actually. I'm still trying to get up to speed. In fact—"

He frowned. She'd stopped so abruptly that she gave the impression of a tape recorder suddenly being stopped. "What's wrong?"

She cleared her throat and looked abashed. "It's just—it's just that I actually brought some work with me." She cringed a little. "Sorry."

He laughed then lifted his wineglass in a toast. "You haven't changed, Cleo. And I'm very glad."

They clinked glasses, and he realized that he was happier at that moment than he'd been in a long time. It had been the right decision to send Cleo the card. This felt good. *Perfect.* At the moment, he could imagine no place he'd rather be, and no person he'd rather be with.

"It's my turn to ask questions," she said. "You're heading up Goodson Mining, I know that. But what about Harvard? When are you going to go? The company must be in a pretty good position by now, isn't it?"

"The company's doing great," he said. He ignored the question about Harvard.

"So you're focusing on expansion now? I remember that's what you and your dad always wanted for the company."

"It was his dream," Josh said, stating the truth as much as he was avoiding it.

"So tell me about it. What's the first step? Have you got the geological surveys from potential locations? Where are you thinking about expanding first?"

Her words hit him like a battering ram, each one reminding him of the walls he'd encountered, the ideas he'd let go, and it made him feel as if everything he'd done over the last five years—all the localized growth and revenue increases in the company that he was responsible for—was nothing but a failure. He stood up and started for the kitchen.

She stopped him with a hand on his arm. "Josh?"

"Sorry. It's just that I've been living and breathing mining for years—do you know this is my first vacation since my dad died? I think I should go on a conversational vacation, too. No mining talk."

He saw her brows rise, and her expression was an odd mixture of shock and something that he would have thought was irritation if he didn't know better. The she laughed, and her expression cleared. "You're right," she said, letting go of his arm. "We have an entire weekend to talk business. Right now, we need to discuss more important things."

"Dessert," he said.

"You read my mind."

She got up to help him with the cheesecake he'd brought back from the deli. She put slices onto plates for each of them while he uncorked another bottle of wine and took it to the coffee table in front of the fire.

He settled himself on the couch, and she did the same. They each reached for a napkin, and their hands brushed. He felt that *zing* again, and she jumped. He hid a smile, certain she'd felt it, too.

"Sorry," she said, smiling sheepishly. "I guess I'm a little jumpy."

"Maybe it would be better if we admit the situation's a bit awkward," he said.

"Is it?"

"We haven't seen each other for five years," he said. He took a sip of his wine and commented on the elephant in the room. "And the last time we were together, we were naked."

"Well, not *the* last time," she countered. "You drove me to the airport. I distinctly remember wearing clothes. I'm pretty sure the airlines insist upon it."

"Still—"

"Yes," she agreed. "There's still something between us, isn't there?"

"Is that bad?" He held his breath, fearing her answer. Knowing he couldn't accept it if she said that there was no chance.

"No," she said softly. "It's not bad."

He felt as though he was conducting an orchestra, and all the players had to come together in harmony. This holiday wasn't about getting her in bed—well, not entirely. It was about getting her back into his life. It was about courting her. *Dating* her. And even though they'd known each other forever—even though he'd tasted every naked inch of her—it was also about starting over.

He'd made over the kitchen and re-created their first date for a reason. This was a beginning, and he wasn't going to push. In the end, he would win. He would get Cleo back.

And he intended to thoroughly enjoy getting there, one small step at a time.

"Do you remember how we used to play Monopoly?"

She cocked her head, her mouth pursed in amusement. "I do remember. Are you quizzing my memory, or is there a nefarious purpose to your question?"

"Entirely nefarious," he said. "I saw Monopoly in the cabin's games closet."

"Monopoly and dessert," she said. "And, of course, the wine. Not bad."

"And good company," he added, watching her eyes.

"Yes," she said without any hesitation, and in a voice that made him think that his plans were going to work out just fine. "Excellent company."

Half an hour later, he owned half the railroads, Boardwalk and was comfortably tipsy from all the sips of wine he'd taken when passing Go. She rolled, got six and landed on Chance.

"Something good," she said, then drew a card. "Yes!" She moved her piece to Go. "Two hundred dollars, please."

He held out the money, but waited for her to do

her part. She picked up her wine and took a sip. "Do you have any idea how wasted we're going to be if we drink every time we pass Go for an entire game?" she said.

"We've done it before."

"Yeah, in college. When you're genetically programmed to drink like a fish."

"Feeling a bit light in the head?"

She shook her head then nodded. "I didn't eat a whole lot today. I don't think the pasta soaked up much of the wine."

"Want to stop?"

"Nope," she said.

"Why not?"

She looked him straight in the eye, and he saw something flirtatious in her gaze. "Because I'm having fun."

He laughed. "In that case..." He picked up the bottle and pretended he was going to top off her glass. She squealed and backed away. "Stop! It's your roll! If you don't play, how can I achieve my goal of world domination?"

"Isn't that Risk?" he asked, mentioning another game they used to play.

"Do the Vickerses have Risk?"

"Didn't see it. But they do have Twister."

"Do they? Interesting..."

He recognized the suggestive tone in her voice, and he wanted to give a whoop of joy. Instead, he played it cool. "Could you settle for domination of only Manhattan?"

"Is the Monopoly board based on Manhattan?"

He frowned. "You know, I'm not sure. I could get my phone and look it up on the web."

She reached for his hand, held his fingers tight. "Just roll."

"Right." Since he didn't want to let go of her hand, it was an awkward roll, but he got a seven, which put him on Park Place.

"Don't you dare!"

"Bwahahaha!" He twirled an imaginary mustache as he bought the property, thereby ruining her chance of blocking his efforts to put a hotel on Boardwalk.

She yanked her hand back, and he regretted the move. At least until she smacked him with the pillow and he realized he needed his hand to defend himself. After a few minutes, he'd been backed into a corner of the couch and she was leaning over him, a pillow in hand and a smile on her beautiful face. Her green eyes sparkled, and she was so close he could count the smattering of freckles that dusted her cheeks and nose. She hated them, but he'd always thought they were sexy as hell.

She was breathing hard and she dropped the pillow, her chest rising and falling. Time stopped, and it was just them. The world no longer turning. "Josh, I…" Her lips were red and moist, parted just a bit, and he could feel her breath on his face. He silently prayed that she'd go with it. That she'd lean forward just a little more and kiss him. He could taste her in his imagination, peanut butter mixed with wine and just a hint of chocolate. *Please*.

And then the moment shattered.

She bolted back, her expression a mixture of surprise and desire. And, he saw, regret. "Sorry, I—"

"It's okay," he said. *Really, really okay.*

"All this wine. I'm getting a little tired. Maybe I should crash."

He glanced at his watch. "It's only eleven."

"It's later in D.C.," she said.

He hadn't even considered how exhausted she must be. "Right. Of course. You take the bed. I'll stretch out here on the couch."

"You sure?"

"Of course. It's totally comfortable."

She stood. "Okay." But she didn't walk away. "Maybe I should just have a cup of coffee. I'll probably get a second wind."

He jumped on the suggestion. "I'll make you an espresso. The Vickerses just brought the machine up."

"I pull late nights all the time. I shouldn't be such a wimp." She smiled. "It's just jet lag."

He remembered her being a night owl, going to bed when many folks were just getting up. "If Monopoly's getting old, we can always roast marshmallows." The fire had started to fizzle, but another log would bring it back to life again.

"Marshmallows?" she repeated.

"I'm up for alternative suggestions." Like her body

slick and naked beneath his. Probably best not to mention that idea, though. He shifted as certain parts of his anatomy responded to the prurient turn of his thoughts. *Don't think about it.*

"Marshmallows sound like fun," she said.

"Great. Excellent. You go find a couple of wire coat hangers, and I'll get the coffee and marshmallows."

"Do you have chocolate and graham crackers?"

"You read my mind," he said. S'mores had been a special treat when he and his dad went camping. And, yeah, he'd shared them once with Cleo on a camping trip, too. She'd been new to the roughing-it thing, but she'd loved it, and they'd told ghost stories around the campfire and fed each other gooey marshmallows, which had led to some rather gooey sex, as well. She had to remember. The question was whether she was remotely interested in an encore performance.

But he had to stop anticipating things that might not happen. Better to just live in the moment and appreciate what did.

By the time he returned to the living room, she'd straightened out two hangers and was kneeling in front of the fire. She'd set the grate to one side, and he put the plate down on the hearth and settled in next to her. "I'm going to burn mine to a crisp," she said. "Don't laugh."

"You're supposed to gently brown them."

"No way. Burned is better." As if to prove the point, she shoved a marshmallow on the makeshift skewer, stuck it into the flames and pulled it out.

The white ball of fluff flamed like a meteorite, and she turned the skewer, making sure that all of it got charred. Then she blew it out, waited a few seconds for it to cool and popped the whole thing in her mouth. "Mmm," she said through a mouthful of gooey goodness.

"Heathen. Let me show you how it's done." He put a marshmallow on his own coat hanger, then held it over the fire until it was toasted a perfect brown. "Ta-da."

"Not bad. But not gooey enough for a s'more." As if to demonstrate, she flamed another marshmallow and smushed it in between the cookies and chocolate. She took a big bite, and ended up with a clump of chocolate and marshmallow in the corner of her mouth.

He reached out and brushed his thumb over it, then brought his thumb back to his mouth. "You're right. Your way tastes great."

"Josh, I—"

Before he could talk himself out of it—before she could think to stop him—he moved in for a kiss.

He was right, she did taste like chocolate and wine.

Her response was hesitant at first, but finally she opened her mouth under his, and he thought he was going to lose it right there. She was everything he ever wanted, and she was right there in his arms. That was all that mattered. There were no second-guesses, no fear that this was going to end and she'd bolt from the room. Just *this moment*. Only this.

She pulled away, and his heart twisted. "Josh—"

Her breathing was as tight as his, and he could see the desire in her eyes. It was in the way she rubbed her palms down her jeans, the way her lips were parted. And the way her nipples peaked behind her T-shirt, so hard he could see them even under her bra. "Josh," she repeated, and he leaned closer, wanting to take her. Wanting only to hear her name.

"I—I'm sorry." She got to her feet, her expression confused and frazzled. "I think— I'm going to take a shower and crash."

And then she was gone, and he was left sitting there wondering how he'd gone from having the woman he craved melting and willing in his arms, to sitting alone in front of a fireplace littered with graham-cracker crumbs.

CHAPTER FOUR

CLEO SHUT THE BATHROOM DOOR behind her and leaned against it, breathing hard, her mind in a muddle. *What am I doing?*

She'd come to talk business, not to rekindle romance. Not even for fabulous reunion sex. And yet she'd almost let herself get carried away and surrender to her desire. And why? Because Josh called to her. Because, of all the men she'd ever known, he was the only one who made her feel open and alive. Who made her feel as if sex was an extension of the fun they were having with each other. An expression of unity rather than just exercise and heat between the sheets.

She wanted him, plain and simple.

But she'd walked away because she knew she had to. The re-creation of their first date, the candles, the tone of his voice—all these things told her that it would be more than reunion sex to Josh, more than just fun.

She had to tell him why she'd come. And yet, if she did, then the chance to have Josh in her arms would evaporate. She'd never expected that to be a complication, and yet, damn her, she wanted to feel him against her again. She'd realized just how much she wanted that when he'd kissed her. A kiss that had worked its way down to her toes and into her soul. Making her forget common sense and reason. Making her remember only him.

She'd done the only thing she could do to prevent herself from hurting him—she'd pushed away and ran. And probably hurt him anyway in the process. Smooth, very smooth.

So now he was in the living room stinging, and she was in the bathroom, tipsy and more than a little turned on.

So go out there and sleep with him. The truth will still be there in the morning.

She wanted to—oh, how she wanted to.

But she couldn't bear the thought of making this any harder on Josh than it already was. Which meant that she and her raging libido were going to take a nice cold shower, then climb into a nice warm bed—alone. Not the most enticing of plans…but she couldn't argue with its practicality.

She ran the icy water and tried to get in. But she couldn't deal with the cold, much as she might need it. Instead, she twisted the temperature-control knob and slid under a stream of warm water, letting it sluice over her, letting it warm her.

Her skin was already sensitive with desire, and she closed her eyes, letting her mind wander, imagining Josh's hands on her breasts, following the path of the water down her stomach and lower. Her own hand dipped between her thighs, and she moaned as she touched herself, wishing it could be Josh, but nonetheless wanting the release.

Stop it.

She opened her eyes. This really wasn't the way to get her libido in check. Shower. Sleep. That was the plan. Getting hotter and hornier was really not the smartest thing to do.

She turned the handle to increase the hot water, then looked around the shower. No soap, no shampoo.

Well, damn.

Her own travel bag was in the living room, but surely there was some outside the small shower. She pulled the curtain aside and peered around. Sure enough, a few feet away a small table stood, topped with bottles of shampoo and conditioner, a bar of soap and what looked like a delicious body gel.

Fab.

She slid back under the water and cranked the hot up a bit more. She should be turning the cold up, but that was okay. She was determined. Confident. Completely in control.

She could take a hot shower without succumbing to the demands of her libido.

Of course she could.

SINCE JOSH COULDN'T JUST sit there wallowing in disappointment after Cleo bolted for the shower, he started to clear the dishes. Only he accidentally dropped the dessert plate onto the hearth, and, as he was picking the pieces up and tossing them into the trash, he managed to slice his thumb.

It didn't hurt—well, not a lot. But it was bleeding. *Damn.*

He wrapped a tissue around it, which promptly turned red. He was on his way to grab his car keys so he could snag the first-aid kit from the trunk, when he remembered the Check Engine light that had come on as he'd followed Jillian to the cabin. They'd backtracked and left his car at Guy's Auto Shop in exchange for the promise that it would be good as new on January 1, despite Josh's protests that Guy didn't need to work on a holiday.

Which meant any bandages he was going to find would have to be in the cabin.

He scoured the kitchen first and came up with nothing. Then he searched the games closet and the bedroom. Nothing, and nothing.

Of course, most people kept first-aid supplies in the bathroom.

But Cleo was in the bathroom, naked, and he couldn't exactly go barging in there.

But he didn't want to bleed out on the rug.

He glanced at the closed bathroom door. His thumb throbbed.

Okay. He'd go in. If he made no noise, he might not even disturb her. There was a flowered curtain around the tub, after all. It wasn't as if he was going to get an eyeful. And too bad for that...

He opened the door gently, paused just long enough

to make sure the shower was still running, and walked in, closing the door behind him so that the steam wouldn't escape. A mirrored medicine cabinet hung over the sink. He opened it and found himself staring at a box of Band-Aids.

Perfect. He opened one, tossed the tissue, rinsed his thumb and performed some quick first aid right over the sink. Behind the shower curtain, he could hear the water pounding, and it didn't take much imagination to picture her in there, sleek and sexy and warm and wet.

Go.

He went, but he paused at the door to look back, letting his imagination carry him to heaven one last time.

And that's when it happened. The curtain pulled aside and a very wet, very naked Cleo was standing right there, her eyes wide.

"Oh!"

"Sorry! Sorry!"

"What are you doing?" She pulled the shower curtain so it hid what he'd already seen. What was burned in his mind forever.

"I needed a Band-Aid. I was on my way out." He held up his bandaged thumb, and realized how lame he must look since he was obviously still in the bathroom. And obviously staring in her

"Ever heard of the power of speech? A simple 'hey, I'm in here' would have done just fine."

"Sorry. I—"

"What?"

He shook his head. "I thought I could slip in and out without disturbing you." Although part of him wondered if secretly he hadn't been hoping for a moment exactly like this. Him in front of the tub, and her slowly pulling back the curtain.

"Josh? Hello?"

"What?" He blinked and realized she'd said something to him.

"I asked if you could bring me the soap and the shampoo." She cocked her head toward the table.

"Sure." He grabbed the stuff and took it to her, knowing full well he should just pass it to her and go. Fast. That was what a gentleman would do.

Except he wasn't even remotely interested in being a gentleman.

He reached out with the soap, and when she took it, he brushed his thumb over her hand. She gasped. Such a soft sound, it was almost swallowed by the sound of the running water. But he heard it. He heard it, and he knew.

"Cleo…"

She ran her teeth over her lower lip.

"You want help?" he asked. And then he waited, bold and silent, holding his breath.

She let go of the shower curtain, and it seemed to fall in slow motion. Suddenly, Josh could breathe again.

"It can't mean anything," she whispered. "It's just…I just want you."

"I know," he said. But she was wrong. It meant everything. And before the weekend was over, he'd prove it to her. "I want you, too."

She smiled with the words, reaching for his waist-band and tugging him close. Her fingers fumbled at his button and fly, and he helped her along, stepping out of his pants and socks, and then climbing into the tub with her. His T-shirt was soaked immediately under the warm spray, and she peeled it off him, her hands sliding over his chest, making his heartbeat pick up tempo and his cock take notice. She noticed, too, and her hand slipped down between them. "Where's that soap?" she whispered.

"You put it in the dish."

"Right."

She released him long enough to lather her hands, then passed the bar to him. He tried to concentrate on working up a lather, but it was hard with her expert fingers gliding over him. Lord, how he'd missed her touch.

He was tense and tight and ready to explode. He reached down and eased her hands around to his back. "Too fast," he murmured, and she made a satisfied little noise, as if her goal of tormenting him had been soundly met.

He slid his hands over her belly and breasts, making her body slick with soap before pulling her close. The water beat down on them, drenching them, heating them, and he used the soap as an excuse to explore every inch of her, refamiliarizing himself with a body he'd once known as intimately as his own.

He lifted her arms, soaping them and then closing her hand over the shower rod. Then he eased to his knees and slid his hand between her legs, touching her lightly, feeling her tremble in his hand. Her soft moans mingled with the splashing of the water, the small bathroom making the sounds echo, so it felt as though he was lost in her passion.

He bent close, desperate to taste her, and brought his tongue to her clit. She gasped, and he held her steady as she soared higher. And he was the one who was taking her there. He didn't let up, stroking and teasing, his fingers sliding up to stroke her nipples, his cock hardening with every moan, every little squeal, every desperate, needy thrust of her hips.

On and on it built until he could feel her body tighten, the tension mounting higher and higher and higher, more and more, until finally she grabbed his shoulders and he realized he was holding her up because her knees had given out.

She slid down into the tub, now half-full since his soaked T-shirt was blocking the drain.

"Heaven," she whispered, her mouth finding his.

He kissed her, wanting to share the taste of her. She clung to him, her body soft and ready. "More," she whispered.

"Oh, yeah."

"Not here," she said. She lifted a hand to the shower spray. "It's gone cold."

He hadn't noticed, but she was right. They'd used up all the hot water.

"Not a problem," he said. He got out of the tub and wrapped a towel around his waist, then helped her out. Slowly, methodically, gently, he dried her off.

"Have you seen the bedroom?"

"I haven't. Want to show it to me?"

"I do," he said. And at the moment he couldn't think of anything he wanted more.

SHE DIDN'T HAVE A CHANCE to be chilled from the cold water because Josh scooped her up, pressed her close to his warm naked chest and carried her to the bedroom. He deposited her in the middle of absolute decadence: a soft velour bedspread that caressed her already aroused and sensitive skin.

For one moment while he was carrying her, reason had tried to slide back into her mind, screaming that she had to take it back, to stop this. That she never should have let desire win out over reason.

But somehow the words couldn't come. She wanted this, *needed it*. She'd missed what she had in Josh—a friend, a lover, a teammate, all rolled into one. When she'd been with Perry, she'd always had the feeling that he was performing. As if after every date, every kind word, every orgasm, he expected her to lift up a scorecard or something. And the truth was, he'd never ranked a perfect ten.

Not the way Josh had, just by being himself.

Was it too much to ask to want to be blown away this weekend, just one last time?

Beneath her, the bedspread was soft and warm. She writhed against it, wanting him. Only he'd gone back to turn off the water.

She ran her fingertips over her sensitive skin, her eyes closed, her nerve endings on fire.

"That's an enticing sight."

"Do you want to look?" she teased. "Or touch?"

"I'll admit to enjoying the view, but I think I'll take door number two."

"Good choice," she said. She reached up as he came over her, then she hooked her arms around his neck as he straddled her. With a low moan, she lifted her mouth to his, desperate to taste him. His hands slipped down, fingers stroking her already sensitive sex, and she trembled in his hand, hot and wet and ready.

His mouth closed over hers, and she devoured him, all chocolate and sweet and oh, so male.

Ignoring his protest, she broke the kiss and trailed her mouth to his ear, biting and teasing and tasting, remembering that drove him crazy. It seemed some things never changed, because with only a few nips and licks, he let out a rough growl and flipped them over.

She settled herself again, laughing as she straddled him this time. "Nice trick," she said, leaning forward as he reached up to cup her breasts. "Got any others?"

"Plenty," he promised.

She stroked his chest, relishing the sensation of his skin against hers.

The fire had kept the living room warm, but the air in the bedroom was cool, and she shivered as it whispered against her overheated body.

"You're so beautiful," he said. "I've missed looking at you. Talking to you."

She'd missed it, too, but she didn't dare say it out loud. Missing implied emotions, and that wasn't what this was supposed to be about. Instead, she leaned over and kissed him, speaking through touch instead of with words.

He twined his fingers in her hair. It felt nice, but that wasn't where she wanted his hands. She wanted palms on skin. Heat on heat. Body against body.

And so she boldly moved his hands to her breasts.

She moaned aloud when he squeezed her nipples, rising up so that he could close his mouth over one and tease it with his tongue. She twisted with the pleasure of it, wanting him to take more, to increase the violent heat of pleasure that was ripping through her. Wanting not just his mouth, but all of him. "Josh, please. Inside me."

In answer, he slid his hand down, his fingers teasing her, making her even slicker, giving her a tempestuous preview of what was still to come.

"Let go," he whispered.

She did, letting him stroke and tease her until she trembled against him, her orgasm ripping through her as he cupped her gently with his hand.

She rolled off him, sated and happy.

But at the same time she still wanted more. So much more.

"That was wonderful," she said, turning onto her side. "But you know I'm not done with you."

"I'm happy to hear that, actually."

She grinned. "Make me the happiest girl in the world and tell me that you have some condoms handy."

"Prepare to be ecstatic…" He reached over and pulled open the drawer on the bedside table. "I like to be cautiously optimistic," he said as he removed a box.

"Thank goodness for that." She let him take the coin from the package and sheath himself, because she was woefully out of practice and she really didn't want to waste any time. Not when she wanted to feel him inside her. Not when she wanted Josh to take her all the way to the stars and beyond.

"I've got to warn you, though," he said. "I don't think I can play this out much longer."

"Thank goodness for that, too," she said. She was ready. She was desperate. And if he wasn't inside her soon, she was pretty sure the world might end.

He straddled her, and with one powerful thrust, entered her. She lifted her hips and met him. She wanted it hard, wanted to be claimed. Wanted it hot and wild and *Josh*.

His hips pistoned with hers, and she felt that wonderful climbing tension as her body headed toward heaven, splitting wide and then reforming in a cascade of stars and colors. Soon, soon…

They said anticipation was part of the pleasure, and they were so right, but at the moment, she just wanted the explosion.

And then it came—he tightened, arching up, and that was the trigger for her body to lose it. She melted into his arms, a thousand points of light and a tumble of stardust. Pleasure so intense she didn't have the words. *Spectacular* seemed so completely inadequate.

He rolled away and pulled her close. She burrowed up against him as he pressed soft kisses to her ear. "Wow," he said, and she seconded the thought.

But it was late, even later in D.C., and she was sated, barely able to keep her eyes open. But as she drifted off, she worried that even though she'd warned him not to think this meant anything, she had to tell him about her real reason for coming. But not now. Now, she'd drift off in Josh's arms, lost in this sea of pleasure and contentment.

Everything else could wait until tomorrow.

CHAPTER FIVE

CLEO WOKE UP IN JOSH'S ARMS, her back against his chest, the heat their bodies were generating more than enough to warm the entire cabin.

It felt damn good.

More than that, it felt like old times.

She closed her eyes and silently cursed herself. She should never have said yes in the bathroom. She should have told him the truth about why she was truly here.

With regret weighing heavily on her, she slid out of bed, shivering the moment she broke contact with him. But it was for the best. She wanted to be up when he woke. Doing normal stuff. Routine. And then she'd tell him that the nostalgia and the reunion and the wine had messed with her better judgment. She'd tell him they had to talk.

They'd be adults.

They could do that.

Since her bag was still in the car, Cleo grabbed a T-shirt from Josh's open suitcase and pulled it on. She'd change into her own clothes before he got up…but first she'd deal with her growling stomach. She went into the kitchen, scrounging around in the refrigerator and pantry for food. She wasn't an amazing cook, but even she could do up a few eggs.

Josh stumbled into the kitchen before she had a chance to run out to the car...but not before she'd put together a plate of scrambled eggs, a plate of fried eggs and a stack of toast that almost reached the ceiling.

"Are we expecting the French Foreign Legion?"

She gave him a rueful smile. "Sorry. Distracted. I wasn't paying attention. Hungry?"

His smile was wicked. "For a lot of things, actually. Food, and then..."

"Right." She spun away from him, wondering if he could hear the way her pulse was pounding in her chest, kicking herself for not making clothes a priority over food. She opened the refrigerator, stared blankly inside for a moment, and then pulled out orange juice. "OJ?"

"Sure."

When she turned back around with the carafe and a glass, he was eyeing her, concerned.

She forced a perky smile.

"Cleo." His voice was flat with just the hint of a questioning intonation.

"Hmm?"

"What's wrong?"

"Nothing," she said, then immediately hated herself. At the very least, she owed him honesty. Time to face the music. "Okay, it's not nothing."

He sipped his orange juice. "Do you want to tell me? Or should I guess?"

She drew in a breath for courage. "I have a confession to make."

"I know," he said.

She frowned at him. "You know?"

"Are you feeling guilty about Perry?"

Her gut twisted. Josh thought Perry was her confession. Only, Perry was so far out of her head and she didn't feel the slightest bit of remorse about having shoved him away. "No, it's not that. Perry and I are completely over."

"Then what is it?"

"Josh," she said. "Last night was great, but—"

"One step at a time," he said. "I know."

"Josh, I didn't come here to the cabin with this in mind," she said, gesturing between the two of them.

"That's okay. After five years, I get that you'd be in 'just friends' mode. But I'm glad you moved past that."

"It wasn't just friendship," she said. "I had an ulterior motive."

His brows lifted with amusement. "Did you?"

"The case I mentioned? The one with the Argentine mine? I need to hire a consultant. Someone who knows the mining industry inside and out. I came because I wanted you. Professionally, I mean. Not personally." She managed a little smile. "And I should have told you that before we—well, before we got into bed."

He was still for a moment, and she held her breath. Afraid this was going to be it. That he was going to ask her to leave. And she would have no defense.

Instead, he simply looked at her. "A consultant? I'd like to do that. But is it a conflict of interest? Can you hire me if we're together?"

Together.

The word gave her a surprising little tingle of pleasure. She savored that thought for a moment. Was that what he truly meant? And if it was, did she want it, too?

Yeah. I do.

She knew that every day away from him would be a day she'd miss him. She'd miss sharing the details of her day, the failures and triumphs.

So yes, she wanted to be together. At the very least, she wanted to try to make it work.

But was it a conflict of interest? Not technically, but it could be awkward, of course. If a consulting expert was dating an attorney and then they had a bad breakup, things could get nasty. And Leon wouldn't approve. He liked things in the law to be clean, with no complicated personal relationships to potentially muck up the work.

But Josh was the perfect consultant. Was she really willing to toss aside the professional coup of finding the perfect expert for the theoretical possibility that she and Josh could get back together after five years apart? After all, they'd only been reunited for a day.

How could she be expected to make a decision about both her life and her career after only a few hours?

And yet it wasn't. Because she knew. She and Josh fit. She'd always known it—and, yes, she'd always believed it.

Considering the romantic restaurant theme Josh had surprised her with upon her arrival, she had to assume that he believed it, too.

"Cleo?"

"No," she said. "It wouldn't be a good idea. Not an official conflict, of course, but my boss wouldn't approve."

"I see." But there was a hesitancy in his voice. He understood the problem; he was still waiting to see what side she came down on.

She looked hard at him. "Can you recommend someone else to consult?"

He cocked his head. And slowly, very slowly, she saw him smile. "Cleo," he said. "Are you sure?"

"If I wasn't," she countered as she slid easily into his arms, "then I'd already have my consultant. Look at all the trouble you're causing me. I came here thinking I was combining work with pleasure, and it turns out I still have to do the work."

"I'm terribly sorry." His lips brushed against hers. He didn't seem sorry at all.

"That's okay," she said, more at home in his arms than she could remember feeling for a long time. "I guess you'll just have to make it up to me."

JOSH HAD NEVER BEEN HAPPIER about anything in his life. *She wanted him.* But it wasn't a feeling of relief that came over him. More like realization of a truth long buried. They were right for each other—they always had been. And finally, life could mirror reality. They really could be together.

He grabbed the hem of the T-shirt she was wearing and yanked it over her head, delighted when he revealed her naked body underneath.

She practically purred, and he felt himself stiffen with need. "Were we really apart five years?" he whispered.

"We weren't ever apart," she answered. "Not really."

The answer almost made him come undone. "Come with me," he said, taking her hand and leading her back to the bedroom. She fell back, laughing, onto the bed. He'd pulled on boxers, but now he left them in a heap on the floor, consumed only by her, the soft body outlined by the soft bedspread.

He straddled her, trembling as the steel length of him brushed against the soft flesh of her thighs.

She exhaled, her body quivering as she spread her legs. His balls tightened, and when he slipped his hand down, touching her, finding her slick and ready, he almost came on the spot.

He sheathed himself quickly. "Wider," he said, and when she complied, he held on to her waist and thrust himself into heaven. She arched her back, a breathy moan escaping as her muscles contracted around him, drawing him in, milking him as he moved in a sensual rhythm above her. "Cleo," he moaned, his body clenching and need building.

She rose to meet his thrusts, and, as the pressure built and built, he held his breath, fighting release, wanting it to last almost as much as he wanted the explosion.

He was on the verge when she shifted, pulling free of him. His body protested, but she only smiled that smug grin and urged him to roll over so that she could straddle him.

His eyes closed, wanting simply to feel, to experience. He knew the moment she came, her muscles tightening around him like a velvet fist, sending him over the edge only seconds behind her.

He locked his arms around her, pulling her down against him, letting their heartbeats mingle as one as they lay together for an eternity.

When time started up again, she slid out of the bed and held out her hand. "Shower?"

He wasn't about to protest, though they did need to talk. He followed her into the tub, this round doing a much better job of getting clean.

She kissed him under the spray. "So what do we do now? If neither one of us believes that any time has passed, it's not like we need to catch up."

He smiled in agreement. "No catching up required at all."

"So?"

"We could continue to burn calories in bed—best

way I can think of to spend New Year's Eve until the fireworks—but how about adding a little variety to the mix?"

"Sex in front of the fire?"

"Not bad," he conceded. "But I thought we might take a walk."

He watched her face, searching for signs of disappointment. He feared that, despite the words they'd spoken, Cleo only viewed what was going on between them as a purely physical thing. And while he wouldn't deny the appeal of losing himself inside her, he wanted more than that. He wanted the whole package, and sex was such a small part of who she was and who they could be together.

But there was no hesitation in her enthusiasm, and they were out of the shower, dry and dressed in under half an hour.

The snow the night before had been light, and today the sky was clear. Neither of them knew the area around the secluded cabin, so they just took off walking down a path through the forest, watching the snow melt in the trees, trying to catch sight of winter squirrels, listening to the sound of the snow melting and falling from the trees.

Josh had wanted to talk about their future, to make sure they were on the same page this time. But as she slipped her hand into his, he decided to enjoy just being with her for a little longer. The future could wait. They walked hand in hand, chatting about nothing, snow crunching under their feet. For over half an hour they moved down the secluded lane, twisting through paths cut through the trees, until Josh feared that they should have left a trail of bread crumbs.

He was about to suggest they turn around and either head back to the cabin or try to find civilization in another direction, when they heard squeals of delight. They hurried a few more yards forward and found themselves at a hill where a group of four kids were plowing down a hill on inner tubes.

They watched for a few minutes, their noses cold, until Josh finally decided that you only live once and approached the kids. The oldest, acting as spokesman, told Josh that their parents owned another tucked-away cabin, and they came up every Christmas. This hill had become their secret hideaway. So long as Josh and Cleo didn't blab the location, they were welcome to share the tube.

Josh and Cleo both performed an elaborate cross-your-heart routine to seal the deal, then they crawled onto the tube and went down together. Not a smart move—they had no control whatsoever and ended up crashing into a massive snowdrift, much to the delight of the kid who'd lent them the tube.

Josh didn't care, he and Cleo were laughing too hard themselves. They dug themselves out, dragged the tube up the hill, gave it back to the kid and continued their walk.

"We're going to need a hot bath after we get back," she said. "We'll be soaked through after this. Not that I care. I haven't had as much fun as this in ages."

"Hot bath, hot cocoa."

"Hot sex," she added. "And, of course, fireworks." She grinned. "It's New Year's Eve, after all."

He laughed. "And here I thought you meant a different kind of fireworks. Still, you plan an excellent agenda," he said. "Are you ready to go back?"

She shook her head. "No, I'm fine. Unless you are?"

"I'm enjoying the walk." He reached out and took her gloved hand in his again, the normalcy of the action making him light-headed.

"You still haven't told me about your plans," she said. "For expansion, I mean. What's on the agenda for Goodson Mining?"

"Expansion's been my top priority," he admitted. "But it's not as easy to accomplish as you might think. Not in a family-owned company."

Her brow furrowed. "Why on earth not?"

"Everyone has a say, and everyone's afraid the company will go under if I'm not there to run it."

"Will it?"

He hesitated. The question was so direct, so completely to the point, that it almost seemed too intense. As if she was breaking some unspoken rule in asking it.

"Do you have to stay to keep the company stable, Josh?"

"I did," he said. "If I'd left five years ago, the company would have collapsed." He glanced at her face, knowing by her expression that she realized he hadn't truly answered the question. He drew in a breath and took the plunge, getting to the heart of what she was asking. "Now, of course, there are so many other paths I can take. I've been interviewing geologists and lobbyists, hoping to put together a team to work on negotiating the various deals necessary for expansion."

"That's wonderful!"

He looked sideways at her, wondering if she truly meant that. It had taken him a long time to accept that the only way the board would approve expansion was if he farmed out the real meat of the job to new employees, while he stayed in Nevada.

It wasn't what he wanted—he wanted to do the traveling and the negotiating. But the board was fighting him every step of the way. And maybe his mother was right—if he had a family at his side, his business regrets would fade fast. Hell, he couldn't imagine having any regrets if he was with Cleo, their children playing in the yard, the woman he loved in his arms each night.

Thankfully, she was in one of the most portable professions on the planet. All she needed was to be admitted to the Nevada bar, and she could open up shop in Carlin, in Reno, wherever she wanted. And if she was already doing mining work, she could have Goodson Mining as the first of many lucrative clients. He had the connections, after all.

Within a year, she could be one of the top attorneys in the field. And they would be together.

He took her hand, squeezing her fingers as his

heart swelled with happiness. She was his missing piece. His better half. The yin to his yang.

She always had been, and she always would be.

And he was so certain of that fact, that he didn't notice her silence, or the odd, still way she was looking at him.

CHAPTER SIX

"No! No! YOUR LEFT FOOT on blue." Cleo tried to stay still so she wouldn't fall as Josh shifted slightly to the right and tried to thrust his leg between hers to get to the blue circle on the Twister mat.

"Well, don't move. You're going to—*agh!*" He grabbed her arm, and they went tumbling, with Cleo ending up on top of Josh, their faces close together, and him smiling a devious little smile.

"This shouldn't be that hard with only two people," she said.

He pressed a hand over his heart. "Are you suggesting I might be exaggerating the difficulty of these moves? I assure you, it's not true. I'm just a klutz. Pure and simple."

She laughed and scooted off him, sliding back onto the couch. He did the same, and she slipped her feet onto his lap, her toes warm and snuggly in thick wool socks. After their walk, they'd spent the day doing nothing much around the cabin. A little Monopoly, a little Twister. A lot of talking. It was great. Cleo couldn't remember the last time she'd felt so relaxed around a man.

Actually, that wasn't true. She could remember exactly—five years ago. And with this very guy.

She resisted the urge to sigh as she took a sip of the hot cocoa they'd made before playing Twister, now finally cool enough to actually drink. Being with him brought back so many feelings. Good ones. Comfortable ones.

Certainly she'd never felt this content around Perry. With him it was as if there was some sort of film between them. But with Josh it wasn't there. No—that wasn't quite true. There was still one thing hanging between them. One mystery that she didn't understand, and about which Josh was still being evasive.

She needed to know, though. She needed to understand why Josh was still in Nevada. Why he hadn't gone to grad school. Why he wasn't opening branch offices, traveling the world, negotiating land rights with foreign jurisdictions. Why he wasn't reaching to attain his dreams.

"Josh, is your mother ill?"

He looked at her in surprise. "She's fine. Where did that come from?"

She allowed herself a grin. "I'm psychoanalyzing you."

"Must be some analysis if the end result is that my mom is sick."

"I'm very glad she's not," Cleo said. She thought about asking the next question, but decided to wait. This was New Year's Eve, after all. Serious questions could wait for the new year. She eased toward him and slipped her hands around his waist, arching against him until she had the satisfaction of hearing him moan and feeling the hard length of him press against her thigh. "Guess what I'm thinking now," she whispered.

His breath tickled her ear. "You're thinking that the hot tub on the back porch sounds incredibly tempting."

"You know me so well," she whispered.

"I'm amazing," he said. He kissed her then eased away, holding a hand out to her. "If we go now we can watch the sunset from the warmth of steaming hot water."

Since that sounded too good to pass up, she followed him out. The hot tub was on the back porch, secure under a vinyl cover. "Do you know what to do?" she asked.

"I think so," he said. He peeled back the cover, then found some controls that made the water start to bubble. She didn't have to ask if it was already hot; the rising steam answered that question.

"Come on," he said, stepping boldly out of his clothes and leaving them on the patio.

"It's freezing!"

"Thus the hot tub."

"We're going to turn blue when we get out," she complained, but she tugged off her socks and started to peel off her jeans. At the very least it was an adventure, and she had a feeling Josh would happily warm her up after they raced from the hot tub back into the cabin.

They settled on opposite sides at first, just looking at each other. They couldn't actually see the sunset, not with the hills and trees, but the sky turned a beautiful orange color, and Cleo sighed, losing herself in the beauty of the mountains.

"We forgot the wine," Josh said.

Cleo lifted a brow. "Then you brave the cold to go get it. I'm staying right here where it's warm."

"With you there," he said. He got up and moved closer to her, their feet meeting on a footrest under the water. They sat that way for a moment, just enjoying the quiet and the company.

It was Josh who finally broke the silence.

"We should talk about tomorrow," he said.

She nodded. "We probably should. But—can we not? Not yet." She slid closer and eased up onto his lap. She wanted him. She wanted *them*. And she was certain that he wanted it, too. But she couldn't shake the feeling that they were at cross-purposes. And if she was right, she wanted to postpone the inevitable. When she and Josh had parted before, she'd been catatonic for weeks. She feared parting with him again would kill her.

"We do need to talk about tomorrow," she said. "About mining and litigation and you and me." She pressed her palm to his face and met his eyes. "But you know what? Right now, I don't care about any of that."

"No? What do you care about?"

"What do you think?" she teased.

"Hmm. Let me guess." He slipped his hand between her legs, and she arched her back, losing herself as his fingers found her cleft even as his cock pressed hard against the inside of her thigh. His mouth nipped at her ear as one hand traveled up to stroke her breast, the other finding and teasing her clit.

"Is that what you were thinking?" he asked.

"You know me too well," she said, and she meant it. He knew exactly how to touch her, body and soul. And right then, his fingers were wreaking havoc on her ability to speak. His fingers gently stroked her swollen clit, and she kept her eyes open, her face in front of his, as he brought her closer and closer to the brink.

Her body bucked, but she didn't look away. She let the orgasm take her, let it send her spiraling up and over, and all the while she looked into his eyes.

"Cleo," he whispered.

"Make love to me," she said, the word soft and full of meaning. *Love.* Not sex.

Gently, slowly, he kissed her, and she opened her mouth to his, exploring and tasting, even as she slowly and gently spread her legs.

He eased inside her with tender thrusts, each one pulling her a little more into him, tying the connection between them tighter, until, when he was fully inside her, she couldn't tell where he ended and she began.

Still, she didn't close her eyes. She wanted to see him. To see *them*. Herself reflected in his eyes. As he thrust rhythmically into her and she rose to meet him, she saw passion there like she'd never seen before, and it humbled her.

"Cleo," he whispered again. It was as if her name was a trigger. She exploded beneath him, crying out his name as her body clenched around him, pumping and claiming, draining him dry with the force of her passion.

When the orgasm subsided, she pressed up against him, hugging him tight, lost in a sensual swirl of satisfaction...marred only by the fear that something dark waited on the horizon, something that would work to keep them apart again, even when the thing she most wanted in all the world was to spend the rest of her life in his arms.

"CLEO," HE WHISPERED AGAIN, moving slowly inside her. He never wanted to let her go. Never wanted to lose her. Blindly, he cupped the back of her head, kissing her hard. Claiming her.

He was still inside her, and he moved slowly now, watching her as she moved with him, lifting her to exactly where he needed her.

"Josh." Her voice was soft, dreamy, and the passion in it made him even more desperate to possess her—and even more aware of what he would lose if she left. He couldn't tell her with his words, so he tried to tell her with his body. Tried to convince her that this was real and necessary and something that couldn't—shouldn't—be broken. Not again.

She was right in his arms, and he didn't want to let go, afraid that if he did—if he stopped kissing her or touching her—she'd disappear.

She made a sweet, desperate noise that was a cross between a moan and a cry, and the sound of it made him harder, if that were even possible. Because he recognized that sound. It was the sound of need, and it was washing over both of them, filling them and teasing them, both a plea and a promise.

He clung to it like a lifeline, certain that her need matched his own as he thrust inside her, again and again, until the doubts that tormented him disappeared and all he could do was bask in the feel of her and the knowledge that this moment was one they shared fully and completely. Sex and love and, yes, a future.

They came together, their minds and bodies soaring then crashing back down into the warm water of the hot tub. They clung to each other, and he reveled in that. He reached up to brush an errant strand of hair from her eyes. She smiled and his heart did little flip-flops.

She pressed a soft kiss to his lips and then slid off him. "We should get inside before we melt," she said.

"We probably should."

They both hesitated, because of course they hadn't bothered with robes or towels.

"You first," he said.

She laughed. "As if. You go."

"On three."

She narrowed her eyes at him and then nodded. They both crouched on the step, mostly underwater, but ready to spring. "One," she said.

"Two," he said.

"Three!" she finished. They took off with a flurry of water and raced inside, both with the same idea. They practically dived onto the bed and burrowed under the warm, dry sheets.

"We're getting everything all wet," she said, but her laugh suggested she was less than concerned.

"We'll do laundry when we thaw," he said. "If we don't get out of bed, we'll miss tonight's fireworks."

She rolled over and propped herself up on her elbow. "I'm only interested in our own fireworks."

"Me, too," he said. "Thank goodness for Jillian."

She laughed. "Jillian?"

"When Jillian offered me this cabin, she said it has a history."

"Really?" She sat up, the sheet held tight to her chest. "Tell me."

He sat up, too, facing her. "Apparently, Jillian and Ken had a rough patch in their marriage, and spending time here helped to heal it."

"That's sweet. I'm glad they patched things up. They're a great couple."

"Apparently they're not the only couple it's worked its magic on."

"Magic?"

He shrugged. "Or whatever. The point is, they study it now. Couples come, they leave with their relationship rekindled, the bumps smoothed out. Single folks come, they leave having found love. They're tracking it, recording it, like a study."

"That's ridiculous. They're scientists. A house that rekindles love?" Her words were dismissive, but he saw something else in her expression. Recognition, maybe? "Why did you mention it?"

"Because, from my perspective at least...the house did its job." He eased back, reaching for the nightstand on his side of the bed. He'd been thinking about it all day—the one thing he'd put there when he'd come up to the cabin. And now he wanted to give it to her.

He pulled open the drawer and took it in his hand. Then he sat up again and faced her, the gift hidden inside his palm. "You gave it to me, and now I'm giving it to you," he said. "This time for good."

He saw confusion on her face, but also delight. Slowly, she tugged his hands apart, and gasped with pure joy when she saw the pocket watch glistening in his palm.

"You kept it." She picked it up as if it were one of the crown jewels.

"Of course I did."

She opened it and read the inscription. "Forever," she said.

"We had to postpone forever once," he said. "But I don't want to wait anymore."

She met his eyes and he saw love—and relief—reflected at him. "I don't, either." She exhaled. "I just realized what I've been so worried about."

He frowned. "What do you mean?"

"You've been…I don't know…evasive I guess. About your plans for the company. For the future. I guess it scared me a little. I thought maybe you'd given up your dreams." She held up the watch. "But if you're giving me this, then I know that can't be true."

He fought a frown, not wanting her to know her words confused him. How did the watch connect to his plans for the mining company?

"It's going to be crazy for a while," she said. "This trial will keep me horribly busy, but if you're diving into expanding the company, then you're going to be just as busy. So long as we're both prepared for the other's insane schedule, it should work out fine. If you're looking to expand to Argentina, maybe we can even fly there together. And I imagine you'll have a lot of business in Washington. My apartment's small, but—"

He took her hand. "Whoa there, sweetheart. I don't need to go to Washington."

Her brow furrowed and her mouth parted in confusion.

"There's no reason I can't run the whole business from Nevada," he said.

"Isn't there?" She spoke slowly and carefully. She wasn't criticizing or questioning, but somehow he heard both.

"No," he said firmly. "No reason at all. I'm fortunate that way. The business world is so global anybody can run a business from almost any location."

She slid out of bed and stood up, tossing on a T-shirt while she paced. He watched her nervously, noting how much chillier the room suddenly seemed. "Why, Josh?"

"What do you mean, why?"

"Your mother isn't ill. The business is doing well—it's not going to flounder if you're not on-site. In fact, we both know that at this point the best thing for the company is for you to be out there drumming up more business."

"Which I can do by hiring geologists and lobbyists. Executives to run branch offices. It doesn't have to be me."

"Doesn't it? It's your face they need to see at new mines. It's your voice they need to hear in Washington and boardrooms around the globe."

"Cleo—"

"And even if it wasn't necessary for the company, well, what about you? This was your dream. Hell, it was your dad's dream. Have you forgotten?"

"Dreams can change," he said.

She looked at him hard, and it was as if she looked right through him to the lie in his heart. "Can they?" she asked.

"Yes," he said firmly, more to convince himself than her. "The company needs me here, Cleo."

"You really believe that?"

"I know it," he said more harshly than he'd intended. "The board won't approve any expansion plan unless it's a plan that I'm delegating to other people.

The board feels strongly that my presence in Nevada is what keeps the company going. I'm the heart of the company, Cleo, and the board knows that."

"Your mother is on the board, isn't she?"

"She is."

Cleo didn't say anything.

"It's not like that," Josh said. "Her concern is keeping the company intact."

Cleo nodded slowly, almost sadly, and Josh felt something heavy weigh on his heart. "And what about me?" She held out the watch, the case open, Forever flashing in the candlelight.

"We can do the long-distance thing while you work through the Argentina case, and then I thought you'd take the Nevada bar. If you're going to be second chairing a major mining litigation, you'll be well positioned to open your own firm out here. Or you could work in-house with me." He paused, suddenly nervous. "I love you, Cleo. I want us to be together. To work together. To raise a family together."

"That's what I want, too," she said, her voice tremulous. "But not like this."

Her words were a slap across the face. "What do you mean?"

"I mean that you may be right, Josh. I can be a lawyer anywhere. But I choose to be one in D.C. Because I love the work, and I love the people. And, yes, they've become like a family to me. I learn something new every day, and I'm advancing in my profession." She stood up a little straighter. "Could I choose to practice in Nevada with you? I probably could. It's not like it was five years ago when I had to go away to get the best education. I have it now, and yes, my job is pretty portable. But why should I?"

The weight on his heart tightened. "Because I'm here."

"No," she said. "You want me here *because* you're here. I just want you." Her eyes glistened, filled with unshed tears. "I chose Washington, Josh. But you didn't choose Nevada. You're trying to make it palatable, but you didn't choose it."

"Sometimes people don't have a clear choice. It's a compromise." He searched for words that would make her understand, but the words didn't come.

"Maybe," she said. "I don't know. I only know what I see. You shelved your dreams once because it was the right thing to do. But now...now I think you're too scared to reach for them. And it's breaking my heart."

CHAPTER SEVEN

CLEO CURLED UP ALONE on the couch. Josh was still in the bedroom. She knew he was reeling from what she'd said. Hell, she was reeling, too.

But she'd had to do it, no matter how much it broke her heart. Because he'd trapped himself, and even if he couldn't see it, she could.

Except she knew that he *did* see it. He'd been too vague in his explanations. Too pleading in his attempts to make her understand how much sense his plans made. He hadn't chosen to stay at the center of Goodson Mining—he'd been guilted into staying there. And it had caused him to question his own abilities, his own courage.

Eventually, though, he'd realize the truth of it: that the company, the family, wasn't the entirety of who he was or what he wanted to do. And if she moved to Nevada and started a practice and they started a family, well, then he really would be trapped. And maybe he'd start to resent her. At the very least, he'd start to resent himself.

It was all such a mess.

Resolved, she stood up and pulled on her clothes. It was one in the morning, but she couldn't take being here any longer. She'd sleep in her rental car at the Reno airport if she had to, but right then she had to get out. Otherwise, it was just too heartbreaking.

Perry hadn't been the man for her because he wasn't honest about his ambitions. Josh was the man for her because he was exactly the opposite. He knew what he wanted. He knew what he needed to make himself happy, and made no secret of it. And yet he wasn't going after it. He still wasn't pursuing his dreams. Worse, he was letting someone else keep him from pursuing them.

If she stayed, she'd only be party to something she thought was horrible and sad.

She had to go.

Cleo hesitated only long enough to leave the watch on the coffee table. She wanted forever, wanted it desperately. But once again, forever eluded her.

JOSH DIDN'T REMEMBER FALLING asleep, and the fact that he had was testament to his exhaustion, because surely his churning mind wouldn't have shut down otherwise.

He could tell by the sun that it was still early, and he wondered what it was that had awakened him. Then he recognized it. The sound of a car engine.

She was leaving.

He was out of bed in a second. He didn't have a clue what he was going to say to her, but he raced through the cabin anyway. It was a new day, and he'd at least take another stab at convincing her. At apologizing.

Apologizing?

He pushed the word and its ramifications from his mind, telling himself firmly that he had nothing to apologize for. They just needed to talk. To work it out.

But that was a lie.

He did owe her an apology. Hell, he owed himself one.

He just hoped it wasn't too late.

But when he pulled open the door, it wasn't Cleo he saw in the driveway but Guy Brown, the mechanic with whom he'd left his car. The very same Toyota that was now sitting in the driveway.

She was gone. He'd lost her.

"I decided to head down to Reno," Guy said. "Thought I'd drop your car off."

"Thanks," Josh said, still numb.

"You okay?"

"Yeah. I'm fine." He took the keys that Guy held out. "No, I'm not. I'm not fine at all. I just made the biggest mistake of my life."

"Huh? The car?"

"Not the car. And I didn't just make this mistake. I've been making it for five years. *Dammit.*"

Guy cocked his head, looking at him the way folks stare at people in grocery lines who talk to themselves. "You need anything?"

Josh held up the keys. "All I need is to hurry."

He said thanks to Guy and told him to mail him

the bill, making sure the mechanic had a ride before he dashed inside to grab his wallet and cell phone. He didn't have any idea what time the first flight left Reno for Washington, but he didn't care. If he didn't meet her in the airport, he'd follow her to D.C. Whatever it took, he was going to catch her and they were going to talk.

And he knew exactly what he was going to say.

First, though, he had someone else he had to talk to. And even though he knew it was going to be hard as hell, as he drove away from the cabin, he put on his headphones and punched speed dial on his phone.

EASTERN AIR FLIGHT 187 leveled out, and the pilot turned off the Fasten Seat Belt sign.

Cleo kept her buckle on and her hands tight on the armrest. The man in the seat next to her looked down at her hands and white knuckles and smiled gently. "Nervous flier?"

"What? Oh." She forced herself to relax. "Just jumpy today. Don't worry. I won't scream and grab your hand at the slightest bump."

The man laughed and smiled, starting to look a bit too flirty for Cleo's tastes. She pulled out a magazine from the seat-back pocket and pretended to read. A few minutes later, her seatmate stood up and headed for the lavatory. Cleo put the magazine down—she hadn't read a word—and leaned her head back, her eyes closed.

She tried to keep her mind from whirling, but

somehow she couldn't manage it. All she could do was wish that things were different, but unfortunately, life wasn't a fairy tale.

Her seat shifted, and she realized her companion had returned. She kept her eyes closed, hoping he'd think she was asleep.

Then she felt his hand close over hers. *Honestly. The nerve of some people.*

She yanked her hand back and opened her eyes— And found herself face-to-face with a smiling Josh.

"I switched seats with the guy who was here," he said. "I hope you don't mind."

"How—?"

"I drove really fast," he said. "And your plane was delayed. That helped."

"But—"

He pressed a finger to her lips. "I was wondering if that consultant gig is still open," he said, the corner of his mouth tugging up as he fought a smile. "Because I might be in need of a job."

She felt tingly, like champagne, but she squelched the feeling. This seemed wonderful, but if she was wrong, she didn't want to be disappointed. "Why?" she asked simply. "What happened to the job you have?"

"I spoke to my mom this morning. Told her that the board either had to approve my expansion plans—as proposed—or they'd be looking for a new president and CEO."

"Josh." She took his hands in hers. "Are you serious?"

"You were right," he said. "I do love the company, and Goodson Mining has always been my dream. But my dream was to run the company my way, not be chained to it. If the board doesn't get that—if my family doesn't get that—then I owe it to myself to work someplace that does. It was scary as hell, but now it feels amazing. I also realized that I couldn't use you to put a Band-Aid on my broken dreams by trying to tie you to my side. I get now that I was trying to do that. It wasn't fair. Not to you, or to me."

"Where will you work?"

"Anywhere I want to go. Mom and I talked for a long time. She doesn't like it, but she understands. The board won't vote against me."

"What exactly does she understand?"

"That I love my work. That I love my plans, and I have the skills and the confidence to make them happen. That I love her. That I love the company. And," he added, pressing a kiss to her fingertips and then slipping the pocket watch into her hand, "that I love you."

"Josh," she began, but she barely got his name out. She leaned over and took his mouth in hers, pulling him close and kissing him hard. The kiss lasted forever, and when she pulled away, he was smiling as broadly as she was. "I guess you were right," she said. "That cabin was made for romance."

"I'm glad you think so," he said. "Because I made one other call before I got on the plane."

"To whom?"

"Ken and Jillian. I reserved the cabin for next New Year's Eve. If that's okay with you."

She lifted the armrest that divided their seats and snuggled in close to the man she loved—the only man she'd ever truly loved. "Yeah," she said. "I think that's definitely a date we'll keep." She tilted her head and looked up at him, clutching the watch. "Happy New Year, Josh, forever."

"Happy New Year, Cleo." And the kiss he gave her promised many more to come.

* * * * *

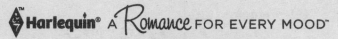

REQUEST YOUR FREE BOOKS!
2 FREE NOVELS PLUS 2 FREE GIFTS!

◊ Harlequin® Blaze™

red-hot reads!

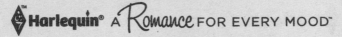